DESERT INFERNO

RAIN TRUEAX

Desert Inferno

Contact information, Works in progress and Author's thoughts at:
http://raintrueax.blogspot.com.
Revised August 2014

ISBN: 978-0-9898075-3-1
Paperback

Prepared and presented by
Seven Oaks
Monmouth, OR.

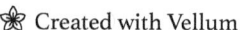 Created with Vellum

CHAPTER 1

June 2000 Southern Arizona

The brush, rich with vermillion oil paint daubed across one edge of a Payne's grey rock. Well that didn't work. Rachel O'Brian scraped the garish color away. Critically, she stepped back to survey the large canvas propped against the rear of her pick-up truck. The lower swoop of shadow across the desert, with sunlight glittering on the hills projected the feeling she had hoped to convey of depth and distance, but...

Her gaze kept returning to the lower right corner. There was something missing, a quality of deadness that ended the canvas at a bad point, drawing the eye away from the cacti and yucca, her intended center of interest. Was the problem a fatal one, or had she lost perspective?

Absentmindedly, she used her wrist to push a long strand of hair behind her ear. She looked from the canvas to the landscape. To her eye what might have seemed barren, to others, was instead lush with yucca, rock, cactus and mesquite. Across the border into Mexico were the rugged, pale purple, Parajito Mountains muted by dust in the air.

"Shoot," she grumbled, "doesn't one ever just work out?" Her fingers nearly itched to take hold of the palette knife and peel off layers of paint beginning again from a raw surface. A more perverse satisfaction would come from taking the knife from her belt and ripping the canvas to shreds. Of course, it would do nothing to save the painting.

She reminded herself that sometimes what at first seemed disastrous had a way of becoming a painting's best point. She wiped her paint smeared fingers with a rag. 'Give it time. Patience, Rachel. Remember. Patience.' From the time she'd been small, her father vainly attempted to explain how it was better to wait for things-- they would be sweeter when they finally arrived. She had never become convinced.

Her paintings all happened in a white, hot heat. She layered on color, shaped the landscape to suit her inner vision-- a feeling she only rarely perfectly captured. If she didn't work quickly-- almost impatiently, the feeling might be taken away. All too easily inspiration could disappear in a myriad of details. Through university training, private lessons, she had learned a degree of patience with her work, learned to temper the heat, to bring the work back to her studio, where she would struggle through the composition, and finally put a signature at the bottom--if it was worth signing and showing. They weren't all.

Again she stared into the distance, pivoting a little, as she reached into the back of her truck, and brought out a thermos of lemon flavored ice water. Squatting beside the truck in the filtered shade of a mesquite tree, she drank directly from the thermos, continuing to stare at the landscape. In another half hour, she would have to leave, as the colors would be washed out by intense sunlight. A faint breeze ruffled tendrils that had pulled out of her long braid.

"So, Matilda," she asked her four-wheel drive truck, "shall we call it a day?" In the way of good, long-standing friendships, the truck listened, not commenting, recommending, criticizing, nor expressing its preference.

Raised in this rugged country, Rachel had learned to crawl with the desert as companion, teacher and friend. Her family's ranch stood in the midst of mountains and desert. Nestling against national forest, the land stretched over rugged hills, grassland, yucca, live oak, and mesquite trees to reach the border. Except for the occasional illegal immigrant group, or less desirably the drug traffickers, it was free of people, a roadless region seldom seen by outsiders.

With the beauty of the cactus, wildflowers, birds and animals, surrounded by the challenge of rugged mountains, its terrain yielded an endless string of paintings that her collectors were waiting to evaluate and often buy.

She knew their secret though, those collectors—what they really wanted. It was the love of the land. She sold love, a love of nature. She herself intensely loved this land, and she was fortunate enough to be one of those who could let it shine through her paintings. It was why as often as possible she painted on location. That's where the energy was. It was what she hoped to transfer to the canvas through brush and paints.

Some feared her land. Some of its denizens were poisonous, some of its people dangerous. As a small child, her papa had given her practical lessons in desert survival. She knew to avoid most of the hazards and appreciate all of the beauties. She had been taught to take nothing for granted, knowing full well the lethal promise for the unwary, the potential for an instant of bad judgment to lead to disaster. But, when her turn came to join her ancestors, she hoped it'd be on her land, with her ashes scattered over possibly the same places she painted today.

At first she thought her eye had been attracted by a jackrabbit or coyote, then realized it wasn't an animal. She squinted but couldn't decide what was out there. Something didn't belong.

Pulling out a pair of binoculars, she studied the terrain. 'A piece of cloth or...' It was white. Maybe a... She shook her head with uncertainty. She had a responsibility to look more closely.

Tucking her shirt into belted shorts, she reached into the glove compartment to retrieve a small 9mm handgun and holster, threw a canteen over one shoulder, and grabbed a soft brim hat. Her feet were already shod with hiking boots and rolled down socks.

It wasn't easy to line herself across the land, down through arroyos, around cholla cacti. Now and then she glanced back to her truck, but kept it in her mind where she had seen the white. "I've got to be crazy," she muttered as the heat of the sun beat down on her shoulders. "Nobody's out here." *But what if there was? Someone in trouble.* She must know.

When she again glimpsed the white, she recognized it as a shirt, ripped and torn, riffled by the faint breeze. She hurried. Closer she could see it was a middle-aged man, hair thin on top, lying on his stomach, his form ominously still.

She knelt at his side. "Are you all right? *Como esta ?*" Was he breathing? Swallowing hard, she touched his neck, finding a barely detectable pulse. His skin was badly burnt and hot.

"Can you hear me?" she asked again. "I have water, but you have to drink." Carefully, she turned him over, trying to prop up his head with her knee to get him in a position where she could dribble water into his mouth. "Drink," she commanded. She poured a little over his forehead to get him aware.

The man made what appeared to be a gurgling sound; his eyes opened for a moment. She doubted he saw her before he closed them. She poured a little into his mouth, hoping he would swallow and not choke. As best she could tell the water was running right out onto the ground. She poured water into her hand and stroked it across his face.

"Try to drink. Can you hear me?" He opened his eyes again, muttered something. She bent closer.

"Dr...uh..."

The light in his eyes was gone. Although Rachel had seen animals take their last breath, she had never been there when a human did. She had now. Before she again felt, she knew the pulse in his neck would be gone. She laid him down. "In the name of the Father and the Son and the Holy Spirit," she whispered as she sketched the sign of the cross over his forehead.

She had to think what to do. She shouldn't move the body, had to notify someone. She shivered as though a cold wind had blown into her heart.

Braking to a stop in front of her porch, not bothering to put Matilda in the garage, she ran up the steps and into the cool adobe. "9-1-1," she muttered, shaking as she tried to punch in the numbers-- feeling grateful for the satellite phone system her father had installed only a year before. If not for that, she'd have had to rely on hoping to raise someone through the CB or drive nearly to Nogales before she would have found enough signal for her seldom used cell phone.

When she finished talking with the operator, she wished she'd seen nothing. It had been hard to make the woman understand what had happened, worse it all sounded so suspicious, reporting a dead body. Or more likely they received such calls all the time. It was old hat, but not to Rachel.

When she was told it could be an hour before anyone could get to her, maybe longer, she took time to shower to remove the feeling of death from her skin and nostrils. Stepping under the cool spray of water, feeling the water running in rivulets down her naked body, brought her a semblance of renewal. "It's all right. It's okay," she whispered, reassuring herself as she sudsed her hair.

Although they had had a few strangers come through, those with insufficient water, mostly they were so far from roads or towns that they weren't seeing the influx that some regions had experienced. This land though had been in her family's lands since 1885. O'Brians had lived on it since 1888. She had heard the stories of how hard held it had been. Most of that was in the distant past or was it still.

Toweling dry, she pulled on white shorts and a loose fitting white top. Restlessly, she braided her long black hair back into a single braid. Barefoot, she walked out onto the long, covered porch, slumped into a wicker chair and stared moodily at the road, willing there to be the telltale dust of a vehicle traveling down it, willing this day to have never happened.

When a truck finally did come bouncing down the driveway, Rachel sighed with relief. Standing at the top of the step, she waited. Still feeling a little dazed by the death she'd witnessed, she realized she should have put back on her boots.

A large man unwound himself from the green Bronco with a Border Patrol emblem on its door. His eyes were hidden behind the brim of a Stetson and reflective sunglasses. Even shaky from her experience, her artist's eye couldn't ignore the sheer grace, with which he moved his long, lean, body, as he strode across her yard. When he reached the porch, he stopped, not climbing the three steps. He looked at her for a moment, perhaps expecting her to speak; then pulled off the glasses.

His face was craggy, with a hawk-like nose, a long scar across one cheek, a square jaw, covered with a day's growth of bristle, and magnificent tawny, almost yellow eyes, rimmed with dark lashes. Nobody could call it a handsome face, maybe some would even see it as ugly, but to her it was mesmerizing. Beneath his Stetson, his hair appeared to be dark blond, a little long on the neck for a Border Patrolman.

"You the one who called?" Those, golden eyes, appeared to look right through her.

"You're Border Patrol?" She could only blame the stupid question on her shock of the morning, because his truck and uniform clearly made it silly.

When he smiled, the expression never reached his eyes. "Jake Donovan." He reached into a back pocket and pulled out ID. "Sorry I look... rough. I've been on an all-night stake-out."

Trying to get control of herself, she looked away from his eyes. She found her gaze traveling down his body. Ignoring the dusty and wrinkled clothing, she saw broad shoulders, muscular chest that tapered to narrow, horseman hips. Swallowing hard, she looked at the only safe place she could think of--the ground. "I didn't expect... that is, yes, I'm the one who called," she answered finally.

"The dispatcher said you found a body." His voice was deep, resonant, the tone carefully politely.

She forced her gaze back to meet his. "Well, to begin with he wasn't a body. That is, he wasn't dead but--"

"You're sure he was before you left him," he tried to finish for her, shaking his head in barely concealed frustration at trying to get a straight story.

"Of course. That is--" She was doing a good job of convincing him she was simple-minded.

"Start at the beginning and take your time."

"Well, it's not like I am used to finding bodies."

"Nobody is supposed to be."

"I expected a deputy sheriff."

"You want to call and make sure I am who I say I am?" he asked. His eyes did look tired, and he clearly was making a concerted effort to be polite.

"No, it's just I thought... I guess the county police or something."

"I was closest. They asked me to stop, and unless there was sign of foul play, it could be our business anyway."

Rachel nodded, satisfied, but still flustered by her strange reaction to this man. She explained then about her painting, about seeing white where it shouldn't have been, then finding the man.

"If you give me instructions, I'll go take a look," he said.

"Well I... It's off toward what we call Alamo Canyon, but I don't think I could explain. I better show you."

He grimaced. "I know this country pretty well. Draw me a map."

She shook her head. "I wish I could. It's just I never think about where I'm going when I'm going, which way is north or south. Matilda and I just drive. I never know where we'll end up."

His eyes lit with interest. "Matilda? Maybe she could help."

"I doubt that." She smiled. "She's my truck."

He looked away, swallowing whatever it was he looked as though he would have preferred to say. He patted his shirt pocket, curling his lips at an unpleasant thought. "Are you sure you can find it again... by this feeling or whatever it is?"

"Yes."

"Get your boots on then and come with me."

"I don't think that's a good idea."

"Huh?" Those golden eyes narrowed, and his lips thinned.

"If I drive, I can retrace my steps. It's not the same if someone else drives. These old dirt roads, well they all look a lot alike." She stopped, shivering as she thought again of those dead eyes. She looked up at him, knowing she felt suddenly near tears. "I'd like it if you rode with me... It would give me something else to think about if I was driving and... well, I'd rather not drive back alone. Would that be okay? That is can you do that?"

It was obvious he didn't like leaving his truck, maybe against regulations. He rubbed the back of his neck, as though fighting off a headache. When he looked back at her, she thought he appeared to be actually seeing her for the first time and not much liking what he saw. Rachel met his gaze and tilted up her chin.

"I'll be right back," she said and ran into the house to pull on

8

socks and boots. She didn't want to give him time to come up with an excuse. She didn't want to make the drive back alone.

Moments later, she was driving up the steep, compacted dirt road, the long, lanky officer squeezed into the passenger seat-- uneasily holding onto the door.

"Does my driving make you nervous?" she asked as she swerved to avoid a narrow, but deeply eroded rut, which was attempting to sever the road in two. On one side of the road a canyon opened up, on the other, a rocky cliff gave the truck barely enough clearance.

"No," he responded too quickly.

"I could slow down," she offered, looking over at him and wishing he hadn't hidden his eyes again behind those reflective glasses.

"Uh how about just keeping your eyes on the road," he suggested in clipped tones.

"My driving does make you nervous." She turned her gaze back to the narrow road.

"Not at all." He didn't let go of the armrest as they slid around a corner.

"Oh, I can see that." She glanced down. "That's why you're trying to put your boots through the floor of the truck. I really do know the ruts in this road, what to expect."

"I'm sure."

Rachel decided the wisest reply to that statement was none and didn't attempt more conversation, until she pulled the truck into the shade of the mesquite.

"I was parked here when I saw something move."

Levering his lanky frame from the pick-up, he reached into the back of the truck for a pack as he looked up. Vultures were now circling high in the cerulean sky, their instinctual radar alerting them to something promising on the surface of the desert.

She felt a desperate urge to get to the body before the

vultures did. "The vultures weren't there earlier." She took a deep breath. "It makes me wonder if he had moved before... before I saw him. I'd been here a couple of hours though not looking that exact way. When I get to painting, I zero in on the subject and... I just wish I had seen him sooner. I think though by the time I saw him he wasn't moving—if he had earlier. The breeze was coming up and it rustled his shirt, don't you think? By the time I got to him, he was near death." She knew she was talking too much and repeating herself but couldn't seem to stop. The combination of the dead man and the *very alive* one was fraying her nerves.

The tall law officer's long legs carried him across the rough desert floor at a faster clip than she could hope to match. By the time Rachel caught up, he was kneeling beside the body, studying first the man, then the ground around him. "Doesn't make much sense," he muttered.

"What?"

He looked up, seemingly surprised to see her. Obviously she wasn't the only one who talked to herself.

"He isn't dressed for a hike, doesn't look to be a worker or a coyote." His gaze moved down the body. "Before it got ripped up so bad by the desert, this was a dress shirt—looks like silk. Those are tailored slacks, no socks or shoes. People have been known to tear off their clothes from heat or sunstroke, but who takes off their shoes to walk in this country?" The thorns and spines of the desert had made a bloody pulp of the dead man's feet.

She had noticed none of that.

"Poor devil never stood a chance. I checked on my way to your ranch. Nobody's been reported missing. My bet is nobody will be... and we won't find ID on this guy."

"What are you saying?"

He smiled coldly. "I don't think he was meant to be found or identified. The desert would have taken care of that in a day or two. I doubt he put himself out here."

Rachel stared at him blankly for a moment. "You mean..." She stopped unable to say the word murder.

"Somebody let the desert do the job for them." Donovan stood, staring in the direction from which tracks showed the man had crawled and dragged himself. "He put up quite a fight to live, but it wasn't enough. He likely had no idea where water tanks or roads were." He looked back at her. "And he was alive when you got to him?"

She forced herself to remember. "Barely. He tried to say something but it wasn't anything... not a word. Just a sound."

"You'll probably be questioned about all this again by the county when they come out."

"Okay. I wish I could help, but I really didn't see anything."

Donovan draped a tarp over the body and then put a string marker around the site. "Maybe more will come to you." Rubbing his neck, he stared off toward the desert. Whatever his thoughts, she couldn't read them. She wondered if anyone ever read Jake Donovan.

After work, Donovan drove straight for a small bar, the Lone Star, chosen not for its name or decor but because it was closest to his home in Nogales. Off in the distance, dark clouds gathered and lightning crackled against the barren hills. It looked like a dry storm that might lead to fires but with little or no hope of a cooling rain for the sweltering valley.

After the last thirty-six hours, he felt the need for a cold beer or three. He'd been up all night on a stake-out on a lonely, godforsaken stretch of desert--where no man in his right mind would voluntarily be--where the only crossers, despite a supposedly reliable tip, had been buzzards and lizards as two agents waited fruitlessly.

Sweaty and dusty, wanting only a cold shower, the call had

come requesting someone to check on a body. Since his partner had a family, Jake had offered to make the side trip-- regretting his generous impulse as soon as he saw the woman standing on the porch.

Maybe he'd seen more beautiful women, but he didn't remember when. Wearing little make-up, she'd taken his breath away, her face and figure the kind they made movies about. He had only to take one look to know she was the sort of woman he would have walked ten miles to avoid. The afternoon had placed her squarely in his path.

Riding beside her in the truck, he had been all too aware of the clean scent of her skin overlaid by womanly fragrance, the softness of her voice, the way long, black tendrils of hair escaped the confines of her braid. By the time he'd gotten to the corpse on the desert, he had been relieved to face it rather than spending longer sitting next to her.

As Jake entered the swamp-cooled bar, the air was almost as hot inside as out. The humid air hung as heavily as the cigarette smoke. Mac, elbows leaning on the bar, looked up and recognized Jake. "Howyadoin'?" he asked, grinning as he whipped a glass from the shelf and filled it with cold beer from the tap.

"Don't ask," Jake responded. Loosening the buttons of his shirt, he leaned back against the bar, turning to let the air from the fan blow across his chest, drying the sweat on his body and offering the only cooling, short of a cold shower, he could expect from the night. At home he had only a small fan to circulate the air.

"Mac, this place is like an inferno. When you going to turn on the air conditioning?"

Mac's face took on an aggrieved look. "Hey that stuff costs money. It's not that bad-- yet."

Krista Bernard walked boldly up to the bar. She smiled up as she sidled her rounded, jeans-clad hips nearly to touch his thigh. "Buy a lady a beer?"

Jake looked around the room. "There one here?" he asked with a faint smile, not surprised when Krista slapped his arm.

Mac brought Krista a beer as Jake reached into his pocket and brought out the fresh pack of cigarettes he'd purchased on his way back to the office.

"Thought you quit," Mac chided with a shake of his head.

Jake lit the cigarette and inhaled deeply. "I did."

"How many times that make?"

"I don't count."

"One of these days they'll make me turn this place smoke free. That talk is spreading."

"When it does, you'll lose business."

"Have a hard day, big guy?" Krista asked, fluffing her straw blond hair.

Ignoring the question, Jake exhaled the smoke.

"I heard a kind of unusual body was found down south. You in on that?" Mac gave the bar a cursory wipe with his cloth.

"What's your source?" Jake asked. He should have been surprised at how fast Mac knew what was going on, but it had long since ceased to amaze him.

"Tony."

Jake took another long drag on his cigarette and felt himself begin to unwind for the first time in what seemed days. "The county's out checking the site."

"Tony said it was a broad found the body."

Jake snorted. "That's the part got your interest?"

"I like the ladies. So's that a crime?"

"Well Tony was wrong for once. She was no broad."

"What other kind is there?" asked Mac grinning. To him, all women were broads.

"No category for this one. Where do you file spoiled, beautiful, rich girls?" Jake asked taking a swig of his beer.

"How do you know all that? Look her up, Jake?" asked Krista.

"Didn't need to. It was written on her tight, little ass."

"You did some looking then?" Mac asked with a chuckle.

"I'm human." Shaking his head, he thought how hard he had tried to avoid looking as he finished the beer in a gulp and ordered another.

"So, the babe was a looker?" Mac probed for more details, hopefully salacious ones. The picture over the bar was one of the sexier ones of Angelina Jolie. It wasn't there for the customers.

Jake surveyed the room casually, noting two men and a woman at one table and a couple at the back booth. He shrugged off Krista's hand, as she tried to pull him to a table. "Not hanging around tonight, kid," he said, shaking his head. "Got a killer headache. It's been a long day. I'm going home to bed."

"That's what you always say," she complained. "When are you and me going to have some fun?" Her large lavender eyes were luminous and demanding as she pulled on his arm.

"Maybe when I'm in the mood for fun," Jake said tersely, stubbing out his cigarette.

"Except you never are," she complained.

Jake looked down at her thoughtfully. The lines and hardness in Krista's eyes told him her life had been anything but easy. She was older than him-- by how many years he could only guess. He knew of at least one husband, but the rest of her life was as closed a book to him as his to her. He shook his head. "I told you before, Krista. Find yourself a boyfriend. That's what you need--a guy who'll be there for you."

"Not you?" she asked with a tight smile.

Jake shook his head. "The last thing I want in my life is a woman--any woman."

"Not even the one from today," she snapped, angrily, the lines deepening around her mouth.

"Like that's an option."

"You're right. No guy who looks like you'd have a chance with a rich bitch." Her laughter at her own joke was loud and piercing.

Jake didn't look at her, not surprised at how quickly she had gone from teasing and flirting to taunting. It wasn't the insult that got to him. It was the vagaries of the female mind. One minute they're coming on to you like you're catnip--the next, spitting venom like a rattlesnake.

Krista smile turned to a frown. "Lordy, Jake, I'm sorry. I didn't mean to say that."

"A woman never does," Jake said.

It was not like he cared. He didn't need complications in his life; and from what he'd seen of relationships between the sexes, they were always complicated. His rule had been to keep the connection under the sheets and never see any of them in the cold light of day. A woman he ran into regularly, like Krista, didn't qualify—even if he had found her sexually appealing, which he didn't.

Jake reached into his wallet to pay for his and Krista's drinks.

"You think that guy was murdered?" asked Mac as he took the bills.

"Didn't Tony already tell you?"

"Just that there was something odd about it."

Jake shrugged. "It's a county problem so far as I can see."

"They doing an autopsy?"

Jake nodded, not volunteering anything. Toxicology would tell them if the man had been under the influence of a drug. It might explain the odd behavior. It wouldn't explain the marks of torture on his body.

CHAPTER 2

U p at dawn, Rachel felt a relieved surprise that she'd slept
well. No more of the nightmares that had plagued her the
first three nights after she'd found the dying man. She wrapped
herself in a robe and took her scone and tea out to the back
terrace.

As always the quiet patio, the desert rejuvenated her, filling
her with healing energy. Summer mornings on the desert were
wonderful. The air was still pleasant; the sky tinged a pale pink
and light blue. Sipping her tea, she watched a cardinal flit from a
live oak to a mesquite. She followed his progress until she lost
him in a brightly colored pink oleander.

As a tiny girl, her mother had taught her that gardening was a
way to connect with nature. Soil had been placed in her pudgy
fingers, and she'd been encouraged to play with it, touch and
know it. "Peace is from the earth," her mother had said with a
smile. Only a few years later, her mother had gone into that same
soil, buried above the adobe house in a family cemetery with all
the O'Brians going back to the ones who had settled this ranch. It
was sacred and precious ground to her. She would defend it with
her life.

She stared into the distance and debated again a question she had been asking herself. How soon would she see Jake Donovan? He had not returned with those who picked up the corpse. She had answered all the questions, and then it was quiet with everything as though there had been no dead man. Nothing had changed. Everything had.

Jake Donovan wouldn't be back. How silly that she had hoped he would. She imagined his face, the long lanky body, and felt a surge of fear and excitement. She couldn't put words to the thrill that she felt in thinking about him-- all the time knowing something in his eyes warded her away. He was like the desert both beckoning and warning.

She had no legitimate excuse to see him. Hank Stryker, the county police officer, had said there would probably be no further questions. Border had nothing to do with it unless it was an illegal entry. It could have been, but the dead man didn't fit any profile for that. He had not looked to be Hispanic.

She let her mind wander back to Donovan. What kind of man was he? Did he ever really smile? Was there a woman in his life? The questions were foolish regarding a man who she'd barely met, but there they were. The very fact that she was interested was a surprise. All her passion had gone into her paintings. What was there about this man to change that?

She leaned forward, her elbows resting on her knees, her chin on her fist as she considered the situation. Given his obvious lack of interest in her, she wouldn't see him unless she made a move. Except, how to do that? She had never chased a man. And this one might be married though he hadn't worn a ring, nor had he the look of a man who belonged to any woman.

So, she asked herself, *what excuse can I use that won't make it obvious I'm checking him out?* Logically she could want to know what they had found out about the dead man. Logically that would require her... going to the sheriff. Well she was just a woman, ignorant of the ways of government. Wasn't curiosity a natural thing? Hadn't he suggested she might be questioned further--of course, not by him, but that was a tiny detail.

She was going to find an excuse to see him again—if for no other reason than to stop fantasizing about him. It likely had been the drama of finding a dying man and then...

That settled it. Meeting him again in a more normal setting would doubtless put an end to this whole business of imagining his unusual face and that tall, rawboned body.

Border Patrol offices were on a busy cross street in Nogales. At the front of the large, warehouse like building, Rachel was directed by a grinning man to a closed cubicle at the end of a long aisle.

When Jake Donovan looked up, she saw instantly she was not to be the favorite part of his day. His golden eyes looked tired, his jaw clenched tight, causing a muscle to throb in his cheek. She wondered if he ever relaxed, ever really smiled.

"Miss O'Brian," he said, "I didn't expect to see you again."

At least he remembered her name, and she could see she'd caught him off guard. That might be helpful.

"I had a few questions... and thought you might want to ask me something more about...you know."

He looked blankly at her, then gestured to a chair across the desk from him. "I don't know what I can tell you."

"Well... I... What did they find out about that man?"

He smiled faintly and leaned back in his chair. "Didn't the police question you?"

She nodded. "But that was several days ago. I thought maybe something new had come up." She realized she was enhancing his original impression of her as a bimbo.

"You seem nervous," he observed. "Feeling guilty?"

She shrugged. "Isn't that the usual reaction of people who sit in this chair?"

"The usual person sitting there is illegally in this country and feeling guilty as hell."

"Everybody's guilty of something. How about you, you guilty of something? You seem nervous too."

His gaze met hers. "Beautiful women always make any man edgy."

She smiled. "Ah and you think I'm beautiful?"

"Don't all men?"

"I didn't think you'd even looked at me."

He was irritatingly aware he noticed just about everything about her, even to the faint fragrance of roses that seemed equal parts perfume and woman. His physical reaction to her was no better than the first morning. To break the connection, Jake stood up and walked to his file cabinet, opening a drawer as though looking for something.

"Are you sure you don't have some questions for me?"

"The incident wasn't Border Patrol business."

"No chance the man was in the country illegally?"

"It's always possible, but we have no proof and sufficient numbers where we do."

She watched him. He decided her eyes were lavender. He wished he could read the expression in them, then was glad he couldn't.

"Mr. Donovan?"

He leaned against the file cabinet and looked down at her.

"Do you ever smile?"

How the hell did you answer a question like that? "When I have reason."

"I've seen you tilt your lips up on the ends in sarcasm, but a genuine smile. Not yet."

"We haven't known each other long."

"True—at least this time around."

"What was that supposed to mean?"

19

"Not much." She leaned forward a little in her intensity, one long leg crossed over the other. "Do you want to know me?"

He shook his head, the smile that unfriendly one, which wasn't what she thought the usual result of flirting was supposed to be. "We're born to what we're born."

"How fatalistic. Are you a fatalist, Mr. Donovan?"

He shrugged. She wanted him to say something more, something that showed he wanted to see her again. She could see he wasn't going to do that. But he had said she was beautiful.

"Did you learn the dead man's identity?" she asked coming back to safer ground.

"Not yet."

She frowned. "No parked cars along a road?"

"Nope."

"Nobody reported missing?"

"Uh uh."

"But you don't believe it was simply a case of a tourist taking a wrong turn?"

"It could be that simple." His tone told her he didn't believe it.

"You think he had come down from Tucson or Phoenix?" She was working hard to come up with questions, so that she didn't have to leave. He wasn't helping.

"The label on his slacks was from New York. His skin was burnt so bad I don't think he'd seen much sun before his last walk."

"Oh... hmmmmm. You know I just realized I could use a cup of coffee," she said abruptly. "How about you?"

His mouth dropped open before he slammed it shut.

"I'm inviting you out for coffee or an iced tea or whatever you want." She smiled. "My dime."

"I have a lot of paperwork to get through."

"No coffee breaks?" She forced amazement into her voice. She had not expected this to be easy. She didn't even know why she was pursuing him, but she had to admit she was. No use pretending it related to questions about the dead man. She would be foolish not to face the truth at least to herself. She wanted to get to know him. She was determined to do it-- one way or another.

"We take breaks if we want them," he answered finally.

"I have a few errands to run," she said. "How about if I come back at the right time for that?"

She could see him trying to think of an excuse. She also saw he hadn't come up with one when he finally nodded. "Sure."

"What time?" she asked, standing and smoothing her white slacks down. His gaze follow the movement of her hands. Maybe this would work out. Except what did work out mean?

"In an hour."

"I'll be back."

He walked to the door of his office, watching as she walked from the building, noting half the men in the building were also watching the sway of her hips. With irritation, he slammed himself back into his chair. Now, why had he agreed to see her again? What had possessed him not to end it right here?

Lighting a cigarette, he tried to figure out what she wanted. Was there some information she thought he had? A woman like her shouldn't have been willing to give a man like him the time of day, let alone invite him for coffee. She was out of his league. He rubbed his fingers along his jaw, trying to think what she could be up to. Maybe she knew more about that guy than she had let on. That hadn't seemed likely, but unlikely things often happened in his line of work.

He'd made it a lifelong habit to assess the situations into which he walked. His work was potentially dangerous enough that in his personal life, he avoided risks. As a child he'd learned the benefits of not being emotionally attached to anything or anyone. A woman meant only trouble, and with Rachel O'Brian, that trouble would be big time. He didn't like the way he thought about her, the way her face and body had forced themselves into his imagination. He didn't want to see her again. So what the hell was he doing having coffee with her?

"Am I late?" Rachel asked Donovan, determined to make him answer her smile but not surprised when she had to accept defeat.

He took a deep breath and, grabbing his Stetson from the file cabinet, walked to the door. "Usually--when I take time to go out--I go to Marty's around the corner. It's nothing fancy."

"Sounds perfect."

The diner was small, dark with a narrow counter and several plastic covered booths. Smoke permeated the refrigerated air. When they were both seated, he tossed his hat on the seat beside him, running his fingers uneasily through his hair. "Mind if I smoke?" he asked, taking a pack of cigarettes from his shirt pocket.

"It's not good for you. Haven't you read the health reports?" she asked with a smile.

"If I was into health, I'd switch professions."

"Well, it's all right with me-- if you insist on killing yourself."

He lit his cigarette, taking a deep draw on it to steady his nerves. "One way or another, we all go."

"Some sooner if they practice unhealthy habits."

"First of all, I am not exactly in a profession to worry about that. Secondly, you aren't one of those health nuts are you?" he asked, blowing out the smoke.

She narrowed her eyes. She wasn't about to admit her foibles to him, not when he was obviously already less than enchanted. "I watch what I eat... generally."

The waitress came up to take their order. "Hi Jake," she said with a grin, looking at Rachel with more than a little curiosity. "How ya doin'?"

Jake raised his brows as he shrugged broad shoulders. "Bring the lady and me a cup of that stout coffee of yours."

"Well, we've done with the niceties," he said when the coffee was in front of them, "now what's this really about?"

She was not surprised at the question. Too bad she hadn't come up with a better answer by now. "Naturally I'd want to know if there is something dangerous going on near our ranch."

"You know that's dangerous country out there. Your family has been there long enough that you know it always has been."

"Well more than the usual lately?"

"I don't have an answer for that."

"You feel something though, don't you? I see it in your eyes. I saw it when you were out there."

He shrugged and took a sip of the coffee.

She looked at her own coffee with distaste. She supposed she ought to drink some of it and wondered if she could do so without puckering up. Another question would delay the inevitable. "What makes you think he wasn't just out hiking, became disoriented and--"

He smiled that humorless smile of his. "It doesn't fit, does it?"

"No, I suppose not." She picked up the cup.

"Not dressed for it. Too pudgy to be worrying about keeping fit. And... how close did you look at him?"

"Well I did try to get him to drink water when I first found him, but he couldn't. He tried to say something and then he was gone."

He stared at her. "I don't remember you mentioning giving him water."

"He couldn't drink it, and he didn't say words or anything I could understand before his eyes went dead."

"No legible words?"

"Just a croak... Kind of a duh. Maybe it was a dying sound-- like a release of breath." She felt just as unable to drink the coffee she was now toying with. Maybe cream would help. Lots of cream. She poured it in, wincing as she looked at the unappetizing concoction. "Why did you ask how closely I'd looked at him?"

"Because--" He hesitated a moment, as though wondering how much to tell her. She realized there was something about this case he was hiding.

"You told me he didn't have on shoes. I admit I hadn't noticed that." The man hid all his thoughts behind an emotionless mask, but she was beginning to see by the tightening of his jaw, the flicker of his eyes that the mask was only that.

"There was that."

"People in the desert go crazy without water, tear their clothing off."

"And their shoes?"

"It's hard to imagine a reason for that other than going insane."

"Trackers tried but couldn't follow his trail because of the wind we've been having."

"You wanted to know from where he had come onto the desert?"

"It would have been helpful."

"There really is no way to drop someone into that area. It's miles with no roads."

"Helicopters could do it. Would you have heard one?"

"Not if it came in low. I don't know. Maybe if I'd been out at the time. Would they go to that much trouble to murder someone? Why not just kill him?"

"Torturers do things like that when they know there is no real hope, like a cat playing with a mouse when he knows the mouse can't escape."

She shivered. "What is it you aren't telling me?"

"What makes you think I am holding back?"

"I saw it on your face."

Jake prided himself on having a poker face, and he didn't like knowing she could see past that. It made him even more uncomfortable when those thoughts were centered on her slender body, when they involved the soft curves of rounded breasts, which the loose cotton blouse didn't conceal, and a curiosity as to how soft her hair might be, and was her skin as silky as it looked?

"So," she asked, "what is it about this man that you didn't want me to know?"

He shook his head ruefully, taking a deep drag on the cigarette as he considered her question. Maybe she knew more than she had told him. If he shocked her, it might come out. "Rope burns on wrists and ankles, other marks of torture."

"I... I didn't see that." She looked down. "Those who do things like that should not be allowed to walk free."

He smiled at the vehemence in her voice. "Unfortunately, that kind is good at not leaving their own marks behind-- coyotes."

"I assume you're talking about the men, who illegally bring others across the border, not the furry songsters who lull me to sleep at night."

His eyes narrowed her as he studied her. No woman he'd ever known considered the eerie yodel of a coyote soothing enough to fall asleep to. Damn. He'd been out of his league since he met her. He glanced down at her untouched coffee "You want that heated up?"

She grimaced as she looked at her cup. "No, I like it this way," she said finally, putting it to her lips and allowing the chalky fluid to flow into her mouth, forcing herself to get it down.

Jake watched her slender throat as she swallowed. Her full lips looked slightly moist. He could encircle her neck with one hand. Viciously, he snubbed out his cigarette.

"If he was a drug merchant, he could have had a falling out with one of the Mexican cartels," he said to distract himself. "When we find out who he is, we will likely have a better idea who set him out there."

"I only wish I'd seen him sooner," she said. "Maybe then we'd have had your answers."

"Life is full of maybes and ifs. They don't do anybody much good." Jake's tone was emotionless. If he had had interest in the conversation earlier, it was gone now.

Rachel watched him light another cigarette. She realized he'd told her more about his own life than he'd intended.

"What kind of artist are you?" he asked before she had a chance to consider further.

She smiled. "Oil paintings."

He drew in the smoke, letting it out slowly. "Seriously?"

"As opposed to?"

"A hobby." She frowned and he smiled. "Rich girls don't usually get serious at anything long enough to work at it."

She bristled and nearly snapped back a sharp retort. For her, art was a driving force, a need as real as food or clothing. She had studied hard at the university to learn design, composition, balance of color, and the skills necessary to transform the ideas in her mind onto canvas. Creating, working with her oil paints, was a part of her so basic that she couldn't imagine life without it. The idea that he would think she didn't take it seriously was irritating. "You don't have much of an opinion of me, Mr. Donovan—as though we've met before."

"You know we haven't."

"Haven't we? Then what makes you think you know me?"

He took a drag on the cigarette, filling his lungs with the smoke before he blew it out. "Just female nature."

"Obviously not nice females?" It was no guess. "And you have classed me with them."

"I didn't intend to offend you."

She laughed at the stubbornly set jaw. "Of course you did."

He wanted to brush her off, forget he had ever met her. She wasn't making it easy.

"You might have known women but not one like me, have you?"

He shook his head.

"So the best way to form an opinion about a person is based on total ignorance?"

He knew he should have quit while he wasn't ahead. "Call it intuition."

"I'd rather call it by its rightful name-- bigotry. Perhaps you should get to know people before you form your hastily, and in this case, ill-conceived opinions."

"Not going to happen--at least not in this case."

"And why not?"

He shook his head. "That's obvious. Women like you don't come knocking on my door." He smiled that cold smile. She wondered again what he would look like if he ever really smiled.

"Would you open the door if one did? How can it be you know so much and yet so little about women?"

He ignored the loaded question and immediately wished he hadn't when her next question probed a little deeper.

"Who was the woman who taught you to hate?"

He ground his teeth. "I have to get back to work."

She rose when he did. Reaching into her purse, she drew out a ten, leaving it on the table.

"You're not paying for this," he growled.

She smiled. "If you make that into a bet, you will lose that one too."

"What do you mean too?"

"You've got all the answers, Mr. Donovan. You tell me."

When Donovan got back to his office, a handsome blond man, in an impeccably cut, gray business suit, was sitting in his own chair, legs up on his desk, waiting for him.

"What can I do for you?" Donovan asked, throwing his hat onto the filing cabinet.

The man put out his hand, as he rose to his full height,

coming closer than most ever dreamed, to looking Jake Donovan in the eye. "I'm David Bannister."

"With?" Donovan prodded as he plopped into his own chair. The man had all the earmarks of a federal agent.

Bannister opened his wallet and flipped an identification card to the front. He watched as Donovan read the name of the agency for which he worked.

"Hmmm I heard of you boys. Kind of a secretive bunch."

"We don't like publicity."

"So what are you doing in Nogales? Wouldn't think we'd have anything big enough down our way to bring you here."

"A body." Bannister folded his long body into one of the chairs across from Jake.

"Any particular one in mind?"

"Winston Joseph Franklin, 55 years old, late of New Jersey. Very recently dead... Found west of here."

"You have my interest."

"I thought I might."

"You got out here fast," Jake observed, putting his boots up on his desk and lighting a cigarette.

"I *was* here. Mr. Franklin was a fence, a very exclusive fence."

Jake raised his brows.

"On a plea bargain over another charge, he had agreed to do a little job."

"So little it cost him his life?"

"We lost track of him until we heard about your dead guy."

"Inconvenient—for him," Jake said, smiling thinly.

"To say the least," Bannister agreed with his own sardonic smile. "Basically this sets our work back to zero, which is unpopular with my boss."

"What was the job?" Jake asked, studying the handsome face of the agent. If the man had an imperfect feature on his face or flaw to his physique, Donovan couldn't see it. For some reason that irritated him. He definitely didn't like this guy.

"Smuggling Mexican antiquities."

"Say what?" Jake asked, drawing cigarette smoke deeply into his lungs before he expelled it.

Bannister grinned. "The Mexican government has been more than a little upset to find some of its most important historical artifacts and treasures disappearing. Most likely across the American border. The most recent incident was last month. A truck, heading for a Mexico City museum with Olmec and Toltec pottery, jade figurines, masks and several ritual vessels, disappeared."

Jake snorted. "Wait a minute with all the drug trafficking, the illegal immigration, possible terrorist bombs, and you guys are worried about frou-frou? You have to be kidding?"

Bannister's expression told him he was not. "We got into it at the request of our government and the Mexicans. Rather than make an international incident out of it--especially since so little is provable at this point--they asked us to find out."

"Trinkets are worth murdering someone?"

"It's a lot more than that. It's a national identity, many hundreds or even thousands of years old. If that doesn't do it for you, their worth can easily be into seven figures. Multimillions for the overall operation. Collectors will pay anything to acquire such rare treasures. When an assemblage like this disappears into private collections, it rarely surfaces. The case became more personal when three months ago we lost one of our guys." Bannister's face hardened; the pretty-boy look was replaced by a hard, seasoned expression, that of a capable, rugged man. "We'll get whoever did it. You can put money on it."

Jake shook his head, still having a hard time believing the scenario. "You really believe this is all over pottery?"

"Any operation is a mix but yes, this went from drugs to antiquities."

"And that's worth murder?" he asked disbelievingly

"There are those who kill for a lot less."

Jake didn't argue with that assessment. "All right, but we're Border, not Customs. What do you want from us?"

"Not *us*. You. You were out there. You saw the body before anybody got to it. I want to hear about it again, maybe something not big enough to have gotten into the report."

"There isn't anything that didn't get into the report. The media didn't play up the fact that he was tortured, but I expect you know."

Bannister nodded.

"Whatever your fence knew about your operation... or you," Jake said with a humorless smile, "whoever killed him knows."

"We assumed that also." Bannister got up from his chair and paced to the other end of the room.

"Who are these men?"

Bannister hesitated. Jake wondered how honest the agent would be with him. His guess was no more than required.

"It's a cartel with one branch south of Mexico City and the other on the border. Yes they do drugs, but this has become as or more important to them. One steals or diverts the artifacts, depending on which is easiest, funnels them up here where they're gotten across the border to dealers who sell them to undiscriminating buyers. We think that part of the enterprise is being fronted by a quasi-legitimate import-export business."

"And Franklin pretended to be one of those dealers?"

Bannister nodded. "One way or another, they must have found out he was connected with us. Whether we've have a leak, or it was bad luck..." He shrugged.

"Whose names have you got?"

"It might be better that you don't know."

Jake laughed harshly. "For me or you?"

"Sometimes the less a man knows, the better off he is."

"In my line of work, that is seldom true."

Bannister was silent a moment, his expression thoughtful. "All right, but I'll have to get back to you."

"Talk to you then."

Bannister's teeth flashed in his handsome face. "You are a suspicious bastard."

"It pays."

"How about access to your files?"

"Anybody able to find anything in those files deserves everything they get," Jake said as he nodded toward the filing cabinet. One of these days he'd get around to putting it all onto a computer. One of these days.

By the time Bannister had finished going through the files and Jake had written his stack of reports, they were both bleary eyed. Jake looked at his wristwatch and saw they'd worked past six. "Time to knock off," he said, rubbing the back of his neck.

"You got plans?" Bannister asked, as he loosened his tie.

"Burger, beer and bed in that order."

"Mind if I tag along?"

"For how much of it?" Jake asked suspiciously.

Bannister smiled. "Just food, Jake."

Jake stood up and stretched, trying to work the kinks out of his back. "If there's more to it than that, you're out the door." He grabbed his Stetson, tipping the brim low over his eyes.

"No problem." Bannister grinned, not intimidated by Jake's scowl.

Jake opened the door to his office, but before he could do more than gape, Rachel walked through. "Hi," she said.

"You can see that we're leaving," Jake said.

Rachel looked up at him. "I came back to..." She stopped seeing Bannister for the first time. "I'm sorry I didn't realize you were busy."

"Never too busy for a lovely lady," Bannister said with an appreciative grin.

"Well, I..." She smiled up at Jake. "I felt bad about the way we had left it. What I said, but I see now is not a good time to talk to you."

"Introduce us, Jake," Bannister said, smiling smoothly.

Her kind of guy, Jake thought as he made the introductions, his mind more on the fact that Rachel was wearing a sleeveless white dress, which draped loosely over soft curves, suggesting more than it showed but implying plenty. Her thick black hair was loose down her back, falling in luxuriant waves. Jake wasn't surprised to see the admiration in Bannister's eyes.

"Glad to meet you," Bannister said, smoothly moving to cut between Rachel and Jake as he took her hand.

She smiled looking up at Jake, the expression in her eyes impossible to read. "I really am sorry I intruded."

"We were on our way to dinner," Bannister put in before Jake could say anything, "and could ask for nothing more than to have a charming, beautiful companion to eat with. It'll make the evening." He smiled broadly, his eyes skimming over Rachel's curves with what could only be described as masculine appreciation.

Jake stood back a little wishing for another cigarette. Rachel looked up at him, "Is that all right?"

"Sure," he said with little enthusiasm and more than a hint of irony. "Why not?" Glumly, he resigned himself to spending a night with Barbie and Ken as they began a flirtation.

Bannister took Rachel's arm as they exited the office. "Where's a good restaurant, Jake?" he asked, looking back as Jake closed the door behind them.

"I usually eat at the golden arches," Jake quipped.

"I think we can do better than that." Bannister wrinkled his nose.

Rachel stopped and waited until Jake came up to them. "A hamburger sounds good to me."

Bannister looked from one to the other. "You're kidding, right? How about Thai food? Not that we are likely to find any. Or..." He shrugged. "You're not kidding. All right, I'm easy. Whatever the lady wants."

Jake studied him through narrowed eyes. He doubted there was anything about the agent that was easy.

Half an hour later, the three of them were seated at a booth in the fast food restaurant with Big Macs, fries and drinks on the table.

Bannister grimaced as he looked at the hamburger, but gamely bit into it. "Actually not too bad--not bad at all," he said as he swallowed. "It is a good sauce."

"You really haven't ever eaten at one of these places," Jake said with disbelief. He found himself, as he had expected, across the table from Rachel and Bannister. Not that it was her choice. Bannister was quick.

"I've missed out on this particular treat, but it's not bad. I may be back."

"It's my favorite hamburger," Rachel said.

"How about the Whopper?" Jake asked with a disbelieving smile.

"Well, sometimes. Actually," she admitted, "you've just found one of my secret vices--fast food."

"Do you call this stuff health food?"

"Don't tell anybody." Her gaze met his; the lavender was like pools drawing him to her or were they looking into his very soul? He didn't like the feeling, and yet it took all he could do to turn his gaze away.

"It's a capital offense," Bannister said trying to draw attention back to himself.

"Could it get me arrested?" Rachel asked teasingly looking at Jake again. He knew she was flirting with him. He might be dense but not so dense that he couldn't read that expression in her eyes. Nothing was making sense.

Bannister grinned. "Detained at least." He shot Jake a glance before he turned back to Rachel. "Tell me where you come from--except heaven, of course." Bannister played with his straw, the action designed to look as casual as the question. For the first time Jake began to wonder what Bannister was really after.

"I live on a ranch out north of the Pajaritos."

"Alone?"

"With my father and a hired man or two."

"Big ranch?"

"A few acres."

"Raise cattle?"

"Not anymore."

"No cattle. What kind of ranch is that?"

Rachel ignored the question and turned her gaze back on Jake. "How many years have you been with Border Patrol?"

He shrugged trying to remember when he hadn't. "Over ten."

"Do you like it?"

"I'm still here." He thought of the kids he had to arrest, the families he sent back across the border to try some other night to make it to the promised land, the drug busts, the long patrols, the waiting for nothing, then the times when there had been trouble, finally the complaints he wasn't doing enough. He didn't always like it, but it was all he knew.

"Aren't you going to ask about me?" Bannister suggested.

"Would you tell me the truth if I did?" Rachel asked.

"Now was that nice?" Bannister laughed.

"She reads right through a man," Jake said pleased for once to see the trait turned on someone besides himself. "I could've warned you."

"You should have."

Rachel glanced at her wristwatch. "Much as I'd like to continue fifty questions, I'm staying in town tonight, and I promised my friend I'd be in early. She feels she has to wait up for me."

They drove her back to the parking lot at Border Patrol where she picked up her truck. Bannister and Donovan leaned against his truck, watching as she drove away

"Now what was that about?" Donovan asked as soon as the truck turned the corner.

"What?" Bannister asked, innocently.

"You know what." Donovan lit a cigarette.

"Just friendly interest." Jake eyed him narrowly through the smoke. "Hey, I didn't realize she was your territory. You jealous?"

"That isn't the kind of interest I mean, and you know it. As soon as you heard her name, you got that wolfish look on your face. You were on the hunt. What for?"

"She's a beautiful woman. Isn't that enough?" Bannister put out his hands with what might've seemed an innocent smile if someone didn't read faces as well as Jake.

"No."

"Okay, I did remember she'd found Franklin's body. Hey, don't be so protective. I didn't ask her about that, did I?"

Donovan took an angry drag on his cigarette. "I know how you boys operate. You look for a connection--no matter how remote--and you milk it. Just because Franklin was found near the O'Brian ranch doesn't mean a thing. It's a big country. Lots of ways into it." For some reason he couldn't identify, Donovan was glad he'd not mentioned in his report that Rachel had found Franklin alive. At the time he'd decided it didn't matter since nothing was revealed; but now he knew the agent would have found some way to use that information, a way that wouldn't bode well for Rachel O'Brian.

"You're thinking this through too much. I know she's not involved in anything."

"Then why twenty questions?"

"Any man would be interested in her. Aren't you?"

Jake swore. "Tell me another one. Rachel O'Brian hasn't had any connection to your little smuggling game and that's the way it's going to stay."

"You're interestingly protective of the lady." Bannister rubbed his jaw thoughtfully. "Personal?"

Jake smiled coldly. "I don't have to be interested in someone to not want to see them used like you boys do. Franklin paid a high price for that."

Bannister flinched. "I have no plans to use her."

"Stay away from Rachel O'Brian."

"Are you threatening me, Donovan."

"Not yet. When I threaten, you won't have to ask."

"So there is something going on between the two of you. I didn't miss how she was watching you all night."

"No more. I know your brand. Everything leads to another question. Just remember what I said."

"If you're not interested in her--that way, you won't mind if I pursue my own interest."

"So long as it's not trying to use her."

Bannister grinned, white teeth flashing in the reflected moonlight. "I wondered if you were going to hit me for a minute there."

Jake threw his cigarette to the ground, grinding it into the pavement with the toe of his boot. "You won't have to wonder about that either."

CHAPTER 3

Rachel sat on a stool in her friend Maria's kitchen. It had been a week since she had seen Jake Donovan, and she felt depressed not to mention confused. She stared into the glass of iced, mint tea in her hand.

"He hasn't called?" Maria asked, stirring cookie dough in a large pottery bowl.

She shook her head with a frown. "He's not going to either."

"So no problem. Call him."

"That would be chasing."

"Girlfriend, what century you living in? Times have changed. Women call men."

"Probably wouldn't do me any good. I tried chasing him. So far it's gotten me zilch."

Maria grinned, sampled the dough and sprinkled in a little more cinnamon. "This is not a problem. It's simple. Make up your mind what you want and go after it. Look, if you give it all you've got and he doesn't respond, then go onto someone or something else. You haven't given it all you have yet, have you?"

"No, probably not. I do have pride."

Maria snorted. "Pride! What's that? Cold comfort in bed, girlfriend. But one thing-- be sure you know what you're getting into. You don't know him very well."

Rachel walked over to where Maria's baby slept in a baby carrier. "You didn't have to worry about any of this. You and Mark always knew each other."

"Not so. He thought of me as a friend, which was complicated by the fact that he had amorous designs on you at the time. If you'd seen him differently, my babies might not exist."

"He was only slightly attracted to me. In the long run, I would have never suited him." She stared at the baby's pink cheeks, the thumb tightly captured in a small rosebud mouth, Rachel smiled against her will. "She's beautiful. I never really thought of having one of my own... until recently."

"You are kidding," Maria quipped throwing her hands up in mock alarm. "I thought you said you didn't want kids ever." She set about scooping the cookie dough onto flat sheets. "I worry about you, sweetie."

"You've been doing that since fourth grade. I always said I didn't need a guardian angel because I had you."

"Someone had to look out for you. You kept taking on the school bullies."

"Me?" Rachel retorted, putting her hand over her heart. "Excuse me, but I may not have heard that right."

"All right we did it together." Maria grinned. "Get busy cutting up the veggies."

Rachel moved to the sink and began scraping carrots. "I gagged down a cup of coffee, forced myself on him for a dinner, which ended up with a third wheel along, and what good did any of it do? I've got the wrong man calling me, and the right man doesn't know I exist." She wrinkled her nose in exasperation.

The kitchen door swung open as a medium-height, slightly balding, mustached man came striding through, loosening his tie.

"Hey, honey," Maria said, "I didn't hear your car." He gave her a quick kiss. "A good day?"

He smiled at Rachel and reached into the refrigerator for a bottle of beer. "We got the extension. I don't know how much good it'll do us, but maybe time to come up with a miracle. Not that I've seen too many of those lately."

"Do the LaToyas deserve a miracle?" Maria asked with a wry grin.

Mark laughed. "Nobody deserves a miracle. That's what makes it a miracle."

"Is this important stuff I am not supposed to hear?" Rachel asked, smiling as he winked at her.

"Not really. Of course, it is important to the ones who have the land disagreement. Amazing that some neighbors, who could go next door to discuss something that could simply be divided, giving ground on both sides, will instead pay lawyers to do their talking." He grinned as he snagged a carrot stick from the bowl before he left to change.

"Suppose it does work for you," Maria resumed the earlier conversation without a miss. "are you sure this is what you want? Domestic bliss? Now, you can do what you want when you want. Devote yourself to your art, run over to San Diego to take a class, down to LaPaz to swim and paint. Take off to Monument Valley on a whim. You get yourself tied down with some border patrol-man, and you'll be stuck like me."

Rachel smiled, knowing Maria had a point but then thinking of broad shoulders, of how it might be at night to fall asleep in strong arms, of having someone come home to her, who would tell her about his day as casually as Mark had just done with Maria. "Yeah right, she said with a laugh, "I've seen how miserable you are."

"So scratch that point. If you are determined to get to know this man, do what the LaToyas should have done, beard the lion in his den."

Rachel didn't pretend not to understand. She'd been considering the very thing herself. "I don't see how I could do that."

"Why not? Not that lady-like business again, I hope. Look, if you want something, you go after it. Doesn't the Bible say God helps those who help themselves."

"I think that was Benjamin Franklin."

Maria giggled. "Okay, well then don't ask my advice."

"Hey, if I didn't want it, I wouldn't ask." Actually she knew she only wanted someone to tell her what she already knew she was going to do. She was looking for affirmation, and nobody but Maria could provide that the same way.

"You will never know if you don't try. What have you got to lose, girlfriend?"

"Pride?"

"That's worthless stuff. Sure won't keep you warm at night— not that we need any heat at the moment. Besides, you know I just said what you were already going to do." Rachel did know.

"Uh oh," Mark, who had changed into shorts and a T-shirt, said from the door. "Is my wife giving you advice, Rachel?" He wagged his finger at his wife who didn't look at all humbled. "No matchmaking, please."

Rachel laughed when she read the logo on his T-shirt--*Yes, I have heard the latest lawyer joke and it's not funny.*

"Stay out of this," Maria warned him. "You're just trying to save another man from the clutches of a woman."

"So who are you plotting against?"

Maria tossed the cut-up vegetables into the sizzling wok.

"You might know him," Rachel said. "Jake Donovan."

"Hmmmmm, with Border?" He snatched a piece of cauliflower from the pan. "Big guy, right? You interested in him, Rachel.

"He hasn't let me get close enough to know."

"Maybe he's gay."

Rachel shrugged. "Do you think he is?"

"If he isn't attracted to you." He laughed.

"Seriously," Rachel said, "what do you know about him?"

"I can't say I *know* him, but I've seen him in action. He was the arresting officer of a client of ours. On the stand, my partner, Alan, cross-examined him, tried to break apart his testimony-- the guy was a rock. I don't usually get involved with affairs of the heart, but it's about time you had a serious boyfriend." Mark's grin was teasing. "So, I'll make an exception. From what I know of that guy, don't play games, take the direct approach."

"You think so?" Rachel asked, trying to make up her mind. "It sounds like you almost liked him even though he was on the other side."

"My client got ten years at Florence and deserved every one." He grinned wryly. "That's the moral conflict when being a defense lawyer. Our job is to get the client off, to assume he is innocent unless we know for sure otherwise. Alan did his best in trying to break Donovan. He wasn't completely sorry when he couldn't."

Rachel stared beyond Mark and Maria, her thoughts mixed. "I wonder if I can."

"Beard the lion in his den," Maria repeated.

"I don't know where his den is," she said wondering how she'd get that information.

Mark grinned. "Turns out I know. I was there once with a friend. What's the address worth to you?"

"Okay, okay. You can have it." He laughingly put up his hands in mock defense when both women turned on him.

Asleep on his sofa, a bottle of whiskey on the table beside him, Jake tried to ignore the insistent knocking at his door. He didn't want to wake up. His week had been a tough one with too little sleep. What sleep he'd had been disrupted with dreams of a violent, chaotic confrontation with an enemy he couldn't see, meshed in crazy ways with visions of a woman he shouldn't want and couldn't have.

Finally he realized whoever was knocking wasn't going to quit. "All right," he yelled, stumbling to his feet. Not bothering to throw on a shirt, he pulled open the door wearing only a pair of worn jeans, unsnapped at the waist. He leaned against the door jamb wondering if he'd had more to drink than he remembered. "What are you doing here?"

"Well, you could invite me in to find out."

He moved aside. Following Rachel, still only half awake, he ran his fingers through his disheveled hair, uncertain of what was going on. He was nearly positive he was not dreaming; and although he'd had a big slug from the whiskey bottle, he was sober.

"How'd you find out where I live?"

"You have friends."

"Some friends."

She pushed newspapers aside and sat on one of his thread-bare chairs. "You look like you were asleep," she said. "I didn't mean to disturb you."

He slumped down onto his old sofa. Oh she was going to disturb him all right. She was wearing pale blue jeans, a sleeve-less, black, loose knit top and sandals. That long black hair hung down her back in a casual ponytail. He felt an urge to reach out and touch its silky length--an urge he sternly stifled.

"I was out all night on a stake-out." Another fruitless night spent looking for ghosts.

She looked around the room. 'You have an interesting home."

He snorted. "*Interesting?* Is that the new word for dump?"

"This house is not a dump." Her gaze went around the adobe walls, small paned windows, the generous use of wood trim. "It's old, territorial in design. They don't make homes with thick walls like these today."

"For good reason."

"It has spirit."

He laughed. "And I thought it was cockroaches."

She avoided looking at his bare chest because it made it more difficult for her to form logical sentences. All she'd surmised about his body had been true. Lean and muscular didn't begin to define those sinewy muscles, the long length of his limbs, the angles and shadows that emphasized masculine hardness. His face was safer-- even though those rugged features had twisted into an expression of irritation. She liked how his unshaven jaw jutted out stubbornly, his brow lowered as he considered her. A smile would have improved it.

"Next question. What are you doing here?" He reached for a cigarette from the pack on the end table and lit it.

The moment had come with still no answers. She had made the decision to come before she had that answer for him or herself. She knew if she took long enough to figure out what to say, she would lose her courage. "Well for starters, I think I owe you an apology."

"Why?"

"I rather pushed myself onto you that night. I knew you didn't want to have dinner with me."

"And so that led you to *push* yourself on me again?"

"Logic is not my forte. The apology was only an excuse."

He took a long drag on his cigarette. "For what?"

"For wanting to get to know you better."

He watched her through the smoke. "For kicks?"

She frowned. "Are you trying to make me mad?"

"Or get at the truth."

"It's obvious you don't have a high opinion of me, but you don't know me-- yet."

"And I'm not going to."

She gritted her teeth. She had not come to fight with him. "Because you don't want to," she said finally.

"Whatever I might or might not want won't be the point."

"And you don't want to find out?"

"Babe, I have been there before."

"Not with me though." She tried to read his expression in the darkening room. "Mind if I turn a light on?" She didn't wait for his approval before she reached for a switch on an ornate monstrosity that sat beside her chair. "Antique?" she asked, teasingly, hoping it would lighten the conversation.

He shrugged. "I don't need lights much."

"Why not?"

"It's cooler, and I like the dark," he said, taking another deep draw on the cigarette and receiving no relief from the nicotine.

"So you lurk in the dark," she said. "Hiding from something?"

"Isn't everybody?"

"What do you have to hide?"

"If I told you, it wouldn't stay hidden." He watched her, not wanting to see the long length of leg, the easy grace with which she crossed one over the other. Even with limited light he was missing none of it.

"What am I hiding?"

"Miss O'Brian, you are a rich girl thinking I am the flavor of the hour." He stubbed out the useless cigarette.

She rose to her feet, angered until she realized that was exactly what he had intended. "Why did you want to make me mad? Is that your defense mechanism?"

He smiled faintly, the expression in his eyes cold. "You'd be smart to leave now."

Gathering her thoughts, trying to keep from losing her temper, she walked to the window, staring at the red orb of the sun as it began to slide behind the mountain. Finally she turned back to face him. "You don't need anything, do you, Donovan?"

"I do my best not to."

"How is that working for you?" She sat back in the old chair.

"Well enough." Suddenly uncomfortable with the intensity of

her gaze, he grabbed a rumpled T-shirt from where he'd thrown it on the floor and pulled it on. "Look," he said, leaning back on the sofa, his head beginning to throb, "you want something. What is it?"

"What if I just want to get to know you and have you know me? Would that be so strange?"

"Writing a term paper?"

She laughed. "Of course, on a man who needs nothing."

"I didn't say I needed nothing." He grimaced. The headache had been there, thinly underlying his day. It seemed now to be coming on stronger, and he blamed that on her.

"Do you get headaches a lot?" she asked with another of her abrupt shifts that left him looking for grounding.

"Who said I had one."

"You did. Hey, I knew you had a stiff neck."

He looked up to see if she was joking. Before he could say anything, she had moved from her chair to kneel beside him on the sofa.

"This always helps my dad." She began kneading the corded muscles in his shoulders and neck. Her fingers were strong, and he found himself reluctantly relaxing beneath their ministrations. "You are so tight, so tense," she whispered, manipulating the large muscles as she rotated his shoulder. "Do you ever relax?"

He tried to tighten his defenses against the feelings she was arousing and found it impossible to do so. He had never had his neck rubbed, never had anyone even notice when he had a headache.

"Is this why you smoke?" she murmured as she kneaded the large muscle in his shoulder.

"I don't need a reason."

"Do you like this?" she asked, her voice low and melodious as her fingers worked their magic.

"How could I say no?"

"Why would you want to?" She had felt his muscles begin to relax. His mind was still tensed against her.

"If you don't know the answer to that, babe, you're not as bright as you look." He reached up and took hold of her hands, removing them from his shoulders, but somehow forgetting to let go of them. They were so small resting in his large palms, such fine-boned, narrow hands. How could they give such a forceful massage?

She sat beside him, nearly leaning against him; yet nothing but the sweet scent of her skin touching him. "Tell me about the stake-out," she said.

He tried to remember and couldn't. Her nearness, his body's awareness of her soft-feminine form next to his, had driven all thought from him. He'd been a long time without a woman.

"It's not been an easy day for me either," she said. "It's not like I've done something like this before... gone to a man's house, practically broken down his door, barged into his living room... and then giving him a neck rub he never asked for."

Abruptly, he rose from the sofa and moved to the fireplace, leaning against the mantle. He looked back at her, letting his gaze drift over her body. "A woman visits a man like this, she's asking for something. Better be sure it's what you have in mind."

Her eyes widened. He shook his head at her apparent naiveté or was it all an act? If it was, he'd never seen better. "You don't know me; know anything about the kind of man I am. How do you know I won't drag you into that bedroom and rape you? There'd be a lot who would say that's what you're asking for in coming here."

"I suppose I was being foolish... No, I wasn't. I knew you. I knew who you were before I came."

"You and I never met until a week ago. You don't know anything about me."

"We both know that's not the truth. You just won't admit it."

"You aren't into that soul mate junk are you?" he asked with a hard laugh. "It's all a lie, babe. There isn't anything but the flesh and the now. You want me. I want you. Then we forget each other's name. That's how it works."

"And you would know all about that?"

"Enough."

"Shall we find out if there is something else out there?"

"How would we do that?"

She walked across the room to stand beside him. She reached out and took his hand in hers. Her fingers were soft as they explored the roughness of his palm, the length of his fingers. "Maybe where it comes to something like this... like us, you're as inexperienced as I am." She reached up and stroked the side of his cheek, ran her fingers lightly along the scar. "How did you get this?"

"Cut myself shaving," he mocked.

Again her eyes met his, their darkness seeming to draw him into her. "You have deeper scars than this one, Jake Donovan. Who gave them to you?"

"You ask the damnedest questions."

"So tell me about this scar. I will learn about the others with time."

He didn't like the sound of that. The facial scar was safer. "It's an old story. Just a fight in a bar. I tried to break it up." He didn't need to tell her it had been his brother, who had gotten him into the fight. Jake had tried to help him... and again failed. "Lucky I didn't have any beauty to lose, wasn't it?" he asked sardonically to distract her and himself from more talk of scars.

"You have beauty." At his smirk, she smiled. "It's an unusual beauty, rough, rugged, like the desert." Her fingers traced the bones of his face. She felt his smile of disbelief against her fingertips.

He shook his head. "In about a minute, you are going to get more than you bargained for."

"Or you will. Look, it's simple. I want to get to know you. Have

RAIN TRUEAX

you know me and not carnally." She grinned. "Something is different here with what I feel with you. I'd like to know what it is."

"You're naive. Any other man and this would have turned ugly."

"But you aren't any other man."

He knew what the smart thing to say would be. No, I don't want to see you again. There is nothing here. But it'd be a lie. Something was there, but it wasn't something he could have. A smart man would end it before it created another scar. He knew how to end it. Except he wasn't willing to do it-- yet.

"Why don't we take it slow? We can start with what kinds of interests we share," she suggested.

He laughed. "Babe, you and I don't share any interests."

"Because our lives have been different, doesn't mean we might not have things we both enjoy. Do we laugh at the same jokes? Do you like cats, dogs or neither? Hot salsa or mild? Do you rent dramas or comedies at the video store? Or do you like the ones where the hero kills everybody by the end of the movie?"

She didn't quite know how it had happened, but they were back sitting on the sofa. He didn't touch her, but she did him as she let her fingers move across his face, feeling the bones under the skin. His face fascinated her. She thought about kissing his lips, but she knew that would start something she wasn't ready to finish... not yet.

"Assuming... I was open to this, not saying I am, how would we do it?" he asked.

She smiled. "How about starting with a bet?"

"You a poker player, babe?" He smiled. It wasn't a large smile, but as close to genuine as she'd seen on his craggy face. His eyes warmed; the gold highlights became more pronounced.

"All of life is a gamble, Donovan; so how about it?"

"What are you asking me to ante?"

She'd gotten more from him than she'd expected. Before he

thought better of all his objections and kicked her out, she decided she would leave. She reached for her purse. "When is your day off?"

"What's that got to do with a bet?"

"We could go for a picnic."

"You are kidding."

"No, I'm not."

He shook his head. "I don't go on *picnics.*" He couldn't believe her even suggesting such a thing. It wasn't just that he'd outgrown them. He'd never been on one, and he had no desire to start with a sexy little thing who didn't know what she did to a man when she touched him that way. The only reason he hadn't kissed her is he knew he wouldn't be able to stop if he started and wasn't sure she'd be able to either. If he had sex with her... He wouldn't think about that.

She stopped at the door, her hand on the knob. "Correction," she said, smiling back at him. "You didn't used to go on picnics. This is our first bet. That you will like it. Be ready... When was that day off again?"

"If I don't get called in--Saturday."

"Good. I know a wonderful place. It's only a short hike..."

He interrupted. "Hiking?" His scowl deepened. "I get enough exercise with my job and working out."

"What about aerobic exercise?"

"A--what?"

"You know, cardiovascular, aerobic. Exercises to clear that unhealthy smoke out of your lungs."

"I don't know about this, Rachel."

"Come on, it'll be fun."

He didn't like the word fun. Nothing that was supposed to be fun ever ended up that way.

"We will go somewhere pretty. We can talk and get to know each other."

"Great," he muttered, "just great." Picnics, hiking, and talking--probably talking about feelings.

"Come on, Donovan. Don't look so glum. I am betting you'll like it."

"And what are you anteing?" he asked as he stood. Rachel was struck again at his size and his sheer masculine presence. Maybe he was right. She had no idea what she was getting herself into. She shivered. How would she deal with a man such as this one? What was she putting up? Yet mixed with her own fear and doubts was her urge to reach out, to touch the muscular chest so clearly outlined under that thin T-shirt. And she knew the shiver she'd felt wasn't of fear.

His eyes darkened, their golden hue almost tiger like in the dimly lit room. He had such beautiful eyes when they weren't narrowed in anger. She wondered what he was thinking. The set of his lips was hard. She could imagine that when really angry, he would look merciless.

"I'll be here Saturday morning, bright and early," she said pushing her doubts aside. "Matilda and I will show you a place I'll bet even you've never seen." With that, she was up and out the door.

As Rachel turned up the long driveway leading to her home, she wondered if her father would finally be there. She wanted to tell him about Jake Donovan at the same time she knew she had nothing to tell and preferred to keep the tenuous possibilities to herself. The decision was made for her when she saw Diego Ramirez's truck in their driveway. She would mention nothing personal when her father's partner was anywhere near. From the time she'd met that *pachuco*, she'd had no trust for him. Those feelings had only grown.

As she crossed the porch, she heard her father call out to her.

She turned and looked down the long porch to see him sitting with Ramirez in the darkness.

"Princess," her father said, pulling her down for a quick kiss. "How's my girl?"

"Fine."

"You have mail on the hall table."

"Anything important?" she asked, wishing she could for once have a conversation with her father when Diego Ramirez wasn't hovering.

Her father shrugged. "One from a gallery in Jackson. I didn't know you had any of your work up there. The other from Randy, *I think.*" He grinned his big Irish grin. A tall man, though not so big as Jake, Michael O'Brian was muscular, his body lithe and strong, his iron gray hair still thick.

Rachel glanced toward Ramirez and made an attempt to be polite, something she didn't want to do but knew pleased her father. "Randy's handwriting is atrocious. It's a wonder any of my cousin's letters ever reach us, and it takes hours to decipher each one." She turned back to her father. "When did you get home?"

"A few hours ago. I wondered where you'd taken off for. No note."

"You haven't been home enough to know when to leave a note," she retorted and felt sorry when she saw his eyes narrow at the hit. Ramirez was as usual watching her, his eyes roaming over her body in a way that always made her feel as though she needed a shower to wash away the taint.

"I've been gone a lot," her father acknowledged, seemingly unaware of Ramirez's leering gaze. "But it seems to me that when I'm home, you aren't. We need to make a date for dinner and catch up."

"Don't forget to ask her," Ramirez prodded, his dark eyes shifting to Rachel's father.

"In a minute. How are your paintings coming? All ready for

the Sedona show?" O'Brian sat back down on the patio chair, ignoring Ramirez's angry grunt.

"All but maybe one or two iffy ones."

Ramirez interrupted. "We heard the cops have been out here."

How Rachel wondered. She didn't see Juna and assumed the part-time housekeeper was still taking care of her daughter after the birth of a baby, which meant she couldn't have told him anything. There had been nothing in the papers linking this ranch to the dead man. She didn't trust Ramirez and was not about to give him more information than required. "That is true. I found a dying man."

"Dying?" Ramirez hissed. "We heard you found a *dead* man."

Rachel looked into his eyes and wished she hadn't. His eyes were reptilian, they seemed to hypnotize as if they were trying to hold her, to see into her soul.

"He was barely alive." She felt irritated at her uneasiness around her father's partner. It wasn't his height, only a little more than an inch taller than hers, no it was in those eyes. This man carried secrets she didn't want to know.

"Did he say who he was?" Ramirez asked.

"He was dying," she repeated. "He couldn't tell me anything."

"Do the police have any idea what happened?" asked her father, looking out into the darkness beyond their yard, his expression hidden.

"From what they told me, no." Rachel considered a moment, then lied, "I assume they think what I do, that it was due to a misjudgment on his part."

"Who did you talk to?" Ramirez asked.

Rachel shrugged with pretended disinterest. "I don't recall names. A sheriff's deputy. Somebody from Border."

Ramirez turned away. He wandered to the edge of the porch, but she knew his ears missed nothing.

"Who is investigating?" her father asked.

Rachel thought a moment before she answered. "Why would

there be an investigation? I think it was just a stupid mistake by someone not used to the desert. It cost him his life."

"I realize you're tired, princess. I'll be up later if you want to talk about your show... or anything."

"Night, Dad. Maybe tomorrow." She felt relieved to escape from the tension she felt on the porch.

Even through the closed door, she could hear their voices-- Ramirez's curse, her father's answering low voice. Both men sounded angry. Had they been arguing when she came home?

CHAPTER 4

Saturday morning unsure if he would even be there, Rachel arrived at Jake's house ready for hiking-- hat, boots, shorts, tank top, a cotton shirt tied across her shoulders, and a light lunch, including water bottles in a backpack in her pick-up.

"Up late last night?" she asked, looking speculatively at the unshaven, rumpled man who opened his door, a pair of probably hurriedly pulled on jeans again his only attire.

Jake shook his head and winced at the effort. "You aren't," he asked as he stood aside to let her enter, "by any chance, a morning person?" His voice reflected the clear suggestion that if she was, it was one more strike against her.

"I love desert mornings, don't you?"

"Not when I can help it." He yawned and ran his fingers through uncombed hair.

"Have you had breakfast?" She grinned at the scowl on his face.

"I don't eat breakfast," he muttered, rubbing his neck.

"How do you expect to have the energy for a hike if you don't eat breakfast?" She pushed past him and into his kitchen.

He leaned against the door jamb as he lit a cigarette, watching her with a wary expression on his face.

"You don't have much food in here," she complained as she pulled out a fry pan and turned on a burner of his stove.

"What are you doing?"

"Isn't it obvious?" She grinned at the disheveled, sleepy eyed man. She felt something move deep inside her at the sight of those sinewy arms, that muscular chest. God, she'd never seen a man's chest with that kind of definition—not even in life drawing classes. She forced a calming breath and looked back into the refrigerator.

"It looks like you're planning to cook."

"You must be waking up."

"But... why?"

"I'm going to fix breakfast."

"I just told you. I don't eat breakfast."

"I know what you said, but you should." She dismissed his protest with a sweet smile. She broke a couple of eggs into a bowl; beat them up before pouring them into the pan.

He started to object again. "Hey," she said looking over her shoulder, "you have time for a quick shower, if you'd like." She pared the mold off the cheddar cheese smiling as she heard the door close and knew he'd given up the battle-- for the moment.

Still shaking his head, ten minutes later, he had showered, was dressed in shorts, t-shirt, and was sitting at his table, eating the scrambled eggs she had fixed, sipping a cup of good, strong coffee.

"I admit it. I am surprised you can cook," he said as he sat back in his chair to light another cigarette. "And even make good coffee."

"Is that supposed to be another thing rich girls don't do?" she asked teasingly, pouring more coffee into his cup.

Uneasy under his gaze, she got up from the table and set about washing the dishes. "If that's all right with you?" she asked cynically, waiting for another barb about rich girls and receiving instead a faint smile but a real one.

An hour later, they were driving up a narrow, dirt road into the Santa Rita Mountains northeast of Nogales. "Have you been here before?" she asked, the wind from the open window blowing her hair almost to him.

"North of my district."

"It's a pretty place. I come when I can; but since it's a fair drive from the ranch, I don't come often enough. My father and I used to bring a lunch and spend the day."

"I've never heard you talk about your mother."

"She died when I was twelve."

"That's sad—I guess."

"I still miss her, but my father did all he could to make up the loss.

"You're lucky then." His tone effectively closed the subject.

Parking the truck at a wide turnaround, she reached for the backpack which Jake took and shrugged into. She put the strap of a large canteen on her shoulder and pointed toward the trail. "That way," she said with a smile at his lack of enthusiasm. "Come on. You'll like it once we get going. You really aren't much for mornings are you?"

"Only when I have to."

"For work?" she questioned as she walked ahead of him on the trail.

He nodded, and then remembered she couldn't see him. "We usually work a month of days, a month nights. When we have a stake-out, it lasts all night. So morning seems like part of night. It's easier for me that way."

The morning air was still cool but it wouldn't be long before, even at this elevation, the heat would make walking less pleasant. The trail wound through scrub oak and tall grasses, along a mostly dry creek bed. "Farther up," she said, turning around to see how he was doing, "there is water in the creek."

Jake was having a hard time keeping his eyes on the trail and off her swaying hips and long, golden legs. *What am I doing up here?* he groaned to himself, forcing his eyes away from the temptation.

He took a couple of deep breaths, reminding himself of all the reasons he didn't want an affair with a woman like this as his loins argued against his logic. She didn't fit any of his criteria for quick sex with no complications. She would be nothing but complications until it was over-- and it'd be over all too soon. Would it be worth what it cost? He knew the answer to that one. So why was he there?

It seemed they climbed for hours, stopping now and then to take in the view of the Tumacacori Mountains across the valley floor. On one of their breaks for the water bottle, they sat on a log and watched the bees buzz around the wildflowers, which still were blooming in the shaded dells. Overhead a cardinal shyly approached then disappeared into the leaves of the oak.

As they climbed, he was impressed by the diverse variety of birds, birds he'd never noticed anywhere in his work. When he was out in the mountains, birds only mattered when they stopped chattering, alerting him to potential danger. Instead of something of beauty, they'd been an alarm system.

Crossing a lush meadow, the air was heavy with the scent of pine and hot summer day, a little brown lizard darted across the trail barely in front of his feet.

When Rachel finally said they were there, it wouldn't have mattered to him where *there* was. The stream had been tiny, as they'd followed it now and then up the trail. Sometimes it had disappeared underground, but here in this little glade, the water tumbled from the rocks dropping into a little pool, its edges rimmed with soft grass and big rocks. Overhead oak, cottonwood and locust trees provided dappled shade. Like many another island oasis in the mountains of the desert, the place was peaceful, Edenic. Better yet, for once he could enjoy it, not wondering if he would be shot by a smuggler with his next breath.

"It is a beautiful place," he said.

"Are you hungry?" she asked, squatting beside him and opening the backpack.

"I could eat."

"Since I didn't know what you liked, I took a chance on the food." She had packed roast beef sandwiches, grapes, wrapped slices of cheese and fizzy water on top of a chunk of ice wrapped in plastic.

"Looks good to me." He took a swig from the canteen before she handed him a bottle of Perrier. He grimaced when he saw what it was but took it. "No beer?" he asked as he drank from the cold but salty tasting water.

"Should I bring that next time?" She grinned as she handed him a thick sandwich.

"No, this is okay," he said, thinking it highly unlikely there would be a next time.

"Tell me, Jake," she said when she had finished half a sandwich, "how did you come to join Border Patrol? I know it's a tough job."

"Do you think these questions up or do they just come to you on the fly?" he asked, reclining on an elbow.

"For someone who investigates people for a living, you seem to have quite a dislike for questions."

"They're okay-- when I do the asking."

She smiled. "You can ask me some questions, if you like."

He pulled up a blade of grass and wished for a cigarette. He'd told himself it was because of high fire danger during the heat of the summer that he'd left them home.

"I guess you aren't. So are you going to tell me how you got into Border?" she repeated.

He shrugged. "No big story with it. It was just there. Growing up, I ran a little wild, in trouble with the authorities, right on the edge of big trouble. Finally, it came down to deciding on which side of the law I was going to land."

"Why Border? Why not a city cop?"

"I like the freedom, being outdoors. Living down here it was easy to see the need."

"And that's the whole story?"

"Most of it," he said, not offering to tell her more.

"So you were a bad little boy," she said with a soft smile. "Do you have brothers and sisters? Were they good or bad?"

"Good god, woman. This *is* an interrogation. Did you get me out here to grill me?"

"I did say I wanted us to get to know each other," she teased. "Truth or dare. Your turn next."

"Geesus, I'd be afraid of the answers," he said liking her quick laughter at his humor.

"Come on," she insisted. "Ask me something. There must be something you want to know."

He thought for a moment. "Why are we here?"

"It's a beautiful place. Where would you prefer to be on a Saturday?"

"Was that another question for me?" he smirked. She was sitting Indian fashion, like a young boy, which didn't make keeping his mind on possible questions that easy. He thought about kissing her but would one kiss be enough? He knew the answer to that one too.

"Where do your parents live?"

He frowned, and she knew she'd landed fully on one of those invisible scars. He stared into the little pool, and she thought for a moment he wasn't going to answer. When he spoke, his voice was husky. "Probably dead."

"Probably?" She quickly regretted the question.

"I have no idea about my father. I am not sure my mother even knew who he was." The words were said emotionlessly, as though they had no meaning. "Mom wasn't around much; then not at all. My brother and I were glad."

That wasn't true. He could still remember the feeling of desolation when he'd realized she was not coming back. No matter how lacking she'd been as a parent, when she'd been there, there'd always been the hope things might improve. She might find a boyfriend who didn't like to knock her sons around. She might find a job that allowed them to have clean clothes for school, enough food to eat. When she was gone, all hope for a normal life was gone. It was hardscrabble after that. Rachel would have no way of understanding.

"Does your brother live nearby?"

"Not too far. He's doing time in Florence."

"You mean prison?" she asked, trying to hide her shock.

"Twenty years--time off for good behavior. I put him there."

"Oh Jake, I'm sorry," she said, reaching out and lightly stroking his arm, "what happened?"

"Not an unusual story. While I was learning how to be a cop, he was learning the ropes of drug dealing. He had a partner. They got away with it for awhile--but then they met someone who told them they could make a real killing. John, like all the fools who think they can beat the system, thought he'd make his fortune and quit. You know they never do. They spend it all and are right back after the easy money again."

He stopped, staring beyond the pool now, at a desert willow. "I was on stake-out that night--pure coincidence. There'd been a tip about a shipment coming across, but I had no way to know it involved Johnny. When we saw them, they tried to shoot their way clear. My brother's partner was killed. John was hit in the leg. The big boy didn't do a day of time. They always walk, keep their hands clean. John was left holding the bag in every way."

"How did the big one get off?"

"No proof. There never is."

"That was tough for you to have to go through that."

"Harder for my brother."

"Was it?"

"He's the one doing time. I'm out here."

She could begin to see Jake Donovan imposed his own penalty on himself, maybe a harsher one than his brother's. "Do you see him often?"

"I'm not on his approved list," he said. "Look, I don't want to talk about this anymore."

"He can't blame you for what he did."

"Can't he?" Jake asked with a smile that was anything but real.

"I don't see how. You were doing your job."

"It's not that easy. He blamed me for being on the wrong side of the law. I don't suppose you can understand any of this."

"I can try."

"Let it go, Rachel. Look, I don't get it." The expression in his eyes hardened. "What's a woman, who looks like you, doing with a guy with a face like mine, a guy whose own mother couldn't stand him, who has a brother doing time? I'm not your kind of guy, Rachel O'Brian."

She leaned forward, reaching out, lightly tracing his face with her fingertips, her fingers wreaking havoc with his resolve to keep everything casual between them. "How do you know what my kind of guy is?" she asked huskily, trying to keep her tone light and knowing she was failing.

"I am an ugly man, inside and out."

Her fingers tipped his chin up and she looked into his eyes. "Obviously," she whispered, "we don't see your face the same way. Know what I see when I see you?" She didn't wait for an answer. "I see a strong face but with too much sadness. Your face is like the desert, craggy and rugged. The desert is not ugly but beautiful."

Before he could respond, she pressed her fingers against his lips. "You've protected yourself all these years by not caring. You figured that worked." She felt an almost unendurable surge of sadness to think of what Jake had said and not said about the little boy he'd been, the man he was. She wondered then why she knew so well who he was inside. She knew it better than he knew himself. She had no answer for why that might be true.

"It does work."

"Does it? Or has it only left a lonely boy inside a lonely man?"

"People do what they have to do. I don't want pity."

She shook her head. "I don't pity you, but can't I feel sympathy for what you've been through?"

"Are you a fixer upper? One of those women who goes around finding people who need somebody to redo them."

She laughed. "So you think I'd want to remodel you?"

"You sure couldn't want me as I am, but I don't want remodeling. I am not here for any woman and that's how it is."

"It's how it has been."

"You don't give up. Listen, I told you about my brother so you'd see this interest you think you have in me is not going to work."

"Because of your past? The past is just that—done and gone."

"It colors today, tomorrow. You see your world in bright, shiny colors. You've grown up to be a princess, surrounded by luxury."

"And what have you grown up to be, Jake?"

He stared at her. "What are you getting at?"

"Back to the start of all this conversation. Why did we meet?"

His smile was faint. "I do a fair amount of interrogations, and that sounds like a trick question to me."

"Not really, but you said you'd never normally have been where you were that day. You didn't have to decide you'd be the one to come out to the ranch. Don't you ever think that some people are meant to meet? It's fate. I won't say why or even know, but there is more going on with human life than meets the eye."

"Babe, it's all biology."

"I don't think it is. I think with you and me there was something there that first day, and we both could have walked away from it. You would have."

"And why didn't you?"

"Because I hadn't felt it before, that magnetic pull to get close to a man, to learn who they were, to follow the trail where it went with them. I wasn't sure I ever would again if I walked away from what was possible."

"What is possible is a dead-end."

"I won't deny that could be, but don't you want to know—for sure? Some things aren't logical. Feelings don't always fit facts. Sometimes though they are strong enough to surmount what might seem insurmountable."

"You think that's what this is?"

"Jake, ours is a story that hasn't yet been written. It could be by us." Her smile was confident and so sexy that he felt as though the wind had been knocked from his lungs. "How would you write our story? If I am the princess, who are you?"

"I wouldn't write a story about us because there isn't an us."

"No imagination," she teased. "Want to hear mine?"

He shook his head.

"The princess looked over the men in her father's kingdom and everyone was found wanting for one reason or another. One was handsome, but so boring. Another was pretty but nothing behind his eyes. She had decided she would have no prince at all, no marriage if they were all her choices."

"Poor little princess," he teased.

"She was very strong-willed. Then one day she heard of a dragon. Several of the princes suggested they would slay him to win her favor. She felt that was very unfair and went out to meet him for herself."

"She does sound like you."

"Be still. Do you want to hear this story or not?"

"If I said no, would you stop?"

"Well, she met him and saw he was indeed fearsome, big,

63

strong, but oh so beautiful in her eyes. She went back to her father and told him that she would have none but the wild dragon."

"I'm sure her father was thrilled."

"Well, what could he do—as we have established, she was very stubborn and so he agreed."

"And then he turned into a handsome prince as soon as they married."

She laughed, the sound went deep into his soul. It was both joyous and so precious that he wanted to find a way to hold onto the memory of it for when it was gone from him.

She leaned against him, her lips inches from his. "God, what a terrible ending that would have been when it was the dragon she wanted. A dragon, who hadn't ever learned how to love, who was powerful but didn't realize how powerful. Who was beautiful but thought he was ugly. He stayed a dragon, but her dragon."

His arms went around her and he pulled her against his hard length. "There would have had to be limitations to their love story," he whispered his lips nearly against hers.

"They would go to bed together in his cave, but then after they went to sleep, they met in the sky every night. They made love as spirits and the love was the best she had ever known or could ever imagine."

"So dragon or human babies? He was grinning.

"She wanted only dragon babies and since she was so used to having her way, that's what they were."

Now he laughed. "You are a nut."

"I know and... I'm not much of a princess either."

"As close as I'll come to one."

"Jake, tell me about your dreams," she said, running her fingers down the large muscle of his back, "and what you want from life."

"I don't dream; there's no point to it." He knew he was making a mistake even as he drew her into his arms. He had been putting off kissing her-- not sure if he was protecting her or himself. He felt her soft body against him, the intoxicating scent of her skin, that blend of woman and flowers. He felt drunk with it. He gave her a moment to pull back, but she didn't. She waited. He pressed his lips gently against hers. At first that was enough but then her mouth opened wider, inviting him within as she pressed against him, her hands on his back pulling him into her.

He wasn't sure how it happened, but the kiss went out of his control. He had never felt anything like it. A desert storm came closest. The power built between them, as though they were becoming one in a way that couldn't be real. Moments were lost to him. All he could feel was her, and the energy that was coming from her to him, maybe from him to her

His tongue delved into her soft mouth, felt its sweet warmth, her hesitant response. When she finally broke off the kiss and sat back, it left him feeling a part of him had left with her.

It was a moment before she spoke. She was watching him when she did. "Someday I'll paint you just like that."

"Good lord, after kissing you think of painting."

"It all goes together for me."

"Pretty ugly painting."

She shook her head. "No, it would be beautiful." She moved far enough away to study his body. He lay back, one leg bent, his arms now behind his head, as he wondered what she was thinking. Finally he felt uneasy at the intensity of her stare. She was sucking him into herself without touching. Her eyes stripped him bare, looked into his inner places, and he knew she saw the things he'd been hiding all of his life. Who the hell was she? With a wary insight into himself, he knew if this didn't end soon, she would destroy him when she left; but he also knew he wasn't going to turn away.

"Looks like that storm that's been building is on its way," Jake observed as they walked back down the trail. The sky was darkening overhead. Rain was falling across the Tumacacoris. He heard the first boom of thunder rumble across the sky. The wind blowing the way it was, within moments it would be all around them.

"We're going to get wet." She grinned up at him. Lightning streaked down, striking near Sardina Peak, followed by the crash of thunder. "I love a desert storm." The wind was whipping her hair all around her face.

"They're better when you're under a roof."

"A roof, a thunderstorm, and someone to share them with. What more could anyone ask?" Her eyes gleamed with excitement. As the first raindrops fell around them, splattering on the dry trail, they began running. By the time they reached Matilda, they were soaked and laughing. The air was still hot, although cooling off fast with the heavy rain.

Rachel crowded in under the steering wheel, while Jake ran around. Within moments, the lightning prongs flashed again, followed almost immediately by the crash of thunder, nearly deafening in its intensity.

He pulled her out from under the steering wheel and onto his lap. His arms were tight around her, holding her against his soaked body. She reached up for his kiss, savoring the taste of the rain water on his lips, then his tongue delving into her mouth. She'd never been kissed like he kissed. She thought it would never be possible to get enough of him. She clung mesmerized by his power, an energy so much greater than the storm raging outside the truck.

"I can't see this working out between us, but I won't say I don't want it. That scares me, babe."

"I didn't think anything scared you."

"Well now you know better." He put his hands to her breast, cupping it through the wet shirt, teasing her nipple, feeling it turn hard under his fingers. If she wanted this, he wasn't going to turn away from it.

"Jake," she said as she pulled away. "I know we are grown adults and all but... can we give this some time before..."

"Some time? Don't you get it, this isn't going anywhere. I can't fit in your world, and you can't in mine."

"Could we find out first?"

"Are you a tease, babe?"

"I... I don't think so. I just want it to be more for either of us than... what's that thing they call it—a quick lay?"

Since he couldn't see it being anything but that, he didn't say anything.

"We could get to know each other first."

"Damn, you keep coming back to that knowing bit. Okay, supposing I went along with it, how would we do that?" He couldn't believe what he had just heard himself saying.

"Well, let's start easy-- with your world. Not your job but your social life."

"Social life," he snorted. He thought of a dimly lit tavern, its air sullen in the heat, of its smoky atmosphere and the people who sat at its tables and leaned on its bar—none of them friends. "You'd love my world."

"Okay, so that's a good start, don't you think?"

"Monday. After work."

"It's a date," she said, ignoring the note of irony in his voice.

Yeah, he said to himself as she started the truck's engine, *it's a date. One you'll never forget and one that will make you shuck this dragon as soon as you can, princess.* He didn't ask himself why he wanted her to be the one to do it.

CHAPTER 5

B ack at the ranch, Rachel went straight into her studio to begin working on a rough sketch of Jake. She didn't need him to pose for her painting; his image was etched in her mind. She could see him smiling wryly, the corners of his expressive mouth barely tilted up, then frowning, his brows lowering with irritation, then those golden eyes widening with surprise, but none of those images was the one she wanted.

She bent over the table, picking out tubes of paint. She already knew the colors, saw the basic composition to use, the expression she would capture on the canvas. She only rarely painted portraits but his would be a portrait of the desert and a man.

The knock at the door didn't stop her work. "Hi, come on in."

Michael O'Brian sat down on a stool as he watched her sorting through the canvases until she found the right size. "What are you up to, honey?"

"Just an idea I want to try." She readjusted the easel for the larger canvas and set it on the support.

"You haven't been home much lately."

She stopped and looked at him. "You were here to notice? It

seems for months you've been on the road all the time. I've been staying with Maria just to... have someone to talk to. Of course, also to have time with my god children." A small lie. "Maybe I will rent an apartment in town... or a little house, like we've talked before."

"Lots of changes," he said with a smile. "Sedona show still set for the middle of next month, right?" He glanced at the framed canvases stacked in neat slots along the wall.

She nodded. "Are you going to be able to come to the opening?"

"If I have to, I'll fly up. I always want to be there for you, princess."

"Well, I've understood that you are busy." She stopped tightening the screws on her easel to look with concern at him. "Are you getting enough rest, Papa? You look tired."

"It's been a grueling six months, but I may be changing businesses soon. Things ought to let up then." He leaned his elbows onto her table, his gaze intent on her.

"Dare I hope that means partners too?"

"You don't like Diego," he said, not asked.

"There's something in his eyes. Something I can't explain, but I wish you'd find someone else to work with."

"Once you begin some things, it isn't easy to get out of them," her father mused.

Rachel frowned. "What sorts of things?"

"I don't want to worry you about my business problems. You get yourself ready for the opening, and let me take care of Diego Ramirez."

"At one time, I thought maybe you hoped there would be a more permanent merger with Mr. Ramirez. One involving me."

"I'd be in hell before I'd let that happen," O'Brian said coldly, "Diego may have hoped that. I can't say. He's an odd bird. I was glad you never wanted to be involved with him, but you are old enough to be finding someone, to think about marriage. I'd feel better if I knew you had a man if something ever happened to me." She looked at him again, aware of the strain in his voice.

"It's been that little problem of meeting the right person." She wasn't ready to talk about Jake. There were so many variables and uncertainties attached to him that she wanted to be sure of his intentions before she said anything.

"Sure you aren't looking for the *perfect* man?" he questioned with a grin. "You know there is no such animal, right?"

Letting her voice deepen, she imitated his. "Men are no good, out for everything they can get and not to be trusted. Always assume they don't mean any of the promises they make. Be careful because they are beasts!"

He laughed. "Now I didn't put it quite that way, but you do have to be careful. There are a lot of men out there who do not have honorable intentions toward beautiful young women."

"Sometimes women aren't honorable toward men either."

"That's the warning fathers give to sons." He smiled. "Get out more, princess. An apartment in town is a good idea. Or maybe even in Tucson, just to meet more people. Go to the right places where you can meet a nice guy, one like Mark Sandoval, a guy who wears a suit, comes home on time for dinner. You won't find a man like that out in these hills."

Rachel smiled, thinking how little Jake would fit her father's criteria for a husband. Remembering Jake's childhood, with no parental love, she felt a renewed surge of gratitude for the stability and love her father had provided especially after her mother died. "I love you," she whispered, moving over to kiss his bristly cheek.

"I love you too, honey. You know I just want you to be happy."

"Hey, you should take some of your own advice; find a woman to be with, to marry."

He laughed with disbelief. "That's different. I'm an old man."

"Hah," she snorted, remembering the power of his body as he hugged her.

He started to leave, but then turned back. "Hear anything more about the man who died out here?"

"No. Why?"

"Nothing. I just wondered. I'll leave you to your work. See you at dinner."

~

"We have to quit meeting this way," Jake quipped as he walked into his office Monday morning to find Bannister sitting on the edge of his desk-- now wearing jeans and a t-shirt.

"Where have you been?" the agent asked, his eyes scanning Jake, as though expecting to find the answer in his face.

"Why?" Jake asked. "Somebody need me?"

"I needed you, tried calling you. You weren't home. I thought Saturday and Sunday were your days off. I need your cell phone number."

Jake smiled. "First of all, I hardly ever carry a cell phone. A lot of where I am they don't work anyway. Second, who appointed you my mother?"

"You were going to take me out." Bannister feigned a look of disappointment.

Jake laughed as he threw his Stetson onto the cabinet at the same time reaching for the pack in his shirt pocket. He lit the cigarette. Bannister reached for one and lit it.

"I didn't think you smoked."

"I quit regularly. This seems like a good time to start again."

"Too much stress? Maybe a change of job?"

"I'm thinking about it."

"Last time I came in, you were in my chair. This time you're just sitting on my desk. We're making progress. And what do you mean I promised to take you out? This is beginning to sound like a serious relationship, and I don't do those."

Bannister moved off the desk and slouched into one of the

chairs in front of it. "You think this is funny. I needed to talk to you," he grumbled sulkily.

Smiling grimly, Jake watched as the handsome agent rose and paced the length of the room. Whatever was bothering the guy had to involve Franklin and that investigation. He could ask, but he'd be in a stronger position if he forced the agent to reveal whatever he'd come to talk about. So he waited.

"I got clearance from my boss to talk frankly with you about our case," Bannister said, sliding down again into the chair as he took a long drag on the cigarette. "I can give you everything we know."

"Why me? It's not like this fits my work parameters."

"There are reasons."

"Okay, assuming I agree what will you want?" Jake asked, drawing deeply on his own cigarette.

"You are a suspicious man, Donovan."

Jake snorted. "You wouldn't be here if you didn't want something."

Bannister looked at him for a moment before he nodded with a faint smile of agreement, his blue eyes amused. "Diego Ramirez." The name was an unwelcome reminder, and Jake leaned back in his chair, watching Bannister through the cloud of smoke they had created. "What do you know about him?"

Jake put his feet up on his desk and stared at the ceiling. "So it *is* me you want-- not Border."

"Yes, it's you."

"Mostly what I know, you already know. Ramirez operates in the no man's land along the border where the Mexicans haven't cared or been able to do much and where we are too busy stopping people coming across to work in the States to concentrate on the guys like him."

"He has no record."

"Nope. He's smart. He lets someone else take the fall. We haven't been able to nail him for even jaywalking."

"You know more than that."

"You want me to tell you what you already know?"

"Maybe we don't."

Jake snorted. "Okay, he has a virtual fortress in the mountains southwest of Nogales, stretching from just south of the border a good fifty miles into Mexico. He is good at what he does. I give him credit for that. He has probably thought up more creative ways to bring drugs across the line than any runner I know. On vegetable trucks, low-flying aircraft, men with backpacks, immigrants. You name it; he's done it, and we've been just behind him. Always too late or in the wrong spot. When we do stop a shipment, it's not traceable to him." Smiling wryly, he added, "However, the last I heard, he was smuggling drugs--not ceramics."

"And now the personal-- between you and him."

Jake clenched his jaw and felt the telltale muscle begin to twitch in his cheek. So Bannister knew that too. "There's nothing personal between that scum and me."

"I never settle for learning what's written on forms. I check newspapers, ask questions. You two have a history."

"Since you already know, why'd you ask?"

"Because I need more. The things that don't get in the papers. I want to know how he thinks, operates. We have every reason to believe he is involved in the antiquities—up to his eyebrows. There is a new shipment coming up. With Franklin gone, we don't know enough to stop it. I want him. I want him real bad. And so do you."

"My involvement with him is old history, too dusty to be of interest. Why would I care about him anymore?"

Bannister leaned across Jake's desk. "Because you never have forgotten and neither has he."

The cigarette dangled from Jake's lips as his gaze drilled into the agent's. He blew out a breath before he took it in his fingers. "Before I answer your question, I have one. What makes you think he's switched from pot to pots and how solidly have you connected him to Franklin?"

Bannister sat back down, his turn to study the ceiling. "A few years ago Ramirez decided he needed a front, something to lend legitimacy to his money. He went into the import-export business with a partner. For awhile, that might have been all it was, but Ramirez can't do anything without looking for the angles, the big money. Artifacts appealed to him several ways. One they are lucrative. Two he already had a network. It only required redirecting it. And three, he's fascinated by some of the artifacts himself—on an occult level. From what we hear, he has an impressive private collection. I'm not saying he doesn't still deal drugs as his main source of money, but antiquities are a lucrative sideline, possibly his source of power—or so he thinks."

Jake shook his head. "This is all a little hard to swallow."

Bannister smiled. "According to what our agent sent before he disappeared, Ramirez thinks he's descended from some Aztec emperor. Maybe old Montezuma himself for all I know. By his reckoning those treasures are his by right of creation and conquest." Bannister cleared his throat. "There was a lot of violence in that culture. It fits right up Ramirez's alley. So, to plunder its treasures and that of the rest of Mesoamerica fits him perfectly. You might say he's become addicted to it. He sells what he doesn't want and keeps building his own collection as a way to become godlike—invincible."

"If that's all so, he's making mistakes—something he hasn't been in a habit of doing." Jake felt a certain sense of satisfaction to think that might be possible. "Addicts lose sight of safety, of commonsense. Their judgment ends up skewed."

"We think he's starting to unravel. One mistake was with the partner he hooked up with. The other with Franklin. Franklin was never meant to be found. Somebody got careless."

"I haven't seen any mistakes yet. If you had, he'd be in jail waiting a hearing."

"Aren't you curious who his partner is?" Jake knew what the answer would be before Bannister said, "It's Michael O'Brian."

"I can't see why he'd do that. Why get involved with a sleaze like Ramirez? The Circle O is worth millions. He doesn't need the Ramirezes."

"It's possible O'Brian was naive, didn't know, let himself get sucked in and then couldn't get out. Maybe the ranch is in hock and cattle won't bring it out."

"You already know that's possible, I guess, or you'd not have said it."

"Their business together is called Montezuma Enterprises."

"Catchy title."

"Fitting also."

"Well, so what? Like you said, O'Brian could be the legit side of the business."

"Could be," Bannister said. "Could be there's a tooth fairy too. The truth of it is I don't know and can only go by what we'd learned before, which is that O'Brian is in it up to his neck."

"Learned?"

"Don't ask me how."

"Sounds like one of your plea bargaining arrangements which are worth exactly nothing so far as truth is concerned."

"I think this one is." Bannister watched as Jake smashed his cigarette into the ashtray. He stood and walked to his file cabinet, trying to give himself a moment to consider what he was hearing. What was it Bannister wanted from him? He watched the agent as he smoked calmly. This guy really never let anything show on his face. Jake could see where this was heading and didn't like any of it.

"O'Brian could be innocent," Bannister said. "We don't know, but you could find out, couldn't you?"

"No!"

"I know you're seeing her."

"You've had me followed?" Jake's gaze narrowed.

Bannister went on as though he hadn't heard the question. "Could be O'Brian is in a trap, maybe an unwilling partner. Ramirez can use very persuasive methods when he wants something."

Jake sucked in his breath as he considered the ramifications of that statement. Was Rachel in danger?

"We have to look at facts," Bannister said. "The facts are the Circle O isn't running cattle these days. Where's O'Brian getting operating capital? We've studied the books for Montezuma Enterprises, and it isn't turning enough profit either—at least not that's on the surface."

Jake felt a headache starting. Bannister was going on. "O'Brian could be in over his head. Maybe he's the boss of the scam. I don't know, and I want to. How much do you know about Rachel O'Brian?" Bannister persisted.

"Enough to know she'd not be involved in any of this."

"We are also assuming that, but her father is and that touches her.

"I won't spy on her family for you."

"I could bring her in for questioning."

"No, you couldn't, not if you didn't want Ramirez to know you are onto him." Jake sat back down. "Run your bluff with somebody else, Bannister."

Bannister shrugged and blew out smoke. "It was worth a try. Her father is and that alone will hurt her. You could prove he isn't. If he is, you might be able to protect her from what comes next."

"I'm going to tell you something, Bannister. The reason I went into Border was it's clean. I don't have to use people. Don't have to spy, and I don't intend to start now. I don't use people like some."

If that bothered Bannister, he didn't let it show on his face. "You know from personal experience what kind of man Ramirez is. He has to be stopped. His killings are particularly disgusting. I've got some photos that would turn your stomach."

"I've seen them for real. It won't work."

"You've gone undercover before."

Jake smiled coldly, as he lit another cigarette, an anger inside him that threatened to get the better of him. "That was a long, long time ago. Give it up. I won't spy for you or anybody else."

"We'll see."

"It's a permanent no, Bannister," he snapped, taking the smoke deep into his lungs. "And stay away from Rachel O'Brian."

"We'll talk about this again," Bannister said heading for the door.

"The answer won't change."

Bannister smiled the cigarette dangling from his lips. "We'll see, won't we?"

The rest of Donovan's day went no better. As a personal favor, a friend asked him to go out to a small ranch house a few miles north of Nogales. An old couple, Frank and Jennifer Morris, had been savagely beaten in their home and left for dead. They had been discovered early that morning. The man had been dead when they found them, but the woman had been rushed to the hospital. It was something with which Border had no reason to become involved.

As he drove up the driveway, past the gate, where Arizona State and Santa Cruz County police cars were already parked around the house, he had to wonder how any violent act could happen in such a peaceful setting. Big trees, a small old adobe home, a few beleaguered flowers struggled to bloom in the summer heat. The house was off the main road, no near neighbors to have heard a disturbance. In the yard, there were lab people looking for tire marks or footprints, any kind of evidence, no matter how faint.

He should have been surprised, but wasn't, to see David Bannister standing talking to one of the forensic experts. "We gotta stop meeting like this," Jake said with a smirk.

"Can't stay away from you, big guy," Bannister retorted. "You just don't realize the power of your magnetism."

"This isn't the kind of thing I would've figured would interest you."

"Nor you," Bannister quipped with a wry grin.

"I'm here for a friend."

"Coincidence, huh?" Bannister waited a moment before he decided he wasn't going to get an answer and smiled.

The two men stepped over the yellow tapes. Donovan leaned, to look at the footprint that was being cast. "Probably a nephew or something," the forensics man said, "but you never know."

Inside the house Jake grimaced.

"A man thinks he gets hardened to this kind of thing," Bannister muttered.

Mixed with the little knickknacks collected over a lifetime-- dream catchers hanging from arches, stained glass animals in front of windows, a Madonna still stood on a piano--were the unmistakable signs of violence and death. Blood splattered the walls, end tables were knocked over, lamps broken, most of which looked to be senseless vandalism.

"What kind of animal would do something like this," he asked, half sickened by the smell of blood and the destruction of a house that had clearly been one of peace.

"Could be trying to make it look like a burglary," Bannister suggested.

Jake shook his head. No burglar bothered with this senseless kind of violence. This looked like a psycho or an expression of violent hatred. It could all have been done to distract anyone from finding the real reason behind what had happened.

The lock at the back door had been broken. It probably hadn't taken much, just a light chain, an old fashioned lock. They weren't people who had expected to be attacked.

Kneeling to study the marks on the floor of the living room, the heavy pooling of blood, Donovan guessed the old couple had been herded into this room, then beaten savagely. It might have been enough to make him lose his breakfast--if he had eaten one.

On the walls were family pictures, a whole history of a life, and it had come to this. There were no words. He too had seen a lot, but it never got easier.

"Hope somebody pays for this," he said half under his breath.

Bannister shook his head. "Usually they don't. There might be a few smeared fingerprints, maybe a shoe print, but..." He shrugged. "If the woman doesn't recover consciousness, we may never know why. Even if she does, maybe not, as she may not know why either unless it was a friend or relative."

Some friend," Jake said, taking one last look. "I can't imagine these people having enemies. More likely stranger to stranger, the hardest thing to catch unless somebody noticed a different car and cared enough to note make, even a license plate; but with no near neighbors, that's unlikely."

He looked more closely at the blood smears on the wall, unsure what made him do so, but a closer inspection led him to believe someone had deliberately put the marks there. "You see this, Bannister?" he asked.

"Yeah, now... Kind of a design?"

Jake shook his head. There were several marks, mostly horizontal and vertical lines, but one appeared to be a kind of distorted cross, maybe a swastika. Could the Morrises have offended some kind of bigot, maybe a Nazi sympathizer?

"Make sure you get some close-up photos, just in case someone figures out what this means later and in case fingerprints show up when under a microscope."

Bannister nodded.

"I know I don't have any official reason to be here, but suppose you could get a copy to me too?"

"Sure, no problem." Bannister stared thoughtfully at the marks.

Walking back to his Bronco, thoughts of Rachel flooded Jake's mind, her beautiful face, the light in her lavender eyes, the gentle curve of her hip, the scent of her hair. He instantly regretted letting the image come to him in this place of death and destruction. Reflecting on her soothed him at the same time it left him more convinced than ever that their worlds could not come together. With the coming night, he would prove that to her and to himself.

∾

"Hi," Rachel called from the doorway of his office. Her long black hair was pulled back in a youthful ponytail. White jeans clinging to slender hips and a loose fitting green jersey top, outlining rounded breasts, made him wonder where it was safe to look.

"Bad day?" she asked in that intuitive way of hers and perched on his desk.

"You could say that."

She leaned over, her lips lightly touching his, nipping his lower lip, then letting out a little squeak as he pulled her onto his lap and gave her what she had clearly been wanting.

"Mmmm," she sighed after a long satisfying moment, her arms around his neck, her lips caressing his temple, "Nice greeting."

"There's more where that came from." He buried his nose in her neck, inhaling the clean, fresh scent of her skin. Perhaps it could erase the scent that had seemed to travel with him all day, the scent of senseless death and destruction.

"Lucky me," she murmured, running her fingers through his hair. "So is this the test? If it is, you can be sure I like it."

He couldn't stop the smile until he remembered again all the reasons it could never happen between them. Tonight would show her too. "No," he whispered, "you have to wait for that."

"Jake."

"What?"

"Just, Jake. I like saying your name. Like the way it sounds when I say it. Jake is a good, strong name. Is it Jacob?"

He smiled. "So they tell me." With a deep breath, he pushed her lightly from his lap. "Come on," he said gruffly, taking her hand, "let's go."

She drove her truck, following him to his house where he took a quick shower and changed. Five minutes later found him parking in the gravel lot beside the Lone Star.

"This is it," he said, glancing over to see what she thought. The front of the building was adobe; at one time, a steer had been painted on its dirty white surface, but now only a horn and hindquarter remained. An outlined neon star, the word 'Lone' at its center, hung over the door. Three old pick-ups and a couple of beater cars were parked in the gravel lot.

"A bar?" she questioned with what he thought looked like a hesitant smile.

"It's where I come after work."

She reached for the handle of the door and was out of his truck before he was. "What happened today?" she asked as they walked toward the entrance. The way she asked it, made it seem the most normal thing in the world to be walking into this bar with her, for her to be asking how his day had gone, as though she'd done it all a hundred times.

"Let's just leave it that it was not a good day," he said, not wanting to talk about Bannister's questions or the blood-filled house. He pushed open the door to the dim interior and allowed her to precede him. A country song about lost love blared through the smoky interior.

The look on Mac's face was almost worth the whole thing. "How ya doin'," Mac asked Jake as they reached the bar and sat on the stools.

"The usual for me. How about you, babe?"

She looked around the bar. Then gave Mac one of those

smiles that still left Jake reeling—and now obviously Mac too. "Corona with a twist of lime?"

Jake lit a cigarette and introduced the two as the barkeep set their beers in front of them. "Actually his name is Damian MacLeod, but Mac's easier to remember after a night here."

"Glad to meet you, Mac," Rachel said. "They tell me bartenders know everybody's secrets. Can I cajole some of Jake's out of you?" She smiled teasingly.

"Nobody knows Donovan's secrets," Mac retorted grinning back at her.

A hand on Jake's shoulder reminded him he hadn't counted on one thing when he had decided to bring Rachel here. Krista looked up at him, and then turned her gaze toward the woman at his side. "What have you been up to, Jake?" she asked, her eyes not leaving Rachel's face.

"Not much," he responded laconically, wishing he could read Rachel's mind as she looked around the room at the kinds of people who were sitting at the tables or leaning on the bar. As he introduced them, Rachel and Krista looked at each other as though meeting someone from another world. Which in a sense, they were. Krista for once, at a loss for words, drifted off.

"Want to leave?" Jake asked Rachel.

"We just got here."

"You can't want to stay," he retorted, knocking ash from his cigarette.

"I can't?" She looked over at Mac who was still gaping at her. "Hot today, wasn't it?" she said conversationally as she sipped the beer he had handed her.

"A scorcher."

Jake leaned against the bar and surveyed the room as was his wont. He never liked being in a room without knowing who else was there. "Strangers?" he asked Mac, gesturing toward three men sitting at a corner table.

"They come in Saturday night for the first time. *Pachucos*," he said with a sneer.

Rachel glanced toward them. "They do look like toughs," she agreed.

"Well, if they're looking for trouble, they won't be here long. I run a quiet, respectable place."

Jake looked more closely at the three men. They were Hispanic, roughly garbed, whispering, and gesturing toward the bar. Their eyes appeared to be on Rachel. This was a problem he hadn't considered. She was an unusually beautiful woman in any environment, but in a place like this, she stood out like a valuable diamond ring in a dime store. For not the first time, he was glad of his own big size, his ugly, mean-looking face. Most men would think twice before approaching her with him at her side.

To his surprise, the men sidled to the bar; one man beside Rachel while the other two stood on Jake's left. "You are a very beautiful woman, señorita," the lone man said.

Rachel ignored him.

"But what are you doing with such an ugly one?" The man gestured toward Jake. "A woman like you, she needs a man who is pretty, more like me. Is this man good in bed?" He gestured toward Jake. "That would be the only reason I could see for you to choose to be with him."

Jake lifted Rachel up onto the bar, standing in front of her, protecting her from all three by his bulk. "Ask me," he said, looking down at the insulting Mexican, then over at his two companions who had remained silent.

"Why would I want to do that, when you are so ugly, *compadre*? It is much more better to talk to the beautiful señorita." He tried to move around Jake but found his way blocked.

"I think it's time for you and your friends to leave," Mac snapped. "Or I'll call the cops." He picked up his bat as an added incentive.

83

The first Mexican man smiled silkily. "I like this place. Give me another beer."

"You heard Mac," Jake said, stubbing out his cigarette, never taking his eyes from the man in front of him.

"We don't need to hear from you, ugly one. I don't much like ugly faces," one of the two who'd been quiet said as he laughed, muttering a crude expletive.

Jake wiped his hands on his jeans. Turning slightly, he spun Rachel around and lifted her over the bar to land beside Mac. He nodded at Mac knowing he'd keep her safe. Unfortunately, Rachel was not cooperating, and he heard her yell something impolite just as one of the Mexicans lunged at him demanding his total attention.

Jake kneed the small man in the groin, his fist dispatching him to the floor where he collapsed in a heap. The second landed a surprisingly solid punch against his jaw, which sent Jake reeling away from the bar.

He could hear screams as he lashed out with his fists at the nearest body and felt a meaty connection just before another fist grazed his own belly.

He wasn't worried about a fist fight, confident he could handle three men the size of these, but when he saw the flash of a knife, he reacted quickly. Fiercely, he spun out with his boot, connecting and knocking one of the men across the room, sending his knife flying.

Jake was nearly stunned by a solid right to the side of his head, but his quick reflexes gave him the moment he needed to soundly pound the man, sending him stumbling away to crumble to the floor in a gasping heap.

And then the first man stood before him, a knife flashing in his hand. Jake steadied himself, smiling coldly at the deadly metal, which gleamed wickedly in the smaller man's right hand.

"Well," Jake grunted, breathing heavily, "what have we got here?"

"Something to cut you down to size, *puto*."

"It's been tried."

"This time it will succeed. You will not look so big with this in your gut."

"You got to get it there first."

The man dove forward and the blade sliced through the air toward Jake's ribs. Smiling tightly, Jake stepped aside, grabbed the man's wrist and brought it down hard across his knee. At the scream, he let go, watching as the man dropped to the ground and rolled into a ball, holding his broken arm.

Feeling winded, his legs spread wide, Jake looked down at the three now sprawled at his feet. "I really got to quit smoking," he muttered.

Mac followed Rachel out from behind the bar. "I called the cops," he said.

"I'd like to get her out of here." Jake wiped his hand across his forehead. Sweat seemed to be pouring from his body.

"Are you really all right?" Rachel asked, reaching up and lightly touching a scrape along his cheek.

He nodded.

"Then why should we let *cadrons* like these three make us leave?"

He stared at her, trying to reconcile what he had been expecting with the reality of the little warrior standing before him. "It'd be easier if you didn't have to deal with cops," he said, still breathing heavily.

Smiling now, she ran her finger down his arm, her own hand trembling. "But what if I like dealing with *cops*."

Jake heard Mac laugh at what he knew was probably a bewildered expression on his face. "This one's on me." Mac pulled three glasses off the shelf, filled them with beer, and chuckled again when Rachel pulled Jake's head down for a quick kiss.

After the police had come and dragged away the three, still-staggering men, one holding his arm, Mac grinned at Jake who was watching with bemusement as Rachel sat at a table talking to Krista. "So," Mac said, "you found yourself a woman after all."

Jake shook his head, drawing on his cigarette. "She's not mine."

Mac grinned. "Well, guess you'll find out about that, won't you?" He chuckled.

Jake shook his head. Not only had she not gotten upset at the fight, or at least no more upset than Krista, but she made a decided attempt to be friendly with a woman with whom she could have nothing in common. He was in over his head.

"So," Krista said intently studying Rachel, as though trying to decide what sort of animal she was, "you with Jake now?"

"Tonight anyway," Rachel said, frowning as she looked over at the big man lounging against the bar, smoking a cigarette and talking to Mac.

"He ain't an easy man," Krista agreed.

"On that we can agree."

"You want to be with him for more than tonight though, don't you?" Krista took a compact from her purse and pretended to study her face in the tiny mirror as though the answer was of no importance to her one way or the other.

"If he survives long enough. Are fights like tonight common here?"

Krista shook her head and put down the make-up. "I have never seen one with knives, but they happen with fists sometimes on the week-end. This is the first time I've seen Jake in a fight though. He's really something."

"Even a big man can be taken down by a knife or bullet," Rachel said, frowning.

"You care about him!"

"You do too, don't you?" Rachel guessed intuitively.

"For all the good it's ever done me." Krista made no attempt to hide her disappointment.

"You two weren't?" Rachel asked, wanting to hear the words, needing to know that there was no one else in Jake's life.

"I could wish, but no. He keeps everybody at arm's length. How'd you get past his guard?"

"I'm not," Rachel reluctantly admitted with a wry smile.

Krista sighed and looked at her narrowly. "Don't hurt him."

"I wouldn't want to do that."

"If he cared for you--began to trust you--and you ran back to where you come from, you'd hurt him."

"Jake and I don't... We don't really know where this is going... if anywhere."

Krista shook her head, looking from Rachel to where Jake stood-- now eyeing them narrowly. "It's an unlikely combination," she said with a short laugh, "the lady and the tough guy."

"Jake agrees with you," Rachel said more stung than she wanted to admit by that analysis, "but I don't."

"This is probably rude but just exactly what do you see in him?" Krista asked, yelling at Mac to bring them two coffees. "You do drink coffee?" she asked Rachel as she turned back to her.

Rachel resisted the temptation to wrinkle her nose. "Now and then, and to answer your question. Jake is beautiful."

Krista laughed again. "You wear glasses or something most of the time. I like Jake a lot, but beautiful he ain't."

"Well, he is to me." Rachel felt irritated at anyone who made fun of Jake's looks.

Krista looked at her with a friendlier smile. "Maybe you do care about him."

"Maybe I do," Rachel agreed as she reluctantly sipped the strong, black coffee Mac set on the table.

"Could we ever be friends," she asked Krista after a moment.

"You and me?" Krista scoffed, laughing again.

"Why not?"

"Us being friends doesn't seem any more likely than you and Jake working out on a long-term basis," Krista mocked.

"*Quien sabe*. Life has a way of taking odd turns," Rachel said with a smile, adding, "actually I make a good friend."

Krista studied her for a moment. "Or a bad enemy?"

"I don't have enemies—that I know of."

"All right, it's crazy, but sure, I like your style, chica. Hell, you got to have guts if you're taking on the big man over there." She chuckled. "Does you and me being friends mean slumber parties?"

"I haven't had one of those since I was fifteen," Rachel retorted, "but we could have tea sometimes." She laughed at the expression of dismay on Krista's face.

"What do you do, when you aren't being a friend to Jake and Mac?" Rachel asked.

"Beauty operator, down at Ruby's. You probably never heard of us. Bet you have your hair done in Tucson or Scottsdale. Or are you one of those who runs over to San Diego on the morning flight, gets her hair done and comes back for dinner." Krista put a hoity-toity expression on her face.

Rachel laughed. "Actually, I never have my hair done. I wash it, condition it, and let it go. I do trim the ends when they get uneven."

"Lordy!" Krista laughed and shook her head. "We'll make an odd combination as buddies. What do you do?"

"I'm a painter, as in pictures."

"I didn't think it would be house painter," Krista chortled and then whistled as the door opened.

Rachel looked up and saw David Bannister walking up to Jake.

"Who the hell's that?" Krista asked. "He's the best looking thing ever come in here... male anyway." She laughed.

"The real question is what he could want here."

"Anything he'd ask for so far as I'd be concerned," Krista joked.

Rachel watched as the two men talked, obviously not happy at what they were discussing. She and Krista stood up and walked over to join them, only hearing the last of a sentence. "...no hope."

Jake shook his head. "Lab come up with anything?"

"Not yet. We'll see if..." Bannister stopped and smiled at Rachel as she came to stand beside Jake. "Ah," he said with a broader grin. "This place is definitely looking more attractive."

Rachel introduced Krista to Bannister while Jake stood back from the group.

"I should be coming here more often," Bannister said.

"I think," Jake said curtly, "that it's time for Rachel and me to leave." He ignored the laughter as he steered Rachel to the door.

Outside, her arm around Jake's waist, Rachel asked, "Okay, that was all fun, but when's the test?"

"You kidding?" he asked as he opened the truck door for her.

She nodded and put her arms around his waist. "You've got a scrape on your cheek and a terrible bruise starting over your eyebrow. Are you really all right?"

"I'm fine."

She stroked his cheek lightly. "You didn't deliberately stage that fight to scare me off, did you!"

"I thought the bar alone would do that." He shook his head at the woman he again was holding in his arms. At no time this whole night had the princess performed according to the script he had made out in advance.

"Do you think I'm such a shallow little thing that I would be shocked at a place like the Lone Star?" She put her fingers over his mouth. "Do not answer that."

"I haven't been thinking clearly since I met you. I think you put a spell on me."

She smiled. "Would it work?"

He grinned and half lifted her into his truck but didn't answer.

"Do you get into such fights often?" she asked as he turned on the ignition.

He shook his head. "Hardly ever since I got to full size." He thought then how strange this one had been. These men had been primed for him, and nothing would have stopped what happened. He had already arranged with Bannister for the two of them to go down to the jail in the morning and ask a few questions. Everything had been too pat.

"So tonight was not typical at the Lone Star?"

"Nothing about tonight was usual for me. How about you?" He grinned at her as he pulled out of the parking lot for the short drive to his house.

"If I was upset by it all," she asked with a teasing grin, "would you give me loving care?"

"What kind of care did you have in mind?"

"How about a cold drink before I have to drive back to Maria's? Did I tell you I am thinking of getting an apartment in town?"

He turned off the engine of the truck in front of his house and looked at her thoughtfully. "Just a drink," he growled, "no playing nurse."

"You did get hurt." Once they were in the kitchen, she made a fuss over him as he had wanted to avoid but found he enjoyed more than he had expected. Feeling her tender hands cleansing and putting ointment on his small hurts, satisfied an inner wound he'd forgotten he received.

When they finally sat at the table with Cokes, she asked, "What did David Bannister tell you that was so upsetting before we came up?"

"Nothing worth getting into."

"Don't con me. I saw the expression on your face. What happened?"

Though he didn't want to, he told her about what had happened to the Morrises. He finished by saying, "She's in a coma and they don't figure she'll make it through the night. I kind of wonder if she'd want to with what she'd have to face."

"Those poor old people. Who would do something like that?"

"That's the big question."

"I didn't know them well but had seen them around. They were always together. So nice to everyone, holding hands. I can't believe anybody would want to hurt them."

"Sometimes life doesn't make much sense." Actually a lot of times but he didn't add that.

"That sure doesn't."

"It might be they saw something... or someone thought they did." He realized he had been thinking out loud.

"You think someone stalked them back to their home?" She shuddered.

He stood up, walking over to the counter before he looked back at her, saw the upset in her eyes and felt irritated for being the one to put it there. If she stayed close to him, it would not be the last pain he would bring her.

"My life is filled with ugliness. It never gets any better than tonight, babe."

"What happened to the Morrisses was just how it is sometimes. Maybe it sounds callous but stuff happens. We both know that."

"I see more of it than most."

She stood up, coming to stand beside him. Taking his arm with both hands, she laid her head against his shoulder. "Pain is life, Donovan. Just because I don't see it, won't make it not be there. Maybe, if you share it, talk about it, the hurt you feel will ease."

"Why would you want to do that?"

She smiled, picking up her purse. "I guess we'll both have to think about that. For now, you're tired; you need sleep, and I better get back to Maria's. She worries about me when I am staying over."

At the door, she stopped. "Oh yeah, I wanted to ask you. The people I am staying with, Maria and Mark Sandoval, are having a gathering, kind of a mixture of friends and business, at their home Friday night. I'd like to go. I'd like you to come with me."

"That doesn't seem like a wise plan."

"Why not? I met your friends. I want you to meet mine. I've told Maria about you, and I want to show you off."

"Are you nuts?" he grunted with disbelief. "Scratch that question."

"I never bring a guy to these parties," she said with a laugh. "I want to shock her that I actually can."

"I wouldn't fit at a thing like that."

"Come with me." She ran her fingers lightly along his arm.

He shook his head. "It's against my better judgment, but then so has practically everything else I've done since I met you."

CHAPTER 6

Donovan had asked David Bannister to go with him to the city jail to interrogate the three men who had attacked him. Instincts, which he had learned not to ignore, warned him the fight had not been a coincidence or simple bad luck. Three men do not come into a strange bar and pick a fight with someone they do not know.

"You think it's because of some case you're on?" Bannister asked as they got out of the Bronco.

"I'm not working on anything that interesting." Donovan lit a cigarette. "For over a week I've been at my desk finishing up reports. It's been my turn to view surveillance tapes. The last couple of times I was in the field, I drew a blank. And no mad relatives out for revenge. Least not who've phoned in."

"What about the Franklin case?" Bannister reached for the pack of cigarettes on the desk and drew out one.

"Don't you ever buy any of your own?"

"I'm not officially smoking. So back to the question."

"Short of being the first officer on the scene, what's my involvement?"

"Somebody might not know that, or it could be all of this is more interrelated than we would think," Bannister said enigmatically, his expression carefully neutral as he blew out smoke. "You were also out at the Morris home, and it was that night when they came to the bar."

"Mac said they'd been there Saturday night too. Looking for somebody he thought. As for the Morrises, how would they know I'd been out there?" Donovan stopped. "Unless there is something you're not telling me."

"Let's go down and talk to your boys, then go someplace and see if we can fit the pieces together."

When they got to the jail, the three were gone, released early that morning. "What's going on?" Donovan grated out.

"On a misdemeanor like disorderly conduct?" the bulkily built sergeant asked sarcastically. "How long did you expect us to baby-sit them?"

"What about assault with a deadly weapon? Or attempted murder," Donovan suggested. He'd listed off those charges to the arresting officer.

"We never heard about an assault."

"So who got paid?" Bannister asked abruptly, a tight smile on his face. The sergeant glared at him, then made a succinct comment about his parentage, which only made Bannister smile more genuinely.

The baking Arizona sun shone down on Jake's head as he and Bannister stood on the sidewalk, frustrated at the snafu or was it? Had there been a payoff involved in the lack of charges? There wasn't much chance those three would be back to complain. Having been around the legal system for a lot of years, Donovan wasn't overly surprised at the turn the situation had taken. It didn't make it less frustrating.

"Let's get a cold drink," Bannister suggested, loosening his tie as they climbed back into the Bronco. "If we look at this systematically, we start with whether they were strangers. You never saw them before, right?"

"They weren't in the bar anytime I've been there, and I always pay attention to who is around me. Mac said he'd never seen them until the week-end."

"It could have been about Rachel but seems unlikely three strangers would go up to you, given your size, and decide to take you on over her."

"I didn't think it likely."

"Well then, let's assume they were sent there by an enemy. Who might that be?"

Donovan lifted his eyebrows. "You were expecting names, addresses and phone numbers, maybe."

"It would be a good start. Do you have enemies?"

"No more than the usual two or three hundred any law enforcement officer collects over a ten year span."

"That shouldn't be hard to check out," Bannister retorted

"Why don't you take on the assignment?" Donovan felt a certain wry satisfaction at the image of the handsome and immaculate Bannister buried chest deep in files, computer read-outs and old microfilm.

"Diego Ramirez."

"You're hung up on that name."

"Could be. Let's see. Let's get into that *personal* history I tried to get you to talk about before."

"It was years ago."

"For some people, there is no such thing as *years ago*."

"Okay fine, but why after all this time? Why now?"

"Maybe something more is going down."

Donovan pulled the Bronco into a parking lot. He followed Bannister into the cafe and let him order the iced teas. When they had their drinks in front of them, Bannister started in again, "Okay, start talking, big guy. Your version's bound to be more colorful than newspaper accounts."

Donovan lit another cigarette before he remembered he'd been trying to taper off. Taking a deep drag on it, he thought, *I'll cut back tomorrow.* "Basically I am pretty sure you know this all. Seven years ago Ramirez had a cocaine smuggling operation shuttling between a ranch he was leasing near Ajo and points south--mainly Guaymas," he said, the memories of all this more clear than he wanted to let on to Bannister. "I was asked to go undercover, which I did not like. It's not my style, not to mention I don't blend in well, but because it was a pool--customs, state and us-- my boss was convinced I was the only one who could carry it off. Maybe because I was younger and stupider, I did it. I worked as a supposed traitor to the Border with Ramirez for five months, two weeks, and three days, until even a shower every hour couldn't make me feel clean and until I thought I had what we needed. Warrant in hand, we raided his operation."

"And..."

Donovan knocked the ash from his cigarette. "Maybe it's true that the devil protects his own because Ramirez wasn't there. We netted enough coke to keep the city of Phoenix happy for a month, but it was a dud, because the bastard got away, no evidence on the place and somebody else held the bag." Donovan stopped, rubbing his shoulder absentmindedly as he stared out the window at the slow moving traffic on the street.

"We both know that wasn't all."

"It never is. The raid did not go down without incident."

"You killed his brother," Bannister prodded.

Donovan shrugged. "A lot of shots were exchanged."

"He sees you as the murderer of his brother and a traitor."

"Most likely."

Bannister ran his finger along the rim of his glass. "He might be thinking it is pay-back time."

Donovan ground his cigarette into the ashtray, only realizing, when it was reduced to shreds, what he'd done. "If I had to worry about every wacko whose feelings I've hurt, I wouldn't sleep nights." As if sexual frustration and erotic dreams about Rachel weren't playing enough havoc with his sleep.

"You're not taking any of this seriously enough, Donovan, and damnitall, you need to. The man is deadly."

"I probably know that better than you. But why didn't he come after me right away?"

"You can't figure out a madman's next move because he doesn't think like you do." Bannister took a pencil from his shirt pocket and began doodling on a napkin. "In trying to get a profile on Ramirez, determine his modus operandi, I talked to a lot of people about what we know." His blue eyes darkened as he stared past Jake's shoulder. "Including talking to a psychiatrist. Using what I knew and suspected, I put together a profile. Psychotics often become fixated. With Ramirez, I think it's the Aztecs, the occult, revenge, and surprisingly numerology."

"Occult as in what?"

"Whatever you want to call rituals and sacrifices in exchange for power."

"You believe any of that?" Jake asked, knocking a fresh cigarette from the pack and digging in his pocket for a match.

Bannister looked at him, a faint smile on his lips, his eyes somber. "I've seen a lot of strange things. I had some experiences in Thailand... Yeah, I believe there could be power in some of it."

"I don't," Jake said, shaking his head.

"Maybe it's when people believe that there'll be power in it." Bannister showed Jake the doodles he'd done. "Recognize any of these?"

Jake studied them. "A swastika, of course. I don't know what the others are supposed to be, but weren't they on the wall of the Morris house?"

"I've been doing some research. Swastikas and symbols like those have been found in a lot of cultural groups but are also used by occult practitioners." He pointed to a series of squiggly lines. "This is a snake and the other we think represents a jaguar.

They were found painted in... blood on a rock at the site of what we believe to have been a child's sacrificial murder two years ago."

Jake carefully put the cigarette down in the ash tray. He heard a lot with the work he did, had seen a lot; but a child, well nothing was as bad as when it involved a child.

"The little boy's body was found just south of the border near but outside Ramirez's ranch. Nothing to connect anyone to it-- except a gut feeling that he's going back to what he sees as his heritage--the ancient Aztec religion. You know the kinds of things they did."

"All right, I believe you. Where it comes to Ramirez, nothing disgusting would surprise me." Jake hesitated. "But there are a lot of nutty groups like that hanging out in the mountains. It could be unconnected."

"It could."

"I still don't see where you link me to any of this."

"So far, it's a feeling, but..." He scowled at Donovan's faint smile.

Donovan lit another cigarette, drawing the smoke deep into his lungs. "Don't tell me you're into ESP too," he said.

"Get serious. We're not talking visions here. We're talking putting together evidence from several sources, a few rumors, gut instincts, and coming up with possibility that this guy is after his pound of flesh. It would not make sense to a logical person why seven might be significant, but for some, everything operates with astrology and numerology."

"I don't doubt he'd like revenge. But Ramirez picks on the weak--people who can't fight back." He thought of a peaceful old couple, a pudgy man tortured and left to die on the desert. Those did fit Ramirez's style. Were they connected, or was he batting at shadows now too?

"Yes, unless he can get you to a place where you can't fight back either," Bannister insisted, reaching out and lightly punching the taller man's shoulder. "I don't want you mysteri-ously disappearing. Watch your back, big guy."

Jake smiled coldly. When had that not been true?

~

When Rachel arrived at Jake's to pick him up for the Maria's party, he was only half dressed and clearly in a rotten mood.

She swallowed hard as she looked at the expanse of muscular chest revealed by the open shirt and the sculptural lines of his torso. She knew, as she looked up, that her eyes revealed all she was thinking, the hunger she felt to touch that hard body, to see him respond to her kiss, to feel his lips soften under hers. Real-izing she was igniting fires that might be impossible to extin-guish, she turned away, but it was too late.

He pulled her hard against him, his arms like bands of iron. He brought his lips down onto hers, first lightly tasting and then searching hers impatiently, his tongue delving into her mouth as she tentatively met it with her own. Her fingers reached under his shirt as she clung to him with a fervor and eagerness she couldn't have denied if her life had depended upon it.

Rachel could feel the muscles in his back as they flexed, the suppleness of his skin, his muscular thighs pressed against her. His hand caressed her breast, bringing her nipple to hot tingling awareness. Feelings of desire and need were being brought to life throughout her body, feelings she'd never known existed apart from this man.

"No." She pushed away, heaving for breath. Despite her feel-ings of increasing need, something about this wasn't right, was all wrong.

"What's the matter, babe?" he asked, his own breath coming fast.

"Just I can't."

"Then quit playing games." His voice was low, husky,

and angry.

"Playing games?"

"You want it. I want it. I'm a good lay. Isn't that what you've been curious about? You push forward and then quickly shove back. You're a big girl, isn't it time you act like one?"

She stared at him, her breasts heaving under the silky white dress, which draped across soft curves hiding and promising at the same time. The damned thing was as seductive as anything he'd seen, yet it was almost virginal at the same time. Not that he believed there was such thing as a virgin by Rachel's age.

"You think I want you for sex, and that's it?" she asked, her mouth set in an angry stubborn line.

"What else?"

"I don't have casual sex."

He looked at her for a moment, his smile anything but real. "That's a problem then, because I don't have any other kind."

"I had a feeling it was that way with you," she said, trying to laugh and knowing she'd failed. "You wouldn't make a commitment to me, could you, Jake?"

"Were we talking about one?"

"No, and that's the point."

"What the hell are you talking about? Tomorrow?"

"Doesn't look like we're going to get past tonight."

He stared blankly at her feeling a little like a fish, which had been hooked and if it didn't break the line soon, would be reeled in.

"You think I'm trying to trap you," she said.

He shrugged and smiled faintly. She had a knack for reading him.

She sucked in a deep breath and stared at him, her mind going in a thousand directions. Finally she knew nothing could be settled now. "Are we going to the party?"

He stared blankly for a moment having totally forgotten the earlier cause of his tension. "You still want me to go?" he asked after a moment. When she nodded, he headed for his bedroom to get his boots.

At Sandoval's, as soon as she got through the door, Rachel was grabbed and hugged by a tall, silver-haired woman who looked up at Jake with undisguised interest. "And who is this?" she asked, boldly appraising him, her eyes raking his long body.

"Jake Donovan, Michelle Rydell."

"Oh, darling!" A blond woman, her hair hanging stylishly loose on her shoulders came up to Rachel, demanding introductions. By the time Rachel and Jake had made it into the living room, he had met five women and no men.

The women seemed particularly predatory tonight, Rachel thought possessively, not wanting to let go of Jake's arm. She had known she found him undeniably sexy, but she had not expected his bold, untamed masculinity to have such a strong effect on her acquaintances.

"Do you want something to drink?" she asked, rubbing his wrist lightly as she held his hand.

"Beer?" he asked with a gleam of interest in those golden eyes.

She shook her head. "More likely white wine, Sangria, juice, or Perrier."

"I'll pass."

He looked around the large house with curiosity. The living room was large with arched windows and doors, Mexican folk art was displayed prominently on the padercita beside the kiva styled fireplace. Brilliant colors ran rampant throughout the rooms. On one long wall a huge landscape of the desert dominated-- its colors bold and impressionistic.

"That's one of mine," Rachel said as he stared at it. She had no idea what he was thinking as his expression was closed.

Maria joined them, smiling brightly with questions in her eyes as Rachel made introductions again. "I've heard much about you," Maria told him with a friendly grin.

"Good or bad?" Jake asked with a faint smile that almost looked real.

"All good, of course," Maria replied with a laugh.

Rachel heard a familiar masculine voice calling her name. Annoyed she scrunched her face as Maria whispered in her ear, "Go talk to Rick. He's been unhappy since he saw you come through the door. I'll keep an eye on your big man."

Reluctantly Rachel let go of Jake. Smiling an apology at him, she hoped he would be all right while she took a moment to prevent Richard Byers from creating a scene. Although she had only dated the man casually, she was aware he'd had expectations of something more between them. She didn't doubt her father's supposed wealth was much of the attraction.

She allowed the attractive, smooth featured financial planner to lead her to a corner of the dining room where they could talk more privately.

"I can't believe you'd come here with another man," Richard complained, running his hand through stylishly cut brown hair. "How could you do this to me?"

"You're drunk, Rick," she observed.

"Not that drunk."

"You and I did not have any understanding."

"We would have," he protested.

"No," she stated firmly, "we wouldn't."

He stared at her. "Why him though? He's a brute. What the hell do you want with someone like that? It's clear he's not your type." he said, his words slurred.

"And what is my type?"

"He looks like a cowboy. Is that what he is, a cowboy?"

"What he is and what he and I are to each other is none of your business."

"Damn it, it was supposed to have been."

"I'm sorry if you had the wrong idea, Rick," she said and walked away.

By the time she got back to Jake, he was surrounded by women, two leaning altogether too close. She caught the tail-end of a sentence as she walked up. "I can certainly see what Rachel sees in you." The woman laughed, as her eyes ran over Jake's body with a look that could only be called lecherous.

The subject was too close to the argument Rachel and Jake had just had. With the wall at his back, he now had the look of a cougar treed by a pack of yelping dogs. Rachel elbowed her way into the group, cutting between Jake and the boldest woman. Leaning back against his hard body, she faced Caroline Rodman. "Did I hear my name?" she asked sweetly.

"You might have," Caroline said with what was clearly meant to be a sophisticated smile and ended up looking merely bored and drunk.

Michelle laughed. "You got back just in time, Rachel. Your man here was in danger of being stripped and raped right here in Maria's living room." Several of the women giggled.

Caroline slapped at her playfully. "Don't be foolish. I'd never really *want* a man like this one. He's just fun to tease. Isn't that right, Rachel? They're fun to play with."

Rachel looked at the cold expression on Jake's face before she turned to Caroline. Her first urge was to slap the woman's face but that would only create a scene. Instead, she took a deep breath, her smile calculated. "Caroline, keep your hands off him."

"What?" Caroline quipped with mock amazement.

"Look but don't touch, darling."

"Well, I never said I wanted to touch," Caroline said petulantly. "He's not exactly our sort, now is he?"

"Well, that depends on who *our* sort is, I guess." She pulled Jake by the hand and led him out of the circle of women.

He whistled. "This place is worse than Skeleton Canyon."

"Skeleton canyon?"

"Just a nickname for a problem spot along the border."

She grinned. "Well, there are some predators here. Maybe you should stick close to me for safety."

His smile reached his eyes. "And I'd be safe then?"

"Would you want to be?" she asked with a grin, disappointed when he stopped smiling. "Let's get a breath of fresh air," she suggested, taking his hand and leading him out to the patio. She sat on the wall. "I'm sorry you aren't having more fun."

He smiled. "I knew I wouldn't fit here."

"You could if you just give it some time."

"Mind if I smoke?"

She shook her head. "It's your lungs."

He lit a cigarette, inhaled deeply. "These people are out of my league, Rachel. Just like you."

"In rudeness. Possibly so."

He chuckled. "I can hold up my own on that."

"I'm sorry she insulted you. I wanted the evening to be a good one for both of us."

He shook his head. "There's only one woman in that room who could've insulted me."

"I just make you mad," she said, taking his large hand in hers and bringing it to her lips. She brushed the rough palm with her lips and then kissed it—then one long finger after another until she rubbed the knuckles lightly against her cheek.

The door to the house swung open, ending the moment with an invasion of bright light and noise of the party inside. To Rachel's disgust, an even more drunken Rick Byers was approaching, weaving as he walked, holding a glass in his right hand and gesturing with his left. "Gonna introduce us, Rachel. I'd like to meet your new boyfriend."

Knowing she had a barely tamed cougar at her side, Rachel hoped the situation wasn't going to escalate into something more than nasty words. She'd seen Jake in a fight but how easily could he be provoked? He'd had plenty of provocation this evening— starting with her.

Jake dropped his cigarette to the ground, grinding it out with his boot. "Introduce us, babe," he said, that angry smile on his lips.

"Jake Donovan, Richard Byers. Rick used to be a friend of mine but not a particularly good one."

Rick gave an unpleasant, obviously forced laugh. "Is that how you see it *now*, darling, beautiful Rachel?"

"It's how I always saw it, darling Rick," she retorted, putting her arm possessively around Jake's waist. She could feel the tense muscles and leaned against him further to defuse his anger or would it increase it?

Maria stood in the lit doorway. "We're just starting dancing."

"Dance with me, Jake," Rachel said relieved at Maria's suggestion.

Jake looked at her with undisguised reluctance. "Dancing?"

"You do dance, don't you?" Rachel pulled him past Richard toward where they could hear music.

Jake shook his head. "A little."

"A little is enough," she said with a smile.

An area had been cleared in what was usually a family room. Surprising to Jake, the music playing was a country duet with two singers mourning a lost love. Rachel looked up at Jake, her eyes dark as she reached up her arms.

The last thing he wanted to do was hold her in his arms again. Moreover, while he felt confused as to what she wanted, he was growing even more unsure as to what he wanted. He might know this thing with her was dangerous, forbidden, would destroy him, but he found himself unable to walk away from it.

He pulled her against him. Her arms entwined up around his neck. The rhythm of the music lulled him into forgetting there was a reason not to enjoy her slim body pressed against his. Just for this one dance, he'd forget this couldn't be. For just this night, he'd pretend some people did stay. And he swayed her to the music as it shifted into a slow ballad.

"Can I cut in?" Caroline Rodman tapped on Rachel's shoulder. Rachel, mesmerized by the music, by Jake's hard body, the musky scent of his skin didn't realize at first what Caroline wanted.

"I thought I made that clear to you," Rachel said, her smile as cool as she could make it.

"Come on. Just a dance," Caroline asked, determined to come between them.

"You're making a scene, Caroline," Maria said coming up to try and soothe the moment.

Caroline glared at them all. "This is ridiculous. Just a dance. I never... Well, just he's got this fantastic body and what's it cost Rachel to give up one dance?"

Jake had paled as Rachel drew him off the dance floor. Caroline Rodman had made no secret as to how she saw him. There'd been women like her before. Women who wanted only one thing and believed a man like him could deliver it-- at no cost. He had been sure Rachel was the same kind of woman. He was finding it harder to believe that and with that hope arose, which for Jake only led to fear.

Rachel looked up at Jake's face, seeming to read his conflicted emotions. "Want to go?"

He shook his head. "No problem."

She smiled. "Maybe not for you, but I'm tired of fighting off women." She'd meant the comment to be taking as a joke, but the hard line of his mouth, the muscle that twitched in his jaw told her that he was clenching his jaw.

Rachel hugged Maria, and it seemed in only moments she and Jake were outside in the night air.

"We didn't have to leave," Jake said.

"I'd had enough. Did you want to dance with Caroline?"

He snorted. "Not hardly."

"Well, I didn't want you to either. It seemed to me it was time to head out. We can dance at your place if you still want."

He stopped and turned her to look at him. "If we dance at my place, you're going to bed with me. Are you wanting that?"

"Not yet," she said.

"Then no dancing."

They got into his truck. "I wanted to tear Caroline's dyed hair out by the roots," she admitted, not sure she should be telling him about her jealousy.

"Dyed?" he asked, amused despite himself, at the tone of her voice.

"Couldn't you tell?"

"Didn't look that close."

Back at his house, he was in no hurry to get out of the truck. He had put off these words too long. Tonight had again shown him all the reasons nothing good could come out of them seeing each other again.

"No point beating around the bush. Tonight was a mistake. We shouldn't make it again."

"No more parties," she agreed.

"No more seeing each other."

"Why? Because I won't sleep with you?"

"Sure. Why not. No sex, no relationship, babe."

She gritted her teeth than realized what he was doing. "I want to go in and talk about this."

"Nothing to say."

She slammed open the truck door and headed for the house. Inside, he pushed open the windows to allow in whatever breeze there was. Warily, he watched her from across the room as she perched on the sofa, her eyes wide and thoughtful. She looked as out of place as he had earlier at the Sandoval's party.

He turned to stare out the window into the darkened yard, thinking of his house, the only home he would have to offer a woman. This place was a dump-- cockroaches in the kitchen, shabby furniture, cracks in the walls.

When he realized why those thoughts had come into his

mind, he felt angry with himself, then with her. Impossible dream indeed. He had to be crazy to have let that kind of thinking float into his head. She *was* bewitching him.

"What are you thinking?" she asked.

He avoided answering and stared back out his window into the darkness. No way was he going to put himself at any woman's mercy.

"You are so pensive." She came up behind him and wrapped her arms around his waist, pressing herself against his back. "You don't need to tell me. I know what you're thinking."

"Rachel," he started to protest but she reached up to put her fingers against his lips.

"This seems crazy to you, doesn't it?" she asked. "It probably is." She stopped, unsure what she could say to explain the urges within her. How she wanted to be with him, to make his house into a home, wanted to sleep in his bed, make him forget all his feelings of being ugly as she taught him how beautiful he really was. How she now knew there was such a thing as love at first sight because it's how it had been for her.

He sucked in a breath at the sensation of her holding him as she was, now her hands free to stroke down his chest to his belly. He wanted to tell her to stop at the same time he wanted to tell her where to put those teasing hands next.

"Definitely crazy," he managed. He tried to turn in her arms, but she clung to him, pressed tightly against his, against his thighs, buttocks and back, making him aware of an ache that would not be alleviated. Her breath seemed to sear his skin through the thin cloth of his shirt.

"Rachel," he said his voice not much more than a whisper.

"What?"

"Damn, do you know what you're doing?"

He heard her smile in her voice. "Not the slightest idea."

"And you think this is fair?"

"No." She kissed his back, her lips moving across his back.

"Geesus, babe."

"Hmmmm?" She asked a smile in her voice again.

"You are a witch." He'd given himself up to the moment. He could've turned at any moment; but if she wanted to play with him, control his strength, he wouldn't stop her. For a moment he would just let this be whatever she wanted.

He felt her fingers at the buttons of his shirt. Surely, she would not, but then he saw she would. Her fingers brushed his skin with an almost erotic torture as she opened the buttons, one by one, pushing his shirt apart as she worked her way to his beltline.

"What now?" he asked finding it maddening and yet at the same time fulfilling to have her controlling the pace of what was happening. He had never had a woman in charge this way. He'd taken what women offered, but they had never wanted more than his strong body. Inside, he knew that might be all Rachel wanted; but at this moment, it didn't matter.

She leaned her head against his back, her hands against the skin of his belly. "I don't know," she whispered.

He tried to remember the question. He turned in her arms, turning her chin up so that he could look into her eyes. In the faint light, they looked silvery, shimmering with unshed tears.

"What's wrong?" he asked.

"I just... I've never," she whispered.

He finally got it. "You've never been with a man."

She nodded.

"You can't mean that. Why the hell not?"

"It was never right before."

"You think it is now?"

She gave a little laugh. "No, just it's harder right now than it's ever been to say no."

He shook his head. He'd never been with a virgin. Hell, he'd never even known a virgin. "Geesus, Rachel," he said with a groan.

"I'm sorry."

"You better get out of here while you still can."

She was crying, but she didn't go. She went to the sofa, trying to stifle tears, which made it all the worse for him.

He cursed and watched her, but he was more afraid of her now than he had been. Damn, a virgin. Who'd have thought it possible!

"I'm sorry," she said finally.

"Geesus, what for?"

"Seemed like the only thing safe to say."

"Well, it's not."

"What would be?"

"Good-bye is a good beginning."

"Sounds more like an ending."

He pounded his fist into his open palm. "Son of a bitch, Rachel. I've tried to tell you since we met that this can't work."

"Why not?"

He swept his arm out. "Look around you, babe. You see this house?" When she nodded, he said, "It's a dump, a pit. You see yourself in a house like this one?" She nodded, and he nearly went to his knees. "You have got to be joking."

"This house isn't that bad. It has charm. It could be fixed up. If someday we decided we wanted a life together, of course, I'd be contributing to the cost of our life."

"Your father's money," he snorted derisively.

"I resent that. I have money of my own," she retorted, stung at his taunt. "I make a fairly respectable living from my painting, and it's more every year. I live with my father not because I can't afford to move out but because it's close to what I paint."

"You make money off your paintings?" he questioned with amazement, distracted from their original argument.

She chose to ignore the affront to her work. After all, it came from his unfamiliarity with the art world. She explained with some patience, "In a few weeks I have a showing scheduled where

I'll introduce the last six month's work. Last time my show sold out within a month--at very good prices, I might add."

He shook his head with disbelief.

"I am a good painter. You should see the canvas I am working on now."

"I'd like to." His voice was hoarse.

"Even when it's of you?" she questioned with a small smile. "Of course, it will never be for sale. I'd never let another woman own any part of you, and it would be a woman who would want to own you."

He stared at her. "Must be ugly as sin."

She could see in her mind's eye the canvas, the tans and browns, the desert background, his wonderful golden eyes staring into the distance, the crags of his face a match for the uplifted hills of the desert behind him. "It's coming along, but isn't finished. Do you want to see it when it is?"

"No."

She felt hurt. "Why not?"

"Because by the time you have it done, we won't be seeing each other."

"You're that sure of yourself?"

"I'm sure of you."

"You think you know me based on other people you have known. You already said you've never known anybody like me."

"People aren't all that different, not in the end."

She saw the hurt in his eyes but also the hunger for her. She knew he'd been aroused, had felt what she did. They'd both taken it as far as they should until things were more resolved. She understood this wasn't the way of today's world, but it was her way. She'd give herself to Jake someday. She was sure she would, but it would be when he wanted her for more than a night. It would be when he didn't feel trapped. Only time would determine when that was to be.

"I'm hungry," she said suddenly aware she was ravenous.

"Me too," he growled, his eyes telling her more strongly than words for what his hunger was.

"Did you eat dinner tonight?"

He shook his head.

"Lunch?" she asked, remembering his habit of ignoring meals.

He shook his head.

"Okay, when was the last time you ate?" She put her fists on her hips, looking at him sternly.

He tried to remember. "Maybe last night," he admitted.

"I can't believe you," she grumbled, switching on the light in his kitchen, "and you probably don't have anything here to fix either."

"I'm not much of a cook," he said, following her into the room and leaning his shoulder against the door jam. "Want to go out for a burger?"

"It's not healthy to only grab fast food, Jake." Looking into his refrigerator she saw that at least he still had eggs and cheese, although the cheddar had another layer of mold on its edges. "That's all you ever have," she muttered, "You need to go shopping."

"I never know when I'm going to be here," he protested, watching her as she began assembling the ingredients for an omelet. By now, he knew how much he liked watching her bustle around his kitchen, having her cook for him--he liked it too much.

"What are you doing tomorrow?" she asked as they sat eating what she felt was a delicious omelet and toast. She'd worry about the cholesterol tomorrow.

"I don't have any plans," he said before he'd thought.

"How about you and me going to across the border?" she suggested.

He sat back in his chair, looking at her skeptically. "What for?"

"Just shopping, lunch. I bet I could find you some things that would change the whole way you'd feel about your home."

"On a dime?"

"Or so," she teased. "You know, you actually need pans too."

He groaned. "Isn't one fry pan enough?"

"If you also had a couple of sauce pans and for heaven's sake. Who doesn't have a broiler pan?"

"You're trying to rearrange my life, Rachel."

"Just a few pieces," she said with a little laugh.

He saw it was not a little piece, and when she left, she'd be taking pieces of him with her. He fought back the only way he knew. "I don't need pans. I don't cook that much."

"You keep at this way and you'll have an ulcer before you're thirty."

"Too late, I'm thirty-two now. Could be I've given them, but I haven't gotten one yet." Not that that might not be changed.

"What about Nogales tomorrow?" she asked picking up the plates to carry them to the sink.

He sighed. "It's against my better judgment but not much since I've met you hasn't been."

Saturday morning when Rachel got to Jake's house for once he was ready but his face wore a scowl as he turned on the truck's ignition and pulling out onto the road and was no brighter as he parked it in a spot near the border where they could easily walk across.

"We don't have to do this," she said.

"It's okay."

"Doesn't look like it."

He forced a smile. "It's fine. My mind was just on other things. I'll get into this when we start doing... Uh exactly what are we doing?"

"Just shopping. Haven't you ever done that?"

"Nope."

"Why not?"

"What the hell would they have that I'd want?" he asked as they walked down the hill toward the arches, which separated the two countries and two Nogales.

"You don't have much fun, do you, Jake?"

"Is this supposed to be fun?"

She gave him a mock glare and took his arm. As they passed through the gates one of the Mexican officials chuckled at seeing Jake. "Hey, Donovan you undercover today?" He gave an appreciative look at Rachel as he casually examined their identification.

"Special assignment for the president," Jake retorted.

"Of the United States?" the guard asked, showing by his change of expression that he had believed Jake's joke.

"Nah. Of the street cleaning union."

The guard looked blankly at him, and then laughed. "Observe carefully, then mi gran amigo."

"Oh I will."

He realized the jokes at his expense would likely be worse coming back. This wasn't his thing and he wondered why he'd let himself be talked into it. Of course, he knew the answer, it was the beautiful woman at his side, who now held his hand and made him feel ten feet tall and as though whatever she asked he could do.

Looking down the street, Rachel interrupted his dark thoughts. "The first things you need are colorful planters."

He frowned with disbelief. "Like for plants?" he asked as she began studying one particular stall with an ample display on the sidewalk.

She nodded.

"I don't have any plants."

"You will."

He grimaced as he shelled out the money for the pots she selected. Just when he thought she must have enough, she found

114

another. Stopping they had to wait while she dickered over the price and finally made an acceptable deal.

Soon, Jake had his arms full of stacked pots, striped serapes and a smiling, terra-cotta sun to put beside his front door. He thought maybe that would be it, but then she had to check out the other side of the street.

He got a cold feeling in his spine, the one that had warned him more than once that he was being watched, but when he swung around, he saw no one even looking toward them. He put the thought from his mind.

"How about a cold drink," he suggested as they passed a sidewalk cafe.

"Later, lover," she told him with a grin, "I want to look at this ceramic folk art. It would look great on your fireplace mantle."

"But--" It was a lost cause. She was in the shop, talking to a heavy-set, older Mexican woman. The two alternated between discussing the fine points of the sculptures and the price. Rachel particularly liked one of a woman carrying an olla. "The colors are nice," she said appraisingly.

"These come from the mountains of Mexico," the woman told her with a smile.

"If I took both the man with a load of wood and the woman," Rachel asked, "what would be the price?"

Now the serious work of bartering began. Rachel almost walked from the shop twice before they agreed on a price satisfactory to both. Jake shook his head, putting down the heavy pots and getting out his wallet. She would bankrupt him and break his back before the day was through, not forgetting bringing about the ruination of his formerly tough-guy reputation.

The figures fit easily into one of the pots. With careful packing, Jake was ready to resume his load, although he was beginning to feel a little like the folk figurine with the pack of wood on his back. Within a block, they had added another colorful Indian blanket, definitely woven by "Indians in the mountains of Mexico."

By the next time he heard the spiel, Jake was skeptically beginning to think more of them looked woven in the mountains of Japan, China or the Philippines, but he kept his observations to himself.

Finally, Rachel, who was also carrying part of the load, began to tire and agreed to stop at a cafe for the cold drink Jake had been craving for the last half hour.

"Fun isn't it?" she asked, sipping on an ice-cold Coke and smiling at him.

Suddenly it seemed that it was enjoyable to be together, to find things, and watch her excitement at what was to her a treasure hunt. He shook at the pile of booty at his feet. "I don't know how much more I can carry."

"I can't believe how much you are carrying." She reached over and stroked his hand. "I've never been able to bring back so much before."

"Nice having your own mule, huh?" he quipped teasingly.

"Or dragon," she said with a grin. She brought his large hand to her lips. Teasingly, she nipped his little finger lightly with her teeth.

"Rachel," he muttered, all his senses instantly aflame, "do you know what you're doing to me?"

She grinned ruefully. "I know what I'm doing to me. Shall I stop?"

He shook his head. "No. Torture me some more." He smiled as she kissed his palm. He could've taken her right on the street and it wouldn't have been soon enough to salve the aching in his loins. Knowing she was a virgin hadn't made this any easier. It was important that she come to him willingly, but when would that be? Would it ever happen? Obviously she had held off on sex for a reason. Would she find one now enough to change her mind? And when she did, if it was with him, would he disappoint her? He pushed the thoughts from his mind. He was moving ahead too fast, worrying over something that likely would never happen. Whoever took Rachel O'Brian's virginity, it wasn't likely to be a craggy Border Patrolman.

Back on the street, she found several small ceramic pieces she couldn't imagine not buying. About the time Jake begin to wonder if they were going to have to buy a mule to pack the stuff, she said, "I think that's it."

Unfortunately, he saw a pair of silver earrings, inlaid with turquoise, that he wanted her to have and found himself buying them when he had finally been free and clear. Shaking his head, he wondered what was happening to him.

When they got back to the border crossing, both he and Rachel loaded with sacks and packages, Jake was hopeful no one he knew would be on duty at Customs. The hope was dashed as he glanced down the line. Although there was no way he could look particularly macho with his arms full of packages, he gave it a vain attempt.

"Well, well," the Customs man said with a hard smile, "what have we here?"

"Stuff," Jake said, putting down his load, digging in his pocket and showing the officer his ID as well as a stack of receipts.

"Sure there's nothing smuggled in these?" he asked, glaring at Jake and not bothering to look at the receipts. He projected the belief he had just netted the head of a major smuggling ring. Any minute Jake expected him to call for reinforcements.

"You can check anything necessary," Rachel said as he looked over her own identification, obviously concerned at the man's tone. "We'd be glad to unwrap the packages."

A heavy-set female tourist behind them got a decidedly worried expression on her round face as the guard glared menacingly at Jake. "I think this might require a strip search, big guy." He fingered his gun.

"That's about enough," Jake growled.

"Was that a threat?" The guard's thick eyebrows beetled up with indignation.

"Whatever it takes to get us through."

"I heard that."

"Good!"

"Jake," Rachel said, taking his arm, "please. We don't want trouble."

"Yeah," the Custom's man said, "listen to the wisdom of the little woman here. Who do you think you are anyway? Some kind of special Border Patrolman who can just waltz through these hallowed gates like you own the place!"

Jake gave him a look of disdain. "Do I look dumb enough to try to guard a border that can't be guarded or like a man who doesn't have anything better to do than harass innocent tourists... at traps?"

"You putting down the work of the fine men of Immigration and Naturalization," the guard snarled, "men who put their lives on the line every day. Sometimes twice!"

"That right there shows a clear lack of intelligence," Jake countered, while Rachel pulled on his arm, trying to get him to stop talking.

"I can agree with that," the agent said, now struggling to keep back a grin.

"I'll bet you can."

"Well, I'll let you through this time without stripping you raw, but it's just because you got this lovely lady with you. She looks like the honest sort, unlike some people. You're just lucky I'm busy today." He handed back their identification.

"Not busy enough obviously."

"Take care of him, miss," the man said, slamming his big hand against Jake's shoulder hard enough to cause him to take a step backward. He turned to Rachel. "Looks like a clear stress problem. Must need some real tender loving care at home." He laughed at Jake's disgusted look and Rachel's shock.

Now Rachel realized that these two men knew each other and were friends. It was at least if you could call what two men sometimes did to each other in bantering--friendship. When they were out on the street, the sun again shining down on their heads, she muttered, "I don't appreciate your humor."

"My humor," he retorted, "I was *not* the one having fun back there, and the worst part of this will be Monday morning." He swore at the vision he'd conjured up. "He's going to make this little incident grow. He thinks he was funny, and he's going to try and convince everybody I know that he was funny, and that this was funny!" He would have slapped a hand to his forehead as a symbolic gesture, except holding all the purchases left him no arms with which to demonstrate.

"Actually," Rachel said with a beginning chuckle, "it was kind of funny."

Michael O'Brian shook his head at the sight of Diego Ramirez shouting his displeasure as Paco Diaz cajoled and begged. As he ranted, Ramirez cradled longingly in his hand a sculpture, a transparent human skull, wrought from crystal and perfectly detailed.

"Please, patron, I tried. We all tried." Diaz's eyes turned humbly downward. "He was too strong for us. Dios, the man is a bull."

Ramirez looked up and saw O'Brian in the doorway. "What are you doing here, Miguel?"

Michael O'Brian entered the room, feeling tension that went to his toes. "What is this all about?"

Ramirez shrugged. "Nada."

"Who did you send your pit bulls after?"

"You take care of your end of our partnership, and I take care of mine."

"What is your end, Diego? Did you put out an order to have the Morrises beaten to death?"

Ramirez gave him a questioning look. "Who are the Morrises?"

"You know and I know you know. Now tell me the truth."

Ramirez's look was one of exaggerated innocence. "You're crazy, Miguel. What are you accusing me of?"

"Quit playing games with me, Diego." O'Brian stared at his erstwhile partner, feeling as though this all had to be a nightmare. Unfortunately it was a living nightmare, from which he feared he'd never awaken.

Ramirez carefully placed the skull on the table and rose slowly from his seat. He stared at O'Brian for only a moment before he walked to a long, narrow window to stare at the stark desert, the barren land that marched to the very door of his patio with no touch of green or lushness. O'Brian knew Ramirez allowed nothing softening around his hacienda, nothing that would give cover to those who might try to sneak up on him at night. This was the Ramirez citadel--a fortress, not a home. Here Ramirez had promised he could hold off an army. O'Brian believed him.

O'Brian slumped into a chair. The room around him was bare except for the huge, ornately carved table and chairs. One wall bore an Aztec feather shield and a knife blade of flaked chert. Beside the window a large font, carved of stone sat as though still waiting for the sacrificial, flesh offerings that at one time were offered it by an Aztec priesthood.

Diaz looked imploringly toward O'Brian, "Please. I beg you, help *el patron* to understand. It was not our fault."

"If not your fault, whose?" Ramirez asked, his eyes feral slits as he stared down at the pleading man.

"I'm going to ask this one more time. What is going on?" O'Brian demanded.

"They failed."

O'Brian took a deep breath to steady his nerves. Any showing of weakness would be a mistake. "Failed at what?"

"Don't worry about it. We let Donovan know we are still aware of him, still remember what he did, who he is."

"Donovan?"

"Jake Donovan."

That was not reassuring. "Anything with him is history, Diego. I've told you before you have to put the past behind you."

"He brought it upon his own head. He put his boots on my ground. That changed the game."

"What the hell are you talking about?"

"Donovan was the border agent who came out to the ranch, who asked Rachel all the questions."

"Hell."

"I have never forgotten him and what I owe him. I have just waited for the time when I would have sufficient power to pay him back."

O'Brian took a deep breath, then waved his hand toward the shaking Diaz. "And you think rabbits like those could've done that?"

"There were three of them. It was meant to be a promise of what was to come." Ramirez glared at Diaz. "Get out of here. Go back to work. Don't let me see your miserable hide until I have forgotten your failure--if I ever forget it!"

Diaz ran from the room. O'Brian sighed and met Ramirez's cruel smile. His partner's face was distorted by anger.

"You expect me to ignore what Donovan has done to me. He stalks the earth as though he rules it. He cannot be permitted to live."

"Forget the past, Diego. The man is nothing to you."

"He's everything to me. I made him my trusted one. He could have--" He stopped and ground his teeth. "And what was my reward for all I did?" he asked, bitterness and self-pity edging his words, "for all I would have done? He betrayed me, and have you forgotten what I told you? He slaughtered my brother."

Ramirez slumped back into a seat at the table. "You think I would let such a man walk the earth free? That I would ever forget? I've waited, waited to fully savor the day I could take my reckoning. Imagining it has given me much pleasure through these years. To imagine how much pain I could cause him helped me endure the wait until the Oracles told me now was the day of retribution. To kill him is not nearly enough. I will have my pound of flesh."

O'Brian watched uneasily as his mercurial partner's mood changed abruptly. Reverently, his eyes dreamily fascinated, Ramirez picked up the carved crystal skull and stared into it, mesmerized by whatever it meant to him. Was it death itself?

"There are risks in breaking the law," O'Brian said, trying to tear the man away from whatever macabre thoughts were absorbing him. "Your brother had to know that. Are you just now recognizing it?"

"You cannot understand," Ramirez murmured. He ran his hand caressingly over the crystal skull, running his finger around the eye sockets. His fingers seemed almost to make love to the inanimate piece, giving it a life that suddenly seemed to glow.

"I understand one thing," O'Brian said, his patience snapping. "Your paranoia will destroy us. When I learned you'd put Franklin out on the desert, I tried to believe you were giving him a chance, but you weren't. You were like a cat playing with a mouse. Still, I reminded myself what Franklin was, so I tried to forget it. Now there has been worse. You are lying about the Morrises. I see it in your eyes. Whether you did it that day or had it done, you were behind it, weren't you?"

Ramirez put down the skull and looked at O'Brian with a sneer on his face. "We had no choice about the Morrises, not after we saw their truck driving away. They'd seen the helicopter after it had dropped off Franklin. Once they saw the papers, how long before they went to the police with what they had seen? It could have led to us."

"Nothing warrants what you did to them. I want no part of this kind of insanity."

Ramirez smiled. "I don't think you have a choice, not if you want to stay healthy... not to mention your beautiful daughter."

O'Brian sprang from his chair. "You dare to threaten Rachel." He could barely control his rage as he paced around the room.

"I didn't say I would do anything," Ramirez corrected. "You knew when you got into this that it was not going to be easy."

"It was a business."

Ramirez chuckled. "Business? Is that what you wanted to think or told yourself?" Gently he caressed the skull before he violently pounded his fist into his open palm. "Whatever you thought, it is what it is now. It is easy for you to say I should forget about Donovan, but betrayal is not something a man forgets."

O'Brian took a deep breath, trying to find words that could penetrate Ramirez's mind. "You will only succeed in drawing attention to yourself. There are many people you can kill but not an old couple like that. They had friends. A fence, well maybe nobody would care about him, but that old couple, the authorities won't stop until they find who did it."

"So maybe I will give them someone," Ramirez said with a feral smile. "The woman is still alive." He stared out the window. "They were both supposed to be dead. Another botched job. It proves again to me that a man must do something himself if he wishes to see it done right."

O'Brian grimaced. "How long before the law starts putting two and two together. It's not hard to figure out the Morrises spent time out on the desert, that maybe they saw something. The law will look for a link and eventually find it. " He swallowed back his gorge as he considered the bloody trail Ramirez was leaving. How had a seemingly innocent business partnership become so twisted? He'd become ensnared in it because he sought to bend the rules thinking what did some pottery matter. What a fool he'd been.

"Ah and if we go back over each thing, what do you think I should have done, oh great one? What should I have done when I learned Franklin was a spy? Should I have let such a man tell his employers what we had to offer? Franklin said he was forced into what he did. Someone else bears the burden for his death. I had no choice but to end his life—although I will admit probably the way I did it was not very smart. If he had been able to talk when Rachel found him, well it doesn't bear thinking about. I don't want her tied into this anymore than you do."

O'Brian realized he was standing by the sacrificial font and looked down at it with distaste. It was as though he could see the blood staining its carved surface. "No more killings," he said finally, moving away from the thing.

"That sounds like an order, mi hermano."

"A prophecy." Michael O'Brian knew he was already entangled in all that would fall upon Ramirez. He had to think about it. Find a way to survive what was bound to fall on them all. If he couldn't free himself from the web, he had to keep his daughter clear of it. More over, he had to keep Ramirez away from her. How the hell could he do that?

"Don't worry," Ramirez said with a chuckle that sent chills down O'Brian's spine. "Whatever happens from now on will be to our advantage. I might have made mistakes before, but I know now what went wrong." He laughed again, the sound echoed in the eerie room. "They know nothing... They can prove nothing."

"They?"

"The feds."

"You think they know nothing?" O'Brian knew it was useless to argue but he tried anyway. "Those hot shots find their pigeon dead. An old couple with no enemies are violently beaten. Donovan is attacked by three nitwits. You think they are so dumb that they won't draw the connections?" O'Brian raised his eyebrows.

"Guessing is one thing. Proving quite another."

"Government men look after their own," O'Brian persisted, determined no more innocent people were going to die. "And I have been told that there is a special unit in here to investigate. They would be men like you and yours, men who don't play by the rules. Who can also be ruthless. You are losing sight of everything, Diego. Your desire for vengeance with Donovan, wanting to hurt him piece by piece, it's going to trip you up and drag me to hell with you."

Ramirez laughed.

"You laugh now, but Donovan is government. If he turns up dead or even missing, they won't quit until they find out what happened. Don't forget the blow-up after they tortured and killed the DEA agent, Camerena. The chafe from that is still coming down."

Ramirez's mouth curled into a cruel line. "The blood of my brother cries out from the grave. He will not rest until he has seen justice. It is in my blood to avenge the wrong that has been done my family."

"What's it going to take to make you see?"

"Don't worry, compadre. I'll find a way that won't hurt our business and may even help it."

Disgusted, O'Brian turned away. It was an effort to keep his voice calm. "You'll destroy us all."

"I can wait, until the day is here," Ramirez murmured, staring into the crystal skull. "As it was with my ancestors, so it will be with me. My enemies pay for their deeds. I will know no peace until I see Donovan on his knees, begging for his life. Until I rip open his flesh, see his blood flow like a river."

O'Brian stared at him, an expression of abhorrence on his face that he didn't need to hide because Ramirez was now into his own world.

CHAPTER 7

F riday night when Jake turned in his driveway, the first thing he saw was Rachel's truck parked along the street. *Okay,* he thought suspiciously, *what's she up to now?*

To his surprise, Rachel was not waiting in the truck. Walking slowly up the sidewalk, he opened the front door, noting it was not locked. In the living room, nothing looked as it had when he'd left that morning. "Uh... Rachel," he called.

"Hi." She popped her head out of the kitchen, "want a cold beer?"

"How'd you get in?"

"Actually, you left the window in the kitchen open. It was easy to unfasten the screen and climb in. Don't you worry about burglars, Donovan?"

He shook his head as he walked through the living room, still trying to decide what she'd done. Colorful red carnations graced the mantle. The objects he and she had bought on their foray into Nogales were resting on tables or draped over pieces of his threadbare furniture. It all made a difference but there was more and he tried to put his finger on what.

The kitchen was bubbling with good smells, a small room air

conditioner in the window was blowing enough air around to make the room tolerable. Over the stove was a wire frame of some sort, and pans he'd never seen were hooked to it.

"What's this?" he asked as he picked up the lid to a pan where a rich tomato-meat sauce simmered.

She closed the refrigerator door and handed him a beer. "It will be enchiladas. Hope your stomach is up to spicy food."

"Hmmm."

"Don't you like enchiladas?"

"I like them... more or less." He took a sip of his beer. The oven was hot and two other pans simmered at the back of the stove. "Looks like a feast."

"Just a few other things. And--" A knock at the door interrupted her. He looked at her with a question. She shrugged-- her large lavender eyes open innocently.

When he opened the door, Krista was standing there. A bottle of wine in her hand. "What's this?" Jake asked as she shoved the bottle into his hand and entered the house.

Rachel was standing at the door to the kitchen and smiled weakly as he glared at her. "Friends for dinner?" she suggested guilelessly.

"Friends? Like who?" he questioned with raised eyebrows.

"Well, you didn't really get to meet Mark, Maria's husband, and I ran into David Bannister, so..."

He grabbed her wrist and with a brief, feral smile directed toward Krista, who had settled on the sofa, he dragged Rachel into the kitchen. "What's this all about?" he asked, loosening the top button of his shirt.

"You look hot and dusty. Do you want to shower before dinner?" she asked, ignoring his question. "There's time."

"Maybe, when I know what's going on."

"Don't be so suspicious, Jake." She reached up and pulled down his head for a quick kiss.

"It pays to be suspicious."

"Not tonight. We're having a few friends to dinner. Don't make a big deal out of it."

"Like the way a *couple* have friends to dinner?" he asked, cynicism lacing his words.

"Maybe," she smiled back sweetly. "I have a few more things to take care of in here. Go take your shower."

By the time he showered and changed into T-shirt and shorts, Bannister was working his charm on Krista, and Mark and Maria Sandoval had just arrived.

After the introductions had been done, Rachel disappeared into the kitchen to reappear with a big tray loaded with wine glasses, Perrier, beer, a bottle of Merlot, the bottle of wine Krista had brought, and quesadilla appetizers. She set it all on a small table.

"Jake would you fill the glasses to order?" she asked, smiling and disappearing back into the kitchen with Maria and Krista.

After he'd filled the glasses, Jake looked more closely at Mark Sandoval who had been standing beside David Bannister.

"Do I know you?"

"I was briefly at your house once with Jerrod Otis when he came to pick up something you said you'd loan him. Can't remember what. I've seen you in court too-- on opposite sides."

"Hmmmm, I'm trying to place the case."

When Mark told him, Jake smirked. "It's all coming back to me. The guy was a louse."

Bannister chuckled.

"Technically correct," Sandoval agreed with a chuckle of his own.

Jake shrugged as he took a swig from his own beer. "Guess none of us do what we like all the time."

"Some come closer," Bannister said. "I'm definitely thinking of making a career change myself."

Jake narrowed his eyes. "Soon?"

"After a certain issue has been resolved."

"You two working on a case together," Sandoval asked with interest.

"Just dating still," Jake said.

"But if he lets me get to third base," Bannister added, "it could get serious."

Rachel and the women reappeared with several trays laden with various Mexican dishes. The food was settled onto Jake's large trestle table which he barely recognized under its purple tablecloth, matching napkins, yellow pottery dishes, candles and flowers. Not only were the nicks in the table hidden, but the mismatched chairs seemed to belong together by the way she had placed them.

Looking around the room, Jake finally realized what had changed. There was a woman's touch everywhere. A couple of lamps from a junk store or her attic not only lit the room but gave it an old-fashioned ambiance that suited the age of the house. Colorful throw pillows helped to distract from the threadbare quality of the sofa and chairs, Indian and Mexican blankets added color, and in some way he didn't understand, the combination of color and aura of another culture brought out a charm in his house Rachel had told him was there but that he had never seen. Nothing had really changed, yet everything had--down to the ceramic male and female figures on opposite sides of his fireplace mantle, one bearing a water ola and the other a pack of firewood.

After dinner, despite a shortage of chairs, they settled into the living room. Rachel smiled and said she'd leave space for someone else and plopped onto Jake's lap. Bannister only smiled wryly as she put her arm possessively around Jake's shoulder.

"Someone told me today," Mark said, his own arm around Maria, "that Jennifer Morris died."

"She never regained consciousness," Bannister said with a nod.

"That was an awful thing," Krista said with a sip of wine. "You think they'll nail who did it?"

"Not a lot to work with right now," Bannister said.

"Any idea of why?" Maria asked. "Maybe when they know why, they'll get the person."

"You a lawyer's wife or something?" Jake joked.

Maria grinned.

"There is nothing specific," Jake said, "but they were ones who liked to spend a lot of time out on the desert."

"What could that mean?" Rachel asked. "I do too."

He didn't remind her that her seeing a dead man had come from that. "There are some places that a person can see too much. Or someone can think that they did."

"And what might they have seen?"

"No way to know for sure, of course, but we've learned from family that one of their favorite spots was out your way."

She grew quiet. "You think it related to the man I found?" she asked finally when she saw he wasn't going to offer more.

"I remember when I was in high school," Maria reminisced. "They came to school events, the concerts, stuff like that even though they didn't have kids. They'd always waited around afterward to talk to the performers, say something nice. My junior year, I sang a solo for a Christmas program. I lost the high note at a crucial point in the song. I felt awful until Mrs. Morris took my hand and told me how much the song had meant to her, how she'd loved the feeling I put into it. I forgot I'd blown the notes then."

"I'd like to get my hands on whoever killed them," Mark growled. "I'd show them what it felt like. Maybe I'd even leave enough for the cops."

"You guys know how to kill a party," Krista complained.

"Sorry," said Bannister with a smooth smile. "What can we talk about that will be more pleasant?"

"How about Rachel's art show in a few weeks? You ready for that?" Maria asked her.

"Two more watercolors to frame, and I will be."

"I remember you saying you were an artist," Krista said with interest. "What kind of stuff do you paint? Any of that weird, new modern stuff with skulls and corpses walking around."

Rachel laughed. "Obviously you keep up on the latest trends."

"I go to some of the shows."

"My work is mostly landscapes. Occasionally people. I guess it's somewhat modern, in that I don't paint exactly what I see. I paint what I feel. It's not photographic, but you can usually figure out what it is. The only times I painted skulls though was when I went through a Georgia O'Keeffe phase at twenty."

"Do you show your stuff in Nogales?"

Rachel shook her head. "But you could come up to the Sedona gallery for the opening. Actually I did bring something with me tonight. It's not framed, but I wanted to show it to Jake."

"Hey, I'd love to see it."

Rachel looked at Jake who seemed to be a million miles away, his expression somber. "It's of you," she said, bringing him back quickly from wherever he'd gone.

"Me?" he quipped. "Didn't that canvas self-destruct?"

"You painted our Jake?" Krista asked. "Definitely I want to see it. Can't imagine a painting of Jake though." She giggled.

"Bring it out," Maria said.

"Is it okay with you?" Rachel asked Jake, smoothing back his hair in a casually affectionate gesture, which told more about the state of her feelings than any words could have done.

"I'd be strung up if I said no," Jake said, his voice reflecting his lack of enthusiasm.

She got up and brought the big painting from its hiding place in the extra bedroom. She propped it in front of the fireplace and stepped back. She heard them all talking at once, commenting on the way it captured Jake and the desert, about how much they liked its energy and the colors. Everyone except Jake. She looked at his face as he stared at the likeness of himself. She wondered what he thought and received no clue from his stony face.

The man in the painting dominated the ground on which he stood and even the mountains beyond his head. Strength, character and even a kind of beauty were evident on his rugged face and even more so in his eyes--the eyes of an eagle surveying his domain.

"Hell, if that's how you see him," Bannister said with a reluctant smile of defeat. "No wonder you preferred him to me."

"I don't know if I believed you were really an artist," Krista said, "I do now."

But Jake said nothing. Rachel was uncertain of whether it was because he liked it or hated it. She became anxious for the evening to end so she could find out.

When everyone had finally gone, Rachel couldn't wait to ask the question. "About the painting—didn't you like it?"

"I just... What were you trying to prove tonight?" He walked to the mantle, leaning one elbow against it as he turned to look at her.

"Huh?"

"Fixing up my house, cooking all that food, having over friends, the painting. What were you trying to prove?"

She rose from the sofa as though from a hot coal. Angrily she thrust the hair hanging loose around her face behind her shoulders.

"Prove! Prove! What on this good earth is the matter with you, Jacob Donovan? Why are you always looking for something under a rock?"

He turned away, looking at anything but her or the painting. He knew what was wrong. He was scared. But he couldn't admit that to her. It was hard enough to admit it to himself. He stood six foot five in his stocking feet, weighed two hundred and ten pounds, and he couldn't tell her that a little thing like her scared the living hell out of him. He had always protected himself or thought he had, but now, he had no weapons against this.

"Do you think I'm trying to trap you?" she asked, hands on her hips, her eyes flashing lavender fire.

"You'd have no reason to do that," he said, the muscle pulsing in his jaw.

"Jake, can't you ever just take something for what it is, without looking for the negative side? I fixed a dinner because I like to cook and I thought you'd enjoy sharing it with friends. People do things like that." She knew her voice had risen, but she had no desire to get it or her anger under control. She not only wanted to yell at him but also to hit him. And right after that, she wanted to tear the shirt from his back, have her way with him, and forget all the reasons she shouldn't.

He sat back on the sofa running his fingers through his hair. "Nothing in my life has shown me how to be with a woman like you. I tried to warn you."

She went to her knees and lifted his head so that she could look directly into his eyes, "Donovan, don't you know, nobody knows how to love until they do."

"Were we talking about love?" he asked coldly.

"We could be."

He stared at her. "All right, you tell me this. babe. What do I do when you decide this has all been a mistake? How do I go back to what I was before you?"

"Life is full of risks," she whispered, lips against his temple. "I know fear too--fear of losing my one chance for a certain kind of relationship that I could have with you. It's all tenuous, uncertain, scary. I don't understand where this kind of feeling came from or why but the alternative to not taking risks is sterile loneliness."

He took a deep breath. "I do like the painting."

She smiled, cuddling down against his side. His arms came around her. "I'm glad because I was afraid you didn't."

"Not that I think I look like that, but I was proud as hell it's how you see me, and I appreciated everything today." With a jolt, almost a kick in the stomach, he realized how much he had appreciated everything. How much he liked having her lying against him. How good it had been to walk through a door with warmth and a woman waiting. A day that included friends sharing a meal. And how had he rewarded her? With suspicion and accusations.

He kissed her, the kiss slow and gentle, as he tried to make it right. She smiled, kissing his earlobe, running her lips along his cheek. "Well, I was wondering," she whispered against the edge of his mouth.

"What?"

"I want you to come to the art show opening in two weeks."

"Uhh, as in Sedona?" He grimaced.

"Uh huh."

"I've never been to an art gallery." Defensively he prepared to line up reasons why he never should go to one.

"Past experience isn't required. All you have to do is stand around and look bored."

"I don't know, babe," he protested, running his hand along the back of his neck. "I can't believe you'd want me there."

"Why not?" She leaned back to study his face.

"I'm not the kind of guy you take to a fancy art show. Think about this for a minute. You want to impress them, right? You think I'd help you do that!"

"I want you to be with me. I don't care who you impress."

"Rachel, I never finished high school. I got my GED, even some college, but I never got a diploma like everybody else."

"So?"

"So--I'd make a fool of myself. All I know is being a cop."

"And what do you think is required to go to an art gallery?" she asked teasingly, running her fingers teasingly across his lips.

"And there's your father," he went on, ignoring the provocation, "won't he be there?" Donovan was not particularly eager to meet the man who was bound to regard his interest in his daughter as usurpation. Adding to that was his discomfort over Bannister's warnings about the illegal activities in which O'Brian could be involved. A casual meeting at an art gallery didn't seem like a wise plan.

"You have to meet him sometime, and Sedona would be as good as any. I want you with me at the opening."

"Persistent little thing," he muttered, his own lips against her forehead as he also found--not for the first time--that saying no to her was not an easy thing.

"It's one of my better qualities," she said with a broad smile as she used her lips rather convincingly to persuade him. "Come with me."

He groaned until he thought up a new excuse. "I don't see how we could. Sedona's a good five hours from here. It'd be too late to drive all the way back to Nogales after the show." He smiled, his thoughts moving ahead. A motel might not be such a bad idea. If they did that, abstinence would come to an abrupt end. He was no fool in reading a woman's body, and he knew Rachel wanted him nearly as much as he wanted her.

"I've already figured it out. Aunt Florence, my mother's sister, lives in Paradise Valley. It'd be late, but we could get there in time to spend the night."

He groaned. "You would have a relative in Paradise Valley."

"It does happen to be convenient."

He wasn't so sure about that. "I still don't think..."

"I want you with me. Please."

"What if I can't get time off?" he equivocated, seriously concerned now that he would not be able to find a legitimate reason not to go.

"You need a vacation, and I'll bet you have months of time saved up."

He groaned again, knowing he had lost another battle and would be going to Sedona want to or not.

"It will work beautifully. We can fool around there on Saturday, swim, whatever and then before we go home, Sunday, go to Mass."

"Mass?" he questioned with a look of pained acceptance on his face. "I don't do church."

"Aunt Flo always goes. She'd expect us to go too."

"This thing is snowballing."

"Do you have a pair of slacks, Jake?" she asked with a grin.

"I can't believe this," he groaned. "You are too much."

"Not for you," she promised, reaching up and kissing him on the chin and working her way determinedly toward his mouth, "never for you."

Mid-way through the week, Rachel took Matilda and went to Sedona to deliver her paintings and haggle with the gallery owner over where the works would be hung for the show. For Rachel, having the paintings grouped as she visualized them was important. She knew the gallery owner also to be an opinionated woman in regards her shows. Unfortunately, they didn't always agree. She brought with her several hundred new, full-color brochures for those patrons who couldn't make up their mind on the day of the opening, something to remind them what a mistake they would be making if they didn't return and make a purchase.

Although she was gone only two days, to Jake it seemed forever. It was then he finally admitted how much a part of him she had become. The night he walked in his front door to the aroma of something good cooking and her coming out of the kitchen smiling, her arms outstretched, he had swung her up into his arms and was kissing her before she could say hello.

"I missed you. I didn't want to miss you," he grumbled as he set her back on the floor.

She sighed, having driven all day just for that greeting. She kissed his chest. "Come out to my ranch this week-end."

He drew back, his eyes narrowed. "Uhhm why?"

Laughing, she unbuttoned the top button on his uniform. "What do you think?" she asked teasingly.

"You tell me."

"I want you to meet my father." She unbuttoned another button. The little witch had gotten all too good at that game. Unfortunately, Jake knew it was one, which would leave him aching.

"Why?" he asked stopping her fingers.

"Don't you think it's time?"

"No." It wouldn't ever be a good time to meet the man who would go into shellshock when he met the man her daughter was seeing.

"It will be relaxed, casual. I thought the three of us could go for a horseback ride. You do ride, don't you?"

"Do I look like the sort of man who wouldn't ride?" he asked distracted for the moment from his concerns over her father.

"You did grow up in town."

"Well, I didn't exactly grow up in a saddle as you likely did; but with the Border, even in this age of airplanes and helicopters, some of the roughest country is covered most easily on horseback."

"Good. Will you come?"

Reluctantly Jake accepted that if he was to continue to see Rachel, eventually he would have to meet her father. He didn't expect O'Brian to be pleased when he saw his daughter's interest in him. But he was learning something else. If Rachel wanted him there, he'd be there.

~

And on Saturday, he was. He drove down the long driveway, feeling as though he was going to his execution. Rachel showed him into her home. "Unfortunately Papa called last night, and he won't be here. Maybe I should have told him about you then, but he was so distracted I let it go."

The adobe house sprawled in several directions. At its center was a fountain and private garden. In the living room a large stone fireplace dominated one wall. Rachel's paintings were on the walls, some abstract, others realistic desert scenes, several bronze sculptures of Native American figures were on stands. "That," she pointed to one, "is an Alan Houser. Isn't it wonderful?"

Jake nodded absently, his interest caught by something else. He walked to the mantle to look more closely at a sculpture that looked like a primitive piece. "What's this?"

"It's the Mayan sun god embracing the moon goddess," she said with unhidden distaste.

"You sound like you hate it."

"That about covers it. It's... got a feel to it that seems violent, as though the embrace is not welcomed to say the least."

"It looks like it'd be expensive *at the most*."

"It's a copy. If it was the real thing, it'd could be as much as six hundred years old and worth about half what this ranch is."

"But it's about embracing. What could be wrong with that?"

She shook her head. "I don't know. Maybe I am blaming it by association. I didn't like the person who gave it to us."

"And that was?"

"My father's partner."

"That's the only reason?"

She shook her head. "You are pushing me. I don't honestly know why I don't like it. Don't laugh at me but those pieces that are copies from another culture, their spiritual traditions, I always wonder what they meant to their creators. Could it be there is a kind of—"

"Bad luck attached," he finished for her.

She nodded.

"You are superstitious?"

"Maybe, a little."

You might have to worry if it was an original, but a copy?"

"Maybe I just don't like the thing because I think it's ugly."

He laughed. "I thought you liked ugly things."

She put her arms around him. "You're not ugly. How many times do I have to tell you that? You're beautiful... almost exotic looking."

"So is the face on that thing."

"There's something different about it..." She stopped abruptly, aware she didn't know why she didn't like the little sculpture but sure now that she wanted it out of her home as soon as she could speak to her father about it. She shivered a little, and then smiled, trying to restore her mood. "Let's go outside. I'll show you the rest of the place before we saddle up."

Out back, Jake saw numerous rustic buildings, a couple of apparently locked sheds and a good-sized barn. All the outbuildings and fences showed signs of their age but were still erect and serviceable.

"I love this place--the birds, the mountains. From my bedroom window I can look south into Mexico; from the back patio I see the Atascosa Mountains; out front I watch the sun set behind Manzanita Mountain. To me, this is paradise."

He nodded his agreement. "Some don't care for the desert, but I've always loved it too."

"For generations my people have cared for this land," Rachel said proudly. "My great-grandparents came here to build this ranch. He had been a marshal in Tucson but decided he wanted a different life. In those days there were still Apache renegades. Blood was shed to hold onto it, but my people did. They brought with them their daughter and four more were born on this ranch."

"Cattle then?"

139

"Yes, the strongest and toughest of the longhorns that could hold their own with all they had to face."

"I'd think a place this size'd still be running quite a few cattle," Jake said, seeing only horses and no other livestock.

"When I was small, it did--too many." Rachel looked at the land beyond the fence. "Because of overgrazing, the grass almost disappeared. Papa took the cattle off three years ago and began a reclamation project. Now, the native grass is returning--the javelina, antelope and deer are flourishing. Eventually there'll be cattle but not so many."

"He could afford to let the land take time off?" Jake didn't want to ask about her father, didn't want to be doing Bannister's dirty work, but the questions were just beneath the surface, his investigative mind unable to resist them.

"I don't think he felt he had a choice. In this part of the country, you can't feed hay year-round and make a profit, unless you grow your own or are raising purebred stock. We have less than two hundred acres of arable land."

"What's Diego Ramirez connection with this place? Is he a partner in the ranch?"

"How do you know of him?"

His smile was dry. "You can probably guess about that. I *am* in Border Patrol."

"I hate him," she spat out the words.

"Why?"

"He's, I don't know the right word. Okay, unclean."

Jake smiled, thinking that about covered it. "So does Ramirez own a piece of this?"

"No, two years ago, he put it into my name on paper. I do not know why he did it as it is O'Brian land, which means his too. Ramirez does, however, own the land right across the border. A few years ago, he talked Papa into going into another business... developing Mexican crafts, then bringing them to the States to sell. Things like that." She pointed derogatorily to the sculpture.

"I have nothing to do with that, but it means he's here more than I like, but Papa promised that soon, he'd end the arrangement."

"Hmmm." There were more questions, but Jake was in no mood to ask them.

An hour later they were on horseback, heading west into the Pajarita Wilderness that abutted the Circle O. Rachel smiled with pleasure at the sight Jake made as he sat easily in the saddle, the picture of a man of long ago, at peace with his environment. With his weathered jeans, worn boots, faded blue cotton shirt, and Stetson, all he needed was a pistol on his hip to complete the picture. Instead, she had seen the shoulder holster and a more modern looking gun. She had stuck a rifle into her saddle scabbard. She had never needed one, but it just made sense in the wild country.

"We should have gone riding sooner," she said. "I didn't know you would ride so well."

"You're a good rider yourself." She sat a saddle as though she'd been in one all her life, which Jake imagined was nearly true.

He pointed to where a coyote was loping across the top of a ridge, heading for its den. "Looks like he's had a hard night."

"Maybe he just doesn't like mornings," she teased.

"Does your dad import any real archaeological goods from Mexico?" Jake asked irresistibly drawn back to his questions.

"That would be impossible," Rachel said. "It's illegal to take Mesoamerican antiquities from their country."

"Meso-- what?"

"Mesoamerican, you know--Olmec, Toltec, Mayan and Aztec."

"You sound like you know what you're talking about."

"I should. It was my minor at the university."

"But you don't like the art."

She smiled faintly. "I like some of it. I admit though I wasn't so sensitive to them then. I thought studying about man's history would be good for my artistic expression, give me a broader feel for design and putting symbols into my work. Mesoamerican seemed a likely choice considering my family heritage. There is actually some Yaqui in my heritage."

"Was studying it good for your... artistic expression?"

"I don't know. Maybe. Some of what I learned was interesting... some a little frightening. Man can do terrible things in the name of his religion."

He let that go but then asked, "If I was looking... like at what you call an artifact, and I wanted to know if it was old and valuable or even where it came from, how would I figure it out?"

"Good question. That's why sites should be left intact. The only real proof is that which is around the artifacts--wood, burnt charcoal, bones, layers of soil. It's easy to create fakes."

"You can't tell by what it is?"

"An expert could make an educated guess, but positive identification—not easily. The Olmecs had a figure they made--half man, half jaguar. They were strongly identified with it, but it was adopted for religious practices by later civilizations too. So-- "

"Hmmm."

"Are you really interested in any of this, Jake?" she asked with amazement.

"What do you think I am, a dummy?" he asked with mock insult in his voice. "I've studied Native American cultures myself. Community college classes."

She smiled. "So then, this is one of those things we have in common that we didn't know."

He hated deceiving her. It wasn't that he wasn't interested in the cultures, but his prime interest had been fueled by David Bannister's questions, which were drawing him to probe for what he could discover. Diego Ramirez was a dangerous man. If Rachel's father was involved with him, he could be dangerous to Rachel.

"What were these cultures again, the ones that make up Mesoamerican?" he asked.

He enjoyed watching the enthusiasm with which she explained to him about the early cultures of Mexico. "Aztecs built probably the most spectacular civilization. They founded Tenochtitlán on Lake Texcoco, which became one of the largest cities on earth at that time."

"You mean in America?"

"No, on the earth. For its time, it was an advanced culture; but if you can know a people by their artifacts, they must have been cruel and warlike. They kept the people around them in subjugation and practiced human sacrifice. Their preoccupation with death showed up in their art."

"Human sacrifices?"

She shuddered. "They liked to cut out hearts as a way to increase their own strength. The practice of dismemberment shows up in their artifacts too."

"So none of them will show up on my mantle."

She laughed. "It can be a little hard to imagine owning when you consider what those images meant to them... It wasn't just imaginary art. They actually did those things as a way to build their power. They also had an obsession with death." She smiled. "Not that, as Krista said the other night, that isn't also showing up in our modern art sometimes too."

"What's the end of the story?"

"For the Aztecs it was Cortez. He was after gold and plundered their cities to get it. Those few who survived were driven into the countryside. You might say they reaped what they had sown."

"Do you believe everybody gets what they deserve?" Jake said staring into the distance and wondering when it would come to him.

"The question, of course, is what do we deserve?" Rachel

asked. To distract him from his brooding mood, she reminded him of his own study of Indian cultures and asked which ones.

"Arizona tribes--Navajo, Apache, Yaqui, the O'odhams."

"I can understand the last three because they ranged through this area. You probably work with their descendants, but how come Navajo?"

"I have a Navajo friend, Ed Begay, stationed in El Paso now. Ed didn't live on the reservation anymore, but it was an important part of who he was. More important, Ed did know who he was. One night we were working a stakeout, he said he could see I had a lot of anger in me and said it wasn't healthy. The way his people deal with inner conflict was through ceremonies. I ought to go up with him and he'd ask his uncle to do a Blessing Way for me. That one pretty much covers it all--religious, social, emotional, physical."

"His uncle was a medicine man?"

"A singer. They don't call them medicine men. Ralph Begay is a wizened up old man, white-haired, but sharp as a tack. He and his wife still keep a flock of sheep. That old man scampers up and down cliffs a younger man'd think twice about."

"And you let him do that for you, the Blessing Way?"

Jake smiled. "Yeah. The words were all in Navajo; so I didn't understand it all, but I think it's their history, kind of an oral reciting, about how they identify with their land, who they are. First a sweat bath to prepare, then stripped to briefs, we went to his hogan and sat on a dirt floor. Begay, blessed the hogan, then laid out what was in his medicine bag--dirt from their four sacred mountains, pollen, flint crystal, a chunk of turquoise, and an eagle feather. "

Rachel frowned. Although she wasn't very religious, Mass only once in awhile, she wasn't totally comfortable with other traditions. What he described sounded occult. But what were all religions when they attempted to manipulate outcome?

Jake seemed oblivious to her doubts as he went on, "He told

me to hold the mountain soil bundle while he prayed and sang. I've heard men pray. Most of the time it comes off meaningless, but not with old Begay. I don't know the word to describe the whole thing, but I guess timeless comes as close as any."

He looked down into the canyon they rode above. Below he saw sycamores and oaks, the setting serene, pure, and untainted. That was something of the way he'd felt about the Blessing Way.

"Blessing Way is to help a man see that happiness is within and blessings are something to look for and see around him. The next day, Begay put a mound in the center of the hogan, marked it with a cross of white corn meal and washed me down hard with yucca suds."

He remembered even now the feeling he'd had after the energetic scrubbing. It was a strange sort of baptism into life. "His singing went on all through that night. A singer has to memorize it all. At first light, he had me go outside to face east and breathe in the dawn four times."

More important than the ceremony in Jake's memory were the two days in the primitive hogan with the Navajo holy man, a man trained and confident in his self and spirituality. And then there was the land itself, the high, plateau country, the beauty of the log and earth hogan beneath a ridge of high red rock, the intense blue of the sky, the scent of sage on the air and in the distance the sound of sheep blatting, their bells tinkling. It had been everything about that time--and yet nothing possible to put into words.

"I'm not a Navajo; and don't want to be one, but up there, I saw the importance of tradition, of believing in something bigger than yourself. Maybe because I had nothing of my own, no creed, not even a set of family traditions, it was the first time I saw that any of that mattered."

"I didn't know non-Navajos were allowed to participate in ceremonies like that."

"Not usually."

She guessed there was more to the story, but since Jake seemed reluctant to talk about it, she didn't pursue it either. There would be time for them to learn each other's secrets.

They stopped for the lunch she'd packed on a hill overlooking the valley. Tying their horses to mesquite trees, they spread a blanket in the shade of a large rock outcropping and sat watching the view as they ate.

"It is peaceful here," he said, leaning back on one elbow.

"I come here sometimes to think--to plan."

"Where it comes to my personal life, I don't plan anything," he said after a moment.

"Why not?"

He shrugged. "I don't know. Maybe I've never been sure there'd be a tomorrow."

"Never?"

He tried to think if he'd ever believed in a future. If he had, he didn't remember when.

"I love to plan, to dream, to consider how something that I want can be."

He didn't want to think about plans, not on such a peaceful morning. Somehow he couldn't see any plan that could join their lives together. To avoid thinking, he reached out, pulling her against him. "Lovely lady," he whispered his lips a caress against her cheek, then her lips.

She ran her fingers through his dark blond hair. Knowing she shouldn't, she resisted only a moment before she reached up and began unbuttoning his shirt, exposing the hard muscular chest to the light and not incidentally, her touch and then her lips.

"Mmmm," she sighed as he lifted her shirt from the belt, his fingers splayed now across her bare back as he explored her mouth with his tongue. He stroked her, pulling her tight against his hardness and laying them both back on the blanket.

In another moment, Rachel realized--with what little part of her mind was still capable of thinking--she would be past stopping, past caring what they did. She had to pull away now. With a will she'd never known she possessed, she sat up, leaving both of them breathing heavily. This was not the time, not yet.

Jake lay back, staring up at the sky as he worked to gain control of himself. "You can't keep doing this to me," he groaned after a moment, his breath coming unevenly.

"I'm sorry." She wanted to touch him but she couldn't do that. She had pushed them both into an unfair situation, but it was because she wanted him so badly, wanted something she sensed only he could give her. She stared at the distant mountain, feeling a frustration that seemed to encompass her being. She was sure though, that for Jake and herself, this was not the time. She was equally sure the time was coming.

CHAPTER 8

At noon Friday when she got to Jake's Rachel suggested he drive her BMW to Sedona. She saw by the gleam in his golden eyes that he wasn't comfortable with the idea. "We don't have to," she said, her own smile uneasy.

"No, it's a fit car for a princess," he said, a sardonic twist to his words that made her know it did bother him.

"I would take Matilda. She was driving okay, but making some kind of noise, and I figured the mechanic better check it out. It might have been nothing, but I didn't want to make it part way and get stalled." He didn't argue with her and got into the driver's seat.

"You don't need to apologize. It makes perfect sense for you to drive a car like this."

"Don't you like how it handles?" she asked as he turned the car onto the highway.

He shrugged as he pulled into the passing lane. The car handled like a dream as he had known it would. His only real objection was in his own inability ever to provide her with such a vehicle.

"Do you like this dress?" she asked, unsure if she wanted to know or just distract him from his moodiness.

He glanced over, although he already knew how the white, simple, yet sophisticated dress emphasized her slender frame, how the turquoise Navajo squash blossom necklace and silver belt made her look a part of this land. "It's not the dress so much," he said with a faint smile, bringing his eyes back to the ribbon of freeway ahead, "but the woman wearing it, and she looks beautiful."

She smiled, settling back in the seat. "I wish Papa could have driven up with us. I hope he flies in as he promised."

Jake kept his eyes on the road, not wanting to think about Michael O'Brian. He'd had Bannister sitting at his desk too many days telling him more of what was coming out regarding Ramirez and O'Brian. Jake had begun to believe there was a real chance Rachel's fairy tale world might soon be threatened. What kind of man was O'Brian that he could leave his daughter in such a vulnerable position? Likely he had some idea of it two years ago when he put the ranch in her name. Protecting the ranch might not be the only threat to Rachel when Bannister found the proof against Ramirez?

For the last week, as the evidence had been building, Jake had thought more and more about something he'd never considered. What if he married Rachel? Got her to move in with him? He knew she was thinking she'd like living with him. He couldn't imagine her doing it without marriage, not with her ideas. If she got an apartment, well that would leave her living alone. He didn't like that at all not with someone running around who liked beating people to death. If they married, he knew it wouldn't last but maybe it'd be long enough to keep her out of the mess he felt sure was going to unroll.

"What are you thinking?" she asked, smiling at his somber expression.

"You do that at the worst times," he muttered.

"Do what?"

"Pry into my thinking." He smiled but he knew she'd taken offense at the attempted joke.

"All right, don't tell me about your thoughts. Tell me about your work this week. Did you finish whatever it is you do with surveillance tapes?"

He knew she was just trying to share his world, but that was almost as bad as talking about his thinking of a more permanent relationship between them since that involved the growing proof of the Ramirez and O'Brian involvement in smuggling. Not just the smuggling either but more. Jake had no doubt about Ramirez but hoped O'Brian was not involved in the rest of it.

"Do you see your mother sometimes, Jake?" she asked from seemingly out of nowhere.

Dark as Jake's thoughts had been, he felt his body tense at this new invasion into his world. Any questions about his past made him uneasy and Rachel always seemed to probe the sorest points.

"Kind of pretty country," he said about the barren terrain through which they were driving.

"You're avoiding anything I ask."

He shook his head. "No. Just..."

"Why don't you ever talk about your family?" she asked her own voice tense.

"Geesus, Rachel."

"I am having a hard time understanding why. When we went horseback riding, you said you'd dealt with past conflicts. Didn't this qualify?"

He shrugged. He knew Rachel well enough by now to know he wasn't going to get away from this until she'd said whatever it was she had on her mind.

"How old were you when your mother left?"

"Uhmmm maybe eight-- the first time. When she left for keeps-- eleven." He knew exactly, knew that the first time he had been seven, a month from his eighth birthday. He didn't want

Rachel to know he could remember to this day what he'd been wearing when he'd realized she wasn't just out but was really gone, the lost feeling inside as he'd looked around the squalid apartment and wondered how he and his brother would live.

"Were you put in foster care?"

"My brother was sixteen when she finally took off. He made sure we didn't get noticed by the system. If you aren't on welfare and don't get in trouble with the law, not too many people care what you're doing."

Rachel looked at him with stunned amazement. "I thought your brother was younger."

"No."

"But... you seemed to feel so responsible for him."

Jake shrugged. "Maybe I figured I owed him." He had only later learned how his brother had paid the bills during those years. Welfare and a foster home would have been better.

"I can't believe the school didn't notice you didn't have a parent in the home."

Jake smiled humorlessly. "There are ways. I wasn't that regular in school attendance, even when she lived with us. My brother got used to forging her name on excuses. Probably they'd have wondered if they'd seen a real signature."

"But the community--"

"Not too many people care one way or the other about a couple of scruffy, kids, at least not so long as they don't get in serious trouble."

"That's terrible."

"We survived."

"Have you forgiven her?"

He felt the muscles tighten in his jaw. "Keep your eyes open for the next gas station. You forgot to fill this beast up."

The desert terrain flew past as they gassed up in Tucson, then drove across the flatlands to Phoenix, and through the city itself.

North, the highway began to climb into scenic hills, covered with saguaro cactus, prickly pear and ocotillo; the dry washes lined with palo verde, desert willow and mesquite trees.

Rachel had thought long and hard about some way to bring back up the subject of Jake's mother, but it seemed there was no easy way. Bluntly, she began, "Jake, it's important you forgive your mother. I can imagine it would be hard, but..."

He laughed harshly. "You can imagine? I doubt that."

"It had to have hurt you a great deal when she left," Rachel said, ignoring his sarcasm. She was beginning to wonder how much of what his mother had done was still impacting Jake's view of women and that meant her.

"Her leaving was a relief."

"How?" He had a closed off expression; clearly she was treading on forbidden territory. An inner prompting told her he needed to air the old hurts, and she refused to let it rest.

She wondered if he was going to answer when he finally said, "She had boyfriends. Sometimes they lived with us. John and I took our share of knocks from our so-called stepfathers. At least when she was gone, so were they."

"That's awful." She reached over, lightly rubbing his shoulders.

"It's nothing now," he said stonily.

Rachel knew that wasn't true. Much of Jake's inability to trust anyone stemmed from his childhood experiences. He had come to believe love led to pain and still seemed to half expect that to be the result of caring for anyone. It seemed if they were to have any chance for happiness, he had to get past that.

"Do you know where your mother is now?" she asked.

"Drop it, Rachel," he snapped. "You are stubborn, like a dog with a bone on something. This all is in the past."

"Is it?" She knew the answer to that question but wanted him to admit it. "Isn't that the real reason you are afraid of your feelings for me?"

152

He looked over at her, his lips set firmly in his anger. "Why are you doing this?"

"What?"

"Nagging!"

"Why is it nagging to want to talk about feelings? It's important."

"Says who?"

"Lots of experts. There are groups where people get together to talk about dysfunctional homes. I've read books that say we have to come to terms with who we've been before we can figure out who we are. It's been shown that-- "

He interrupted angrily. "Son of a bitch. Drop it!"

"Oh I see," Rachel said, frustrated at being cut off and at his unwillingness to share his feelings with her. "You've said enough, and it has thereby been decreed we drop it. What if I still have a need to talk about it?"

"But it's me it's hurting--" He stopped when he realized what he'd said.

"That fact that it hurts you to talk about is proof that there is a wound there that still hasn't healed."

"Damn it Rachel, let it lie!"

"We always reach this point. It doesn't seem fair in a relationship when one person calls all the shots."

"I told you I'd be no good in a relationship--that I wasn't sure how much I had to give."

"But you're not trying."

"I am!" Seeing a sign for a rest area, Jake moved into the right lane to pull off. When he had parked the sedan, he turned to her, his golden eyes narrowed. "Are you looking for a pound of flesh? Is that what this is all about? Well, if it is, you got it." Angrily he yanked open the car door and stalked off, leaving her to fume in the car.

After a moment, she followed, the blazing heat of the summer sun hit her. "What makes you assume the worst in me?" she asked, knowing the answer and wondering if he did.

"Rachel, you have an innocence in you that doesn't get how the world is."

"I understand bad things happen."

"How? Through books?"

"My mother died when I was small."

"So you feel that qualifies you to understand how the world is for families... if you can call it that, like mine?"

"No, of course not."

He stared at the desert below, his teeth clenched as he sank onto a rock wall in the shade of a mesquite. "You take the car. I'll hitch a ride back to Nogales."

"That's illegal."

"I told you where I've come from," he retorted. "A little illegal won't bother me."

"You're the one now being childish. I can't believe your reaction just because I ask a few questions about your family."

He stared beyond her, his expression stony.

"Jake, I'm only asking because I care." She felt tears in her eyes and turned away so he wouldn't see them. She wouldn't use manipulation to bend him to her will. She moved to sit beside him on the wall. "I was wrong to push."

"I shouldn't have blown up," he muttered. She turned toward him and found herself pulled into his arms.

"I don't even know if she's alive now. I haven't seen her in years." His voice was so low she could barely hear his words.

"She did come back then?" Her words were half muffled against his shirt.

"Oh yeah," he said bitterly, "for money. She wanted a loan, at least that's what she called it."

She tightened her arms around him, feeling the pain in his voice, in every muscle of his body. "Oh Jake--"

"Don't pity me, babe. I don't want that from you."

"Jake, I don't pity you. I love you."

"What?"

"You have to have known that."

He swallowed. "No... I didn't." He didn't believe her either, but the words were sweet. He pulled her more tightly into his embrace as his lips crushed hers in a hungry kiss.

Back in the car, heading north again, Rachel thought carefully before she said, "In a way, we share something. With our mothers, I mean. It's different, but my mother left me too. Even though I knew it wasn't her fault, I was still hurt and mad for a long time. It didn't seem fair to me."

"What was your mother like?"

"Beautiful, black hair, coiled high. She was more of a lady than I'll ever be."

Jake snorted with disbelief. "If you aren't a lady, I don't know what one is."

"I don't know how to explain it, but everything around her was beautiful, was done beautifully. Just to watch her weed a garden was seeing something almost ritualistic. She would wear this broad brimmed straw hat, bring a bucket, her gardening gloves and trimmers. Carefully she'd sort through the plants, pulling the ones that didn't belong, throwing them in that bucket. When she was finished, the garden would be immaculate, and she'd carry off the buckets. Me, I never remember to wear gloves, throw the weeds out onto the patio or grass and am lucky if I remember to pick the pile up a week later."

He smiled. "Not exactly a felony."

"Maybe not, but it's not beautiful like the way my mother did it."

"A woman so concerned with beauty wouldn't have thought much of you being with a guy like me."

Rachel reached over, lightly massaging his shoulder. "She understood about love and I think she'd have liked you and thought you were beautiful just as I do."

He raised one eyebrow and looked over at her skeptically.

"Her grave is in the cemetery above our house. I go there sometimes to talk. It's as though I feel like the spirits of my ancestors are there. The last time I felt her approval over my feelings for you. Do you think I'm crazy?" she asked finally after he said nothing.

"I think you're beautiful--"

"You didn't answer my question."

"I know."

~

Sedona, nestled artistically among red rock mesas, was surrounded by colorful rock formations of all sizes. Running through the center of the town, below the main road meandered Oak Creek, large oaks and sycamores lining its banks. On the hillsides, junipers added color to the red earth. The homes were affluent and well kept in appearance. So far as Jake could see, the slogan--bring money--should have been posted on the sign announcing arrival.

The art gallery sat in a Spanish-style building above Oak Creek. Its windows took full advantage of the view, walls lined with colorful canvases, and floor already filled with people admiring the paintings. Rachel had arranged to have large bouquets of sage, mesquite and juniper interspersed throughout the rooms; the scent wafted on the air, reminding the buyers of the wild places out of which these paintings had been born. Native American drumming played from a stereo system.

Jake leaned against a wall, trying to stay out of the way, observing the people as they walked around, listening to snippets of conversation, and watching Rachel mingle and discuss the pieces with potential buyers.

When a tray of beverages came around, he had little hope that beer would be among the choices, and he was right. Reluctantly sipping a glass of white wine, he could see that a beer-drinking man didn't belong here. Cheeses, daintily cut bread, crackers, raw vegetables, Perrier, herbal teas, and white wine were the order of the day.

He began to think how much he wanted a cigarette. This time it had been six days and--seven hours since his last one. He wondered how much longer he could hold out. For a moment he could almost feel the first drag of smoke, the nicotine easing away his tension. For a moment--

A tall, middle-aged man walked up to him. "Boring, huh?" he said, smiling at what Jake knew was probably the glazed expression on his face.

"Not because of the paintings," Jake said defensively. He liked Rachel's work and felt proud of her ability.

"I like the artist's work too," the man said wryly. "It's the blasted openings that are hard to take." His voice was soft and pleasing, fitting his distinguished demeanor. "Everybody talking, making so-called deep observations and nobody's saying anything."

"My problem is I haven't got anything to say... even if it was nothing."

The gray-haired man chuckled. "Maybe the difference is you know you don't. These other folks are still fooling each other."

"I don't belong here."

"It's the pits when your wife drags you out to get some cultural event," the man agreed sympathetically.

Jake smiled but said nothing. He felt no need to inform him that he wasn't married or that he had come here with the artist. He watched as Rachel began talking to a handsome, well-bred looking man. She was so animated, so beautiful that he asked himself once again what she saw in him. This was where she belonged, with a man like that, not in the bar where he'd taken her, not in his dump of a house. Maybe tonight would be the night she saw that for herself.

"You really are uneasy here," the older man observed, his tone sympathetic.

"It's not the people. It's me."

"How come you?"

"Do I look like somebody who belongs in an art gallery?" Jake asked cynically, looking down past new black slacks to the recently polished cowboy boots at the end of his long legs.

"No, you look like you belong on a horse up a canyon somewhere," the man agreed with a laugh.

Jake felt a momentary lift as he thought of how good it would be to be anywhere but here, how much he suddenly craved a breath of fresh air, a moment of quiet.

"Women," the man said with a grin, "you can't live with 'em, you can't live without 'em."

"Tell me about it," Jake groaned.

"You don't look like a white wine man to me. What you need is a cold beer," the man assessed.

"It's not possible," Jake drawled.

"I've been to enough of these things to know the ropes. Follow me."

In a room behind the gallery, connected by a long hallway, a refrigerator revealed bottles of cold, Mexican beer. The man took two of them and led Jake out a door onto a deck overlooking the creek.

"You just saved my life or at the least my sanity," Jake said, swallowing the brew and breathing in the fresh air with almost as much appreciation.

"It's all in knowing the right people." The man chuckled as he took a slug from his own bottle. "You do have a woman here?"

"Maybe." He couldn't believe he was considering that possibility but it didn't matter much what he told this stranger.

The man chuckled. "Well, when you love 'em, you do what you have to do."

The moon was just beginning to rise over the mesas. "I'm learning that too."

"New at love?"

"You might say that."

"It's not easy," the man said, companionably leaning against the railing beside Jake, "but it's worth it. I've never known anything in my life worth so much as the love of a good woman."

"Worth the pain, you think?"

"For every thorn, there's that rose that makes it worthwhile. With time, my friend, you'll find the hurt is more than made up for by the loving."

"You a poet philosopher?" Jake asked with raised brows.

"Even the biggest of fools learns something after a few years." The man set down his half-finished beer. "I wish you luck, friend. I got to get out of here."

Smiling, Jake watched as the man left the deck.

When Jake was alone, he stared into the blackness of the night, wondering for a moment if what the man had said was true. Nothing lasts. He knew that for sure. The thing was would time with her be worth the pain that came later?

It seemed hours before Rachel was finished with the last art patron and ready to get back into the car for the drive south. Kicking off high heels, she wiggled her toes with a sigh of relief. "It was a good show, bigger turnout than I expected. Ardis did a wonderful job in arranging and promoting it."

"That shouldn't have been hard. Your work is great. Each painting adds to the others."

"Mmmm," she said, reaching over and kissing him on the cheek as he pulled the car out onto the dark highway, "thank you."

"It's the truth. I especially liked that one you did of the Babo-quivaris."

"You mean *Lonely Sentinel?*"

"It had a feeling of loneliness all right--kind of a spiritual longing too."

Rachel smiled. "Are you the man who told me you had no education in the fine arts?" she teased.

"It doesn't take an education to feel what you put into that painting."

"It takes sensitivity."

He ignored the compliment. "I also liked your ghost town ink drawings."

"They're some of my favorites," she agreed, yawning. "In a ghost town you feel all the emotions and spirits of the people who've been there before."

"You caught that in the drawings, almost like there was something floating just beyond the lines, but when I squinted, nothing was there."

"I should have you promote my work."

"I believe in your work, babe, but no way would I want to go to these things all the time or try to work the crowds when I was there."

She laughed. "Poor man! Was it so awful?"

"It had its moments."

"Did you meet many people? I tried to keep an eye on you, but it was impossible with all the clients. I didn't mean to neglect you so completely."

"I think for awhile the owner of the gallery thought I was there to steal something," he said with a wry twist to his expressive mouth. "She kept an eye on me for about an hour until she decided I wasn't up to anything."

Rachel chuckled. "She came up to me and pointed you out. I told her you were my bodyguard."

"You didn't!"

"Actually no, I told her you were my lover."

Jake snorted. "She must have liked hearing that."

"She complimented me on my taste." When he looked at her

in disbelief, she grinned. "She asked where I'd found you. She said real men are hard to come by. She requested I order her one if I come across another."

"Do you think I'm going to believe that?" He was amused in spite of himself.

"It's the truth." She put her hand over her heart to emphasize her veracity. "You know how women go for the rough, hard-as-nails, he-man types."

"No," he said, glancing over at her before he pulled the car out onto the freeway, "tell me how it is?"

"Women are putty in their hands."

"Doesn't seem to be working that way for me."

"Ah but it is. I just wish Papa could have stayed longer," Rachel sighed with regret.

"He was there?" Jake asked in amazement. "I didn't see you with anybody I figured could be your dad."

"He couldn't spend much time. I thought about pulling him over to you, but I wanted more time to explain everything; so, I decided to wait." She was beginning to feel that waiting to tell somebody something was the story of her life. Where patience had never been her virtue, she was now bombarded by demands for it. "I think I sold five paintings with three more possible."

"Amazing--" He stopped at her snort of disgust and amended, "I mean, considering the prices you were asking."

"That is a lot the gallery's decision. Every time a show sells out, the gallery believes you should up the prices for the next one. Of course, it benefits the dealer because they get forty percent of the selling price," she explained yawning again. "Between that, failed paintings and promotional cost, there's not quite as much money in it as it might seem. I think I need to start making some prints."

"Maybe then I could afford one," he teased.

"You'll find your supply is unending." She yawned again.

"Take a nap," he told her. "I'll wake you when we get to

Phoenix." He loosened his tie, unbuttoning the top buttons of his shirt, as he settled back to drive through the night.

As he drove and Rachel slept, he began wondering about her aunt. Rachel had told him only that Flo was eccentric and had never married, but other than that, he had no clue what to expect. With a cynical smile, he decided one thing he wouldn't expect would be a joyous greeting.

Was an aunt, an old-maid aunt, going to be proprietary? He couldn't even imagine what family was like--what it meant to have someone older who cared about you, argued with you over your choices, or even cared whether you lived or died.

He found himself wondering if he and Rachel had any chance to form a family of their own. The thought of Rachel as his wife ripped him apart inside. The feelings he had for her-- that she said she had for him were more than he'd ever dreamt, ever imagined. Shaking his head, tough guy, he berated himself, thinking what an idiot he was to dream of something permanent between them. If he asked her to be his wife, she'd laugh in his face. Or worse if she married him, it'd last only a short time before she would realize what a mistake she had made--then she'd leave him just as his mother had.

"What are you thinking?" she asked, surprising him because he had been so sure she was sleeping.

Unable to tell her his fears without putting a knife into his gut, he equivocated. "Wondering about your family. How your aunt's going to take somebody like me showing up at her door."

"You worry about that way too much."

"You and me. It's all a fairy tale, babe. Tomorrow or the next day you'll see that."

"You don't have much faith in me."

"It's not that. It's us together that I don't have faith in."

She smiled sleepily at him. "The princess and the dragon, huh?"

"Something like that, and they don't end up together at the end of the story."

"They did in my fairy tales. I never had much use for the wimpy little princes. I always knew I'd want a dragon. He came to the rescue of everyone, was noble and little appreciated." She smiled with a satisfied purr as she added, her voice a sultry whisper, "Give me a big, virile dragon any day."

He grinned. "It does explain why you're a painter, not a writer."

CHAPTER 9

As the lights of Phoenix came into view, Jake woke Rachel who'd drifted off to sleep. "Which way?"

She told him the exit to watch for and tried to put her hair back into some semblance of order.

"You come here often?" he asked as he switched lanes to turn off the freeway.

"When I was little, I spent a lot of time with Aunt Flo. She's was always there for me. She's great, but consider yourself warned. She is eccentric."

Jake gave her a questioning look.

She smiled. "She either likes people or she doesn't. If she doesn't, she can say some weird things--and if she does, she says even weirder ones."

Rachel directed him to turn up a street that was tree-lined and lazily curved around behind Camelback Mountain. "Ritzy neighborhood," he observed, not surprised.

"My mother's people were in merchandising in early Phoenix. There were some comfortable inheritances, and the investments are still doing well even with the hard times."

"So you do come from money." His voice didn't reflect any of the emotions that went through him when he thought about her wealthy background.

"They were storekeepers, Jake." He snorted with disbelief as she directed him into the next driveway. Even in the dark, it was impressive, a sprawling brick home with lights outlining the driveway and sidewalk, leading to a tall, double-doored entry.

"Maybe she's gone to bed," he suggested hopefully as he got out of the car and walked around to get Rachel's door.

"Unlikely," she said. "Aunt Flo is a night owl. Never goes to bed before two or three. Tonight she'll be waiting for us."

When they got to the front step, there was no need to knock as a tiny, bird-like woman rushed out and embraced Rachel.

"And so--" She released her niece and turned her attention to Jake, her pale blue eyes taking him in from the cowboy boots to the top of his head. "This is the man."

"Aunt Flo, this is Jacob Donovan. Jake, meet Florence Elfrida Barreñca Escondido."

Aunt Flo pulled them both into her huge living room. "Let me look at you," she demanded as she looked into Jake's eyes, then assessed his body, clothing--even the way he stood, legs apart. Jake had to fight the urge to move away from the almost intimate inspection. He half expected the small, dark-haired woman to ask him to turn around to examine his backside. He wondered what he would do if she did.

After a moment, she nodded. "So, Rachel, you got yourself a real man with this one."

"That's what I thought. Nice to hear my opinion validated." Rachel grinned, standing back, her hands on her hips, also looking at Jake, until he felt like a side of beef hung up for inspection.

"When you going to marry him?" the little woman asked.

"He hasn't asked me yet, Aunt Flo." Rachel's eyes twinkled as she met Jake's narrowed gaze.

"Hasn't asked? Are you crazy, girl? No self-respecting woman waits to be asked these days."

"I've hinted aplenty."

"Hinting won't cut it. With a man like this one, a woman has to go after what she wants. He's tough and she better be also."

Jake shook his head, finding it hard to believe the conversation going on beneath his nose, far beneath his nose.

Aunt Flo moved over to sit on her long sofa, patting the spot beside her. "Come here, young man."

Reluctantly, Jake lowered himself onto the sofa, uneasily wondering what questions would be directed at him and not having to wait long before finding out.

"Don't you know what a wonderful girl my niece is?" Aunt Flo asked, looking up like an expectant baby bird for his answer.

"I know."

"Well then--" She looked over at Rachel who had perched on the arm of the sofa above Jake. "Did you cook him a delicious, home-cooked meal?"

"Almost one of my first ploys," Rachel said, then frowned, "but he was on to me right away, Aunt Flo."

"You were huh?" Aunt Flo looked back at him. "Got brains as well as brawn huh?" She didn't wait for an answer to that question but quickly posed another. "You know I've waited a long time to see babies in my niece's arms. Just exactly what excuse do you have for not marrying her?"

Now Jake had a good idea of what family meant--at least weird-behaving family as Rachel had defined it-- but he had no idea how to deal with this feisty little woman. He saw she was determined to wait for his answer.

"I was looking for a woman with a little more maturity. You know anybody who'd fit that criteria?" he drawled.

Aunt Flo laughed, her laughter hearty and deep for such a small woman. "This is definitely the one, Rachel. Don't you let him get away! If you don't marry him, I will do it myself."

"I'm giving it my best shot," Rachel said, laughing.

"Are you hungry, Jake?" Aunt Flo asked abruptly and to his relief, changing the subject.

"Starving," he admitted, unable as usual to remember when he'd had his last meal.

"Don't you ever feed this man, Rachel?" Aunt Flo asked with a smile as she stood up. "No wonder he hasn't asked you to marry him. Come on, let's go out to the kitchen and see what Sara has left us."

Within half an hour, Jake was sitting at a counter in the large, Mexican-style kitchen and polishing off a thick ham and cheese sandwich and to his amazement, a bottle of beer.

"When I heard Rachel was bringing a Border Patrolman, I told Sara--stock up on good beer," Aunt Flo said, sitting back and contentedly watching him eat. "Never known one yet who didn't like his beer."

"Thank you, Ma'am."

"Aunt Flo," she corrected, her eyes twinkling. "I guess I'm getting tired now. Or at least from that look my niece is giving me I know I'm supposed to get tired now. Rachel, you know where the bedrooms are. If I'm not up early enough in the morning to suit you, ask Sara to fix you breakfast. Maybe your young man would like a swim before you turn in. You remember where all the extra suits are, don't you? Nothing quite like a midnight swim." She giggled and with that, left them.

Jake was still shaking his head as he came out of the bathroom, a swimsuit hugging his lean hips. No wonder Rachel was so outspoken. She obviously came by it genetically. He wondered if her mother, Marguerite, had really been the fragile lady Rachel seemed to remember. These women seemed too strong and sure of themselves to be bound too tightly by the codes of delicate society--unless those codes benefited them.

Beyond the sliding glass doors, he saw the pool where colored lights outlined its long shape. As he slid into the cool water, he sighed with appreciation. A good swim would loosen his muscles and make it easier to sleep. At least that was what he thought until a water nymph came up out of the water, grasping him around the waist and pressing her lips against his in such a way that both of them went under the surface.

"Rachel," he managed as he surfaced, bringing her up with him

"What?" Her arms went around his neck, her body floating out from his.

He pried off her arms and began swimming fast laps, determined that if he tired himself enough sleep would be possible.

Feeling pleasantly spent, he swam to where Rachel was sitting on the edge of the pool. Not attempting to pull himself from the water, he rested his arms on the concrete lip.

"You trying to prove something?" she asked.

"Like what?"

"Did Aunt Flo scare you that badly?"

He hadn't wanted to think about what her aunt had suggested or what he'd thought of himself earlier. He stared into the darkness.

"No one can force you to marry someone, Jake. You needn't worry I would try."

"It's not that I haven't thought about marrying you."

"Oh my," she quipped, "did I hear the M word pass your lips."

"Save the humor."

"I like humor. It makes a lot of situations bearable."

"I just can't see it working out between us, not long term."

"Why?"

"We're too different. It wouldn't take you long to figure that out."

"Is that really what worries you, Jake?"

"What do you mean?"

"Maybe you're afraid your own feelings aren't strong enough. Maybe it's not me that you're scared will get tired of being together."

He sucked in a breath. "I do love you," he whispered, his voice barely audible.

"You've never said it." Lightly she stroked along his arm, outlining the muscles with her fingertips.

"You have to have known."

"Maybe, maybe not. It's nice to hear." She kissed where she had touched.

He heaved himself from the pool, to sit beside her, the water running in rivulets down his body. She wore a white one piece swimsuit, which was modest and shouldn't have aroused his desire--but did. By now he was so far gone that just about anything, that she wore, said or did, aroused him.

Swallowing hard, he looked away. "You wouldn't marry me anyway."

"I wouldn't take a chance on that if I were you."

"What do you mean?"

"I mean, don't ask me to marry you if you're hoping I'll say no."

"Babe--"

"Don't," Rachel said, putting her hand over his lips to stop the words. "You don't have to explain anything. I do not want you to feel pressured by anyone."

He laughed. The joke was on him. At this point he was looking for any excuse to marry her, to claim her for however little time he might have with her. "I don't need you pressuring me--to feel pressured about marriage. You think I haven't thought about it? I don't have anything to offer. No money, no nice house. I don't even own the truck I drive. I've got a year and six months left before it's paid off, and by the time it is, I'll probably need another one."

"Hmmm," she said as though considering what he'd said, "but you do love me?"

He nodded. "As much as I understand about love."

"Then you could offer me all I want, Jake. I never dreamed I'd find a man I could feel this way about. If you love me, it's all I need."

She pushed aside her own concerns. Not about what he owned materially but about the coldness in him, that remoteness that pushed her away when she got too close, the places he held closed to anyone, but she loved him. Her kind of love didn't make conditions. She wouldn't ask for more than he was able to give.

"How can you take the risk of marrying me?"

"I think, from when I first saw you, something in me knew you, who you were to be in my life, but don't feel we have to rush into anything now. It's enough for me that you love me. When we get back to Tucson, well, you know..."

He reached out, pulling her into his arms, cradling her against him. "I don't think anything less than marriage will satisfy *me*," he whispered against her wet hair. Maybe if he was married to her, maybe then he could believe in her love. The laugh was on him. He needed the security of marriage perhaps more than she did, and if he married her, maybe he could somehow protect her if her world fell apart. Later when she didn't want anything to do with him, he would deal with that.

"Then?"

"I give up," he groaned. "Make the plans. Whenever, wherever you want."

"Is that a question?" she teased, kissing his wet chest.

There was a long silence.

"Rachel... will you be my wife?"

"Yes." She laughed with a bubble of happiness. "As soon as we can arrange it."

"I just hope you'll never regret this," he said, almost under his breath.

"I love you. I want to make a home for you. I want us to be one in every sense of the word." Her lips sought his as if to prove the truth of her words; and for that moment at least, he believed it.

~

Jake tossed naked and heated on his bed throughout the long night, wondering what he'd done to himself and Rachel. He still found it difficult to believe she would go through with a wedding. Most likely her father would take care of un-arranging it.

With morning, he got an even better understanding of the differences between him and the woman he had finally acknowledged he loved, when he saw Aunt Flo's home in all its glory. It was sprawled out in two distinct wings, the surrounding land a sizeable tract of desert, which shielded the house and its compound from neighbors. Besides the pool and gardens, there was a full tennis court.

"Of course," Aunt Flo said, "I don't use it any more, but you could." She patted Jake on the shoulder as he sipped his coffee, wishing not for the first time that morning for a cigarette.

"I've never played tennis."

Pouring more coffee into his cup, Aunt Flo ignored his curt answer. "You could learn. An athletic looking man like you would be quite good at it." She gave his shoulder a proprietary squeeze. "I can certainly see one of the things that attracted my niece to you." She laughed at the flush he couldn't suppress. "I'm old," she said, "I'm not dead." She laughed again. "Oh my I see I have embarrassed you." She tried to put an apologetic look on her face and failed, causing him to join her laughter.

"It's one of my foibles, I'm afraid," she said with a sly smile. "I don't mean to do it." She paused, then added, "Of course, since I'm always doing it, perhaps I do mean to. Please forgive me. I wouldn't want you to think Rachel's family is a bunch of loonies... even if we are."

He looked up. "I don't know much about families, loony or otherwise," he said, the wistful expression in his golden eyes enough to melt Rachel's heart as she watched them.

"Jake doesn't have much family, Aunt Flo."

Jake stared into the blackness of his coffee not eager to talk about his family or more what wasn't a family.

"Well, if and when you and Rachel marry," Aunt Flo said, "you'll have more than enough. Not only is there me, but my brother, Scott, wife and three kids, live in Flagstaff. Michael has a brother, Robert and his family, so many kids I can't keep track of their ages or where they're at, but they live on a ranch in Oregon."

He realized he needed to clarify his family history. He didn't want this woman to have any illusions about who he was. "Ma'am, my brother has fifteen years left of a twenty year sentence in Florence. My mother, the last time I heard, was in Chico, California. Who knows where she is now or even if she's still alive. The way she played out her nights, it's possible she's dead or ended up in prison herself."

"Is your father dead also?" asked Aunt Flo.

"Aunt Flo!" Rachel rebuked, "don't keep at him that way."

"It's all right," Jake said, leaning back in his chair. "My brother and I had--different fathers. The man who sired me either never knew or never wanted to know the results of his mistake."

"How unfortunate. Your father missed out on knowing what a fine son he had. As for your brother, well, every family has a few black sheep. You'll have problems to accept in Rachel's family too--like me for instance. I was pretty pushy about marriage last night and again just now." She smiled at Rachel's intake of breath. "I wouldn't want you thinking I'd use a shotgun to force you to marry her. Although," she laughed, "since you're the first man Rachel's ever seemed serious about, I might be tempted. That girl's been so wrapped up in her art I thought she'd end up like me. It was a welcome relief, I tell you, when I saw a man like you walk through that door."

"Aunt Flo," Rachel warned sharply.

Jake smiled as he took another of Sara's freshly baked croissants and purposely changed the subject. "You sure have a good cook," he said, smiling at Sara as he bit into his third one.

"It's nice to have a real man's appetite to cook for," the plump cook said as she wiped down the kitchen counters. "We ain't had a man like you here since. Shucks, I don't recollect the last time."

"Michael's been so busy lately," Aunt Flo said, shaking her head. "Did your father make it to your showing, Rachel?"

"A quick flight in and out."

"Everything went well at the opening?"

"Several immediate sales from past customers. A couple of maybes and a lot of admirers with no cash. I wish you could have come."

"Those dratted committee meetings for planning a new church. They schedule them for the worst time; and since this one involved the city commissioners, I couldn't rearrange it, but I'll get up to see it as soon as I can."

"Aunt Flo filled in at school events, mother's teas and just about any place else that a mom might be expected," Rachel told Jake.

"It was a pleasure. I only wish my little sister could have been there, could be here now."

Jake didn't look up. He still had the feeling Rachel's mother would not have been pleased at the man her daughter was planning to marry. "Marguerite would have liked you," Aunt Flo said, as though reading his mind much as her niece did so easily. "She'd have liked the look in your eyes as much as I do."

"I don't have any money to make up for the fact that I'm an ugly man."

Aunt Flo shook her head. "Jake, it's obvious you simply don't understand your own attractiveness."

Rachel laughed at his look of surprise. "That's what I keep telling him, Aunt Flo."

"You sure you didn't prime the pump?" Jake asked, wondering at the looks the two women were exchanging which seemed to deliver messages his masculine mind couldn't read.

Grinning, Rachel ignored him. "He quit fighting the inevitable last night," she told her aunt.

Aunt Flo smiled broadly. "Does that mean?"

"Yep, he's going to marry me, and he even said the arrangements are up to me."

Aunt Flo chuckled. "Complete capitulation huh?"

Rachel nodded happily.

"Nail him down quick then, girl. I'll talk to Father Renaldo. You could be married in my garden," she suggested looking at Rachel's beaming face, then at Jake's look of total surprise.

"As soon as possible," Rachel said, coming to stand behind Jake, wrapping her arms around his neck.

"I'll see what his plans are for Monday."

"I thought--" he started to say. He was cut off, as the two women began discussing wedding possibilities. Not for one moment had he dreamed Rachel could plan a wedding so quickly. The way they were talking, it sounded as though it could be a done deal in a matter of hours.

While Aunt Flo went off to make phone calls, Rachel suggested she and Jake lie by the pool before it got too hot.

Jake sprawled on a chaise, the lines of muscle and sinew clearly revealed in the swimsuit. Rachel swallowed, looking away. It was too easy to visualize him lying there with nothing on. *Oh my*, she thought, *I do love him*, and then was unable to suppress the thought, *how I'd love to paint him nude.*

"How long before it'll be over?" he asked, his voice harsh as it cut into her reverie.

"What?" she asked, amazed at the hint of anger in his voice. "If you don't like the wedding plans, we can work something else out. Did you want to do it with no family around? I could understand that."

"It's not that. It's everything. You, me-- the whole shebang."

She sat up then, quickly flaring in anger. "Jake you don't have to marry me. If you've changed your mind, it's okay. After all, it was your idea, remember."

"I know whose idea it was. I want to marry you," he said moodily.

"Then, why would you ask such a thing?"

"Everybody leaves."

"And you're an expert on leaving, aren't you?"

"I know what happens."

"I think it's time for you to face some truths, Jake." She ignored his jutting jaw, the stubborn glint in those golden eyes. "Did you ever think maybe your mother had her reasons, reasons you and I can't understand, but that made sense to her? And if people have left you since, maybe it's because you drove them away. Is that what you intend to do with me?"

"Of course not."

"You've tried to drive me off more than once." He would've denied it, but of course, she was right. "Can't you believe in me, in what I feel for you?" She shifted to sit on the edge of his lounge, looking down at him, resting her hand on his chest.

"You turn me inside out," he said.

"You do the same to me. I look at you, wearing just that pair of trunks, and I want to possess you every way a woman can a man." She bent and kissed his chest. "I want to know every inch of you."

"I'm open," he said, surprised at how fast she could change his mood. "Wanta do it now?"

She smiled. "I think the wedding night will be sufficient for what I have in mind. Some anticipation on your part will make it all the sweeter."

"Babe, if I anticipate anymore, it'll be over before it starts."

She laughed and he saw that her eyes had turned almost purple with the sensual promise within their depths.

"I love hearing your laugh. I like the stubborn jut of your jaw. What I feel for you is everything rolled into one. I can't explain it, but I do know if getting married makes you unhappy, we won't do it. I will still make love to you when we get back to Nogales."

"Just give me some time to get used to this," he said, his fingers stroking her smooth back. "I want you for my wife. I just don't want to blow this."

Her lips came down on his. Her promises whispered against his lips, against his cheek, but she had no way to know if they reached his heart.

In the afternoon Rachel suggested she and Jake go shopping in Scottsdale. Aunt Flo was immediately taken with the idea. "I'll alert them the treat is on me, one of my wedding gifts to you both. I'll talk to Father Renaldo about the arrangements."

The only one not enamored of the idea was Jake as even Sara chimed in with suggestions on what he should buy.

Rachel drove because, as she put it, she was the one who knew where they were going. Jake looked with consternation as she pulled up in front of an elite men's shop. "No way," he growled, but soon he found himself inside, looking at racks of pure cotton and silk shirts. "This isn't me," he complained to Rachel, but she and the enthusiastic sales clerk clearly thought it was and soon found a white silk shirt and a natural cotton turquoise one. Fortunately it was a shop used to tall men with slim builds.

"White slacks would look wonderful on you," Rachel argued.

"I do not wear white slacks," he protested.

As Jake came back from the dressing room, the young sales clerk sighed, "You're right Ms. O'Brian, they look wonderful on the right body, and Mr. Donovan definitely has the right frame. His proportions are perfect. Unusual on such a tall man."

When it came to shopping, Jake already knew Rachel was not only persistent but stubborn. Eventually it became easier to give in than to fight. Besides, after he'd seen the white slacks on, he had to admit they did look good.

"You can't make a silk purse out of a sow's ear," he growled.

"But you, my dear, are no sow's ear," she purred.

And so the day went as she found several pairs of slacks, a tan jacket, a pair of shorts and two short-sleeved shirts. "I can't afford this," he tried again.

"Aunt Flo is giving us a trousseau as a wedding present. You would hurt her feelings if you refused. She wants to buy you clothes, and she is going to do it--one way or another," she finished, smiling now through gritted teeth.

Recognizing a losing situation when he saw one, Jake gave in with relative grace, at least for him. He admitted to himself that he was not in control. Relief came when the alternations people went off with a bundle of clothing, promising everything would be ready by Monday morning. Anything for Florence Escondido.

It was only a slight improvement to follow Rachel through the women's departments. Everywhere they went, people knew her, and he felt out of place. The one time he dared look at prices, he slammed his mouth shut before he gave voice to his instinctive complaint.

Rachel showed him several things, then at seeing his reaction, thought better of it and shoved him out to wander to a nearby cafe and have something cold to drink.

When Rachel collected him, she had several packages and a plastic wrapped dress on a hanger. He followed her docilely as she said, "Only one thing left."

"What's that?"

"Rings, dummy."

"Dummy? I thought I was your dragon, your darling," he protested as she led him into a jewelry store. Fortunately their taste was similar, and they found simple gold bands, which Jake insisted he buy. With the magic Escondido name, they also would be ready Monday.

Back in Paradise Valley, Sara had prepared a gourmet dinner, and they sat around the pool afterward, admiring a blazing Arizona sunset, highlighted by incredible cloud formations. "Looks like it might thunderstorm tonight," Aunt Flo said with relish.

"You like storms too?" Jake asked.

"Nothing on this good earth like an Arizona thunderstorm to clear the atmosphere. Rejuvenates everything. The more lightning and thunder, the better." She breathed deeply of the air. "I can smell the rain already. Must be falling south of here."

Jake shook his head, remembering Rachel's reaction to electrical storms. "You Escondido women are crazy."

Aunt Flo laughed. "By the way, Father Renaldo promised that although he can't marry you in the church, he will do it here in the yard, or house, whichever you prefer Monday."

Jake felt a band of tight pressure settling around his head. "I might have trouble getting time off."

"Nonsense," Aunt Flo argued. "You have personal time for this sort of thing. If necessary, I can pull a few strings."

"No," he barked, startling Rachel and bringing a pleased smile to Aunt Flo's face, "I'll take care of my job."

When Rachel decided the immediate fireworks were over, she went off to call her dad with the news.

"You look like a man who's been caught in a storm," Aunt Flo observed, "and doesn't know if he likes it or not."

"It's all coming so fast. Nothing like I expected. It's been that way ever since I met your niece. Sometimes I feel it's swallowing me."

"What is?"

He shook his head. "The feelings, this business of love." He frowned as he said the word. He knew he wasn't doing a very good job of explaining the feeling he had of being out of control.

"You don't have to marry her now," Aunt Flo said, coming to sit beside him and pat his hand soothingly. "If you feel like it's coming too fast, I'm sure Rachel wouldn't mind waiting. I've been an interfering old woman rushing the two of you this way for my own selfish reasons. I just wanted to be there is all and wasn't sure I would if it was down at the ranch."

"No." These women were certainly quick to give him a way out. "Right or wrong, I want that woman to be my wife like I've never wanted anything in my life. It makes no sense, but there's no escape for me now."

"It's possible," Flo said with a sympathetic smile, "that it'll be easier for you once you're past the wedding. Men don't usually like the rituals and rigmarole that go with all that. We'll keep this one simple. You know people will probably be suspicious at the rush."

He smiled at that. "They'll find out quick enough they have no reason."

Rachel came back from the house. "Papa isn't home. He went straight back to Mexico. No one answers at the Ramirez place, and the number he gave me in Guadalajara has been disconnected. I wonder what's going on."

"We can wait to get married if you want him to be there," Jake said.

"I don't want us to wait." She looked pointedly at him. "Unless you've changed your mind."

He shook his head. "No."

"Well my father will understand. We can have another ceremony later."

"Another ceremony," Jake choked.

"Just teasing, my love," Rachel said, patting his shoulder, much as Aunt Flo had patted his hand. "Maybe a reception later though--"

He shook his head, trying to decide if she was really worth all she was putting him through, but he knew the answer. By now he'd go through hell itself, to have her. No ceremony, not even two of them, could stop him.

~

Early Sunday morning Aunt Flo, Sara, Rachel and Jake attended Mass as a family. Jake had never been in a Catholic Church. In fact, he realized, as he walked through the open double doors, he'd never been in a church. It certainly hadn't been on his mother's list of priorities nor had anyone in the community thought about inviting the Donovan boys to their Sunday School classes. Later he hadn't seen a reason to go.

"Don't worry about what you do," Rachel whispered as they made their way down the aisle. "Just follow my lead." She grinned at him. "Of course, it's been... Wow, I am not sure how long since I actually went to Mass myself. Maybe you ought to do what Aunt Flo does."

Jake frowned. "I thought you were a church goer."

"Once a year with family... Absolutely always." She smiled.

He gave her a mock look of shock as they slid down an aisle and found a place for the four of them.

She knelt on the bench and then brought her middle finger up to her forehead, down across her chest and across her heart. "Sign of the cross," she whispered.

Jake did not attempt to do what the three women did. He sat back and looked around the large sanctuary. There was a strong scent of wax burning. Two large, colorful tapestries flanked the large crucifix at the front of the church.

Jake felt a bit mesmerized by the pageantry as the service began. The priest, in colorful robes, made his way from the back of the church to the front, following a large cross carried by a boy and the Bible carried by another young man. As the service went on, Jake followed the example of the others in rising, kneeling or sitting, thinking it didn't seem a bad set of rituals, kind of pleasing to the eye and ear.

When the homily was given, everyone sat back. He allowed himself to do a little fantasizing. He imagined Rachel with a baby in her arms, a dark-haired, little girl. And then with a faint smile at his own foolishness, he placed a small, light-haired boy beside himself. He discarded the idea with another moment of thought. That kind of life would never be his.

He was past walking away from Rachel; but sooner or later, she would see what he was, how little he had to give and when she did, she'd go. He had tried to brace himself for it but doubted he could. Most of his life he'd avoided that kind of hurt by not getting too close, but she'd burrowed in under his defenses and left him helpless against her. He would just have to take what came.

The afternoon was spent with the women's heads together as Rachel, Aunt Flo and Sara discussed flowers, food, and got on the telephone to invite close friends and relatives to the wedding the next day. Jake listened but found himself drifting away from the talk.

Father Renaldo arrived and quickly aligned himself with Jake. "You look a little pale, señor," he observed teasingly, in a loud enough voice for the women to hear and stop their conversation. "Are you sure you're going to survive tomorrow?"

"I plan to," Jake drawled, smiling at Rachel's expression of consternation.

"If you faint during the service," the priest went on, "shall I finish it anyway? Or shall I consider that to be no?"

After a moment of pretend deliberation, while Rachel's large eyes raked him with her own unasked question, Jake said, "Marry us. I'd never get up the nerve to go through this twice."

CHAPTER 10

B ecause Rachel had been unable to reach her father, it was
decided they would keep the small wedding a secret until
she had a chance to tell him. Monday morning, Jake called his
office telling them he needed a few more days. Without an explanation, he felt lucky to get three days vacation.

His boss told him David Bannister had been asking for him,
but Jake decided not to call the agent. He was going to let nothing
stop him from marrying Rachel or of taking a few days with her
as man and wife. When they got home, they'd have to face the
issue of where her father had been and whether the man was the
head of a smuggling ring. At least married he could keep her
safe--physically if not emotionally from that mess if the worst
came down.

They went to town for a marriage license. Despite his deter-
mination to let nothing ruin this day, Jake found himself
wondering what Bannister had wanted. A stop to pick up their
rings and another for their new clothing, and they were back in
Paradise Valley by one. Jake still felt uneasy about letting Rachel's
Aunt Flo buy his clothing; but he reluctantly accepted, knowing
he couldn't have afforded anything like them and with a few of

Rachel's relatives from Flagstaff driving down for the quickly arranged ceremony, he wanted to make as good an impression as possible.

Aunt Flo insisted on seeing everything on his body; and because he knew of no other way to repay her, he also put himself through that ordeal. Even Jake could see the difference quality fabric, cut and fit had made, although clothes couldn't hide a craggy face.

When he tried to find the words to thank her, she laughed. "Why do I get the feeling you'd rather have been knocked flat than have me buy you a few little gifts?"

He smiled uneasily, knowing she could have no idea what those little gifts meant to a man who'd never had anyone give him anything. Some of that had been his own doing. He had wanted to owe no one anything. Life was changing for him. Rather than trying to explain any of that, he simply thanked her again.

"It's made me happy," she said simply. "I do have one other little present for you two. I made reservations at a resort in Scottsdale that I think will give you privacy for your honeymoon, short though it may have to be." When she saw the glint in Jake's golden eyes, she added, "Don't you dare argue with me about this."

He clenched his jaw against the emotion that surged through him. Reaching out, he pulled her into a bear-like embrace, which she fervently returned.

Rachel sat in the small den, brushing back her hair, trying to decide if she had forgotten anything. The only unhappy part was wishing her father could have been there sharing this day that she knew would have meant a lot to him.

Her thoughts drifted to Jake, waiting tensely in the living room. This was the man she was trusting with her life and love. She knew how uneasy he was and suddenly she shared his fears. She knelt, closing her eyes, and tried to pray, to find words that would cover how she felt. After a few moments, she stood and took a deep breath as she felt a wave of peace come over her. It was all right. This was the right thing for them both.

She looked at her reflection in the mirror, at the way her hair formed an ebony cloud around her pale face. The ivory lace dress had a scooped neck and scalloped hem-line. It was deceptively simple in its loose fitting cut but with a subtle elegance. She wore small pearl earrings, her only other adornment a large gardenia she pinned behind one ear.

From the living room she could hear a classical melody flowing from a harp. Another element that Aunt Flo had magically brought into her home to make Rachel's wedding special.

Rising, Rachel walked through the door and out into the large, flower bedecked living room. Her eyes were caught and held by Jake's golden gaze. She smiled then as she walked toward him, aware of the pulse beating in his jaw, the tension in his muscles. Tears came to her eyes.

Father Renaldo said the words, and Rachel heard her own voice respond. She heard Jake's deep tones, but the meanings were lost to her. It was as though it all happened in a dream. When she felt Jake reach down and brush her lips, his own soft and caressing, she threw her arms around his neck, meeting his kiss with unexpected passion as he stepped back a pace to keep his balance.

Aunt Flo laughed. "I guess she's got the right man." Then the hugs came, the best wishes and toasts. Everyone seemed to be talking at once and smiles were on all faces. She was Mrs. Jacob Donovan.

In the large dining room, Sara had done herself proud with a spread of cut meats, salads, exotic looking entrees and special breads. The wedding cake stood on a sideboard, not large but beautifully adorned with fresh flowers, and topped with an exceptionally tall groom and dark-haired bride. "Where did you find them?" Rachel asked with delight as she looked at the miniature couple.

"Where there's a will; there's a way," Aunt Flo said with a smug smile.

Rachel hugged her. "You've made this so special for us. Thank you."

Aunt Flo's eyes misted. "It's only what Marguerite asked of me when she knew she wouldn't be here for this day. This is all a gift, Rachel, from your mother."

Several hours later, Jake turned the car through the gates of a luxury resort. Looking around him, he wondered if this was the right place. Overhead palm trees waved. The drive was lined with oleanders, bougainvillea and other exotic flowers blooming profusely. The resort had an elaborate restaurant as its centerpiece with a huge pool and lagoon-like atmosphere surrounding it.

After registering, he drove around to the back where they found their room sheltered among shrubbery and palms. Jake grabbed their bags but put them down at the door. "There's a tradition that's got to be observed here." He swung Rachel up into his arms and carried her over the threshold.

"I like tradition." She wrapped her arms around his neck. "Does this happen whenever we go through a new door?" she teased as he set her down inside.

"Only for the first month. After that it depends on how good you are."

"How about you being good?"

"If I'm good, will you carry me over the threshold?" he asked, putting an end to that debate as he went back out for their bags.

Rachel looked around her with pleasure. "Aunt Flo has always been a connoisseur of fine resorts." The living room was studio-like with bar and refrigerator in the back, plump sofas in the front. Stairs led to what appeared a loft bedroom. Lush carpeting cushioned her steps as she walked through the room. Sliding glass doors opened to a private patio.

Jake threw his jacket on a chair and looked up toward the bedroom. "I never stayed in a place like this. In fact I never knew they had places like this." He realized then Rachel looked uneasy, a little afraid. He decided to give her some space and went into the tiny kitchen to find a note tacked to the refrigerator. "Sara's been here," he said with a grin. He opened the refrigerator to find it stocked with Mexican beer, an expensive bottle of champagne, an assortment of cheeses, meats, fruits and two chilled champagne glasses.

"What do you want?" he asked as he told her the options.

"Champagne, of course... to observe tradition."

He set about opening the bottle without having it explode and brought the filled glasses to where she sat on the sofa, her feet tucked under her.

"A toast?" she asked Jake, accepting her glass.

"To us?" he suggested, knowing that wasn't very imaginative but at this point he was feeling some of her tension. His body was nearly aching with his need. They'd gone a long time with the sexual tension building. Now with relief in sight, he had to hope her first time would not be a disappointment. This would be a first for him also—first with a virgin.

"Look," he said as he sipped the bubbly liquid," we don't have to do anything tonight."

"Are you kidding? I have waited half my life for this and wanted it ever since we met, but I don't want to disappoint you."

"You won't. We'll learn together." He put down the champagne and pulled her into his arms. His lips brushed the nape of her neck, pushing the lush hair aside. She sighed, entwining her fingers in his hair and giving herself over to his kiss. His tongue erotically played with the sides of her lips, then delved into her mouth claiming and awakening her senses. His big hand cupped her breasts through the silken fabric, teasing her nipple into an erect little nubbin. "Something has to go here," he said as he pushed the dress aside to kiss her shoulder.

"What could it be?" she asked with a teasing smile.

They climbed the stairs, kissing, touching, their arms around each other. At the top, she felt almost faint with anticipation. "Jake," she whispered, her lips against his chest.

"Yeah?"

"May I--" She stopped unable to put into words what she wanted.

Even though he had no idea of her request, he spread his hands, signifying his acceptance. When he felt her fingers trembling on the studs of his silk shirt, he swallowed but stood still as she unfastened the front. She pulled the shirt from his slacks and let it slide off his broad shoulders.

She stood back, surveying what she had revealed. Seemingly unconsciously, she licked her lips. When he would have reached for her, she put up her hand lightly against his bare chest. Her breathing was coming unevenly as she shook her head.

Standing still with difficulty, he felt her fingers at the buckle of his belt. She pulled it from the loops. Kneeling at his feet, she unfastened shoe laces. Slowly, lightly stroking his ankle, savoring the moment, she lifted first one foot, then the other, removing socks and shoes.

Jake's fists were clenched now as she rose. He knew now what she was asking of him and gritted his teeth as she worked open the button on his slacks and slowly began pulling down the zipper.

"You are a tease," he managed, amazed his voice didn't break on the words. His desire for her had been a palpitating reality from almost the moment he'd seen her. Now he was swollen with need, with his awareness that whatever she wanted of him, he'd be unable to deny it.

She only smiled, her lips following her fingers as she pulled the slacks down his hips and let them fall to the ground. If he hadn't seen so clearly in her own eyes what this was doing to her, he doubted he could have stood still, but somehow he managed as she finished undressing him.

Nude, he was all she had dreamed, from the broad, defined shoulders, past the almost sculptural chest, to the flat belly and muscular thighs. She had never seen a man in full arousal. She found rather than frightening her, it increased her excitement.

When she reached up to unzip her dress, he put his hand over hers. Tipping her face up for his kiss, he turned her and slid the slider down until the back of her dress gaped open. He didn't remove it immediately, but ran his hands over her back, down her buttocks before he unfastened her bra. His breath was coming unevenly as he reached around to caress her naked breasts, the silk of her dress brushing against his fingers as he teased her nipples into tight little buds.

When he slid the dress off her shoulders, it fell to her feet in a little puddle from which she stepped turning to face him now wearing only silk panties. He looked his fill as she earlier had of him.

"You are so beautiful," he said in a hoarse whisper bending to kiss her lips again. He lifted her into his arms and laid her onto the bed. Her eyes were dark with desire. She was everything he had ever dreamed of in a woman when dreams were the only way he might've imagined having her. Along with the surge of power, that gave him came a fear that he wouldn't be enough for her.

"Touch me," she whispered. "I want to feel your hands on my skin. Make me yours now."

"We're going to take this slow," he said. Using his hands and mouth, he showed her all the places her body could come alive as he stripped her of the filmy panties. He pushed her thighs apart and knelt between them using his tongue and mouth to arouse her to the point she was writhing under him.

"Now, Jake," she cried, knowing if he didn't make her his at that moment, she would go insane.

"Make me," he rasped, barely able to hold control of himself and knowing that in another moment, he'd be unable to stop from doing as she demanded, but he wanted this to be special for her, wanted her to know all it was possible to know about what a woman could feel. He felt of her wetness and then delved within to stretch her a little.

"No," she moaned. "I want you inside me, all of you."

She thrust upward, lifting her hips, and guided him to her. He felt the little barrier and hesitated but she pushed up harder and then he was past it.

"Oh my God," she cried as she again lifted her hips taking him even deeper.

"I hurt you?" he asked, trying to still his movement.

"Only a moment. Now..." She moaned as she rocked her own hips, trying to let him see what she wanted.

His smile was hard, but the expression in his eyes soft as he began to move in and out, gently at first, then increasing the pressure and the speed of the rhythm until Rachel knew only that moment, that feeling. She had never dreamed it could be like this. She felt as though he and she were one on a level that went beyond the wonderful feelings he was causing to grow in her.

When it exploded, there was nothing outside their two bodies.

After a moment, Jake lifted his head. "Rachel?"

"Mmmmmmmmm." She felt as though she was on a cloud, a silky, white cloud that was letting her float above the earth and she didn't want to come back down, not ever.

"Are you all right?"

"Near perfect," she whispered.

"You sure you aren't hurt?"

She smiled, touching his lips with her fingertips. "It was so beautiful. I never knew. If I'd known, I might not have waited."

She heard him laugh and her own smile broadened. Jake wished he had also waited, wished there hadn't been all those one-night stands, that he had come to her without so many meaningless encounters. Then again, maybe he'd have never realized what a gem he had if he hadn't been through all of that.

He couldn't begin to put into words what he had just experienced with her. What had begun a primal need had become instead a desire to unite completely with this one woman. As she had opened to him, he had felt barriers, not just within her, but his own parting and being broken through.

"I've never known what it was like to make love before either." What he'd known before had been sex, and until now he'd never known there was a difference.

She felt him tenderly wash her, then cover her with a sheet and she yielded to the sleep that seemed impossible to deny. She was Jake's at last. There was nothing more to ask from life.

What seemed like hours later, she awoke and saw he was leaning up on one elbow watching her. "Are you hungry?" she asked with a small contented smile.

"You offering?" he queried, a gleam in those startlingly golden eyes.

"I meant food."

"Oh yeah, me too," he retorted with a teasing smile.

They showered. He'd have made love to her again in the shower if he hadn't been afraid she'd be sore. They found long, terry cloth robes on hooks in the bathroom and wandered down the stairs to look with more interest in the refrigerator. At the wedding luncheon, they'd been too high-strung to eat more than a few bites, and so Rachel made them each a sandwich. Opening the sliding glass door, they sat out on the small patio to eat.

"Only in Arizona," she sighed at the warmth of the soft night air, the smell of jasmine that wafted to them from some hidden bush.

"You ever live any place else?"

"No, but I've traveled a bit. Mexico, of course. I spent some time in Southern Oregon when I was a kid, staying on my aunt and uncle's ranch during the summers. I've got a cousin, Randy who is about my age. You'll like him. He's a cop too. He and I had a lot of fun together growing up. It was nice, but it wasn't Arizona."

Jake stared up at the bright stars overhead. "I've never wanted to live anywhere else."

"Well, at least that's one decision we won't have to worry about," Rachel said, eating a bite of sandwich.

"So, what about the ones we do have to worry about? We got married so fast we never really talked about where we'll live." He tried to keep the tone of his voice casual.

"It should be your home, of course. I hope you will let me make it mine. I've a hundred ideas for fixing it up." She smiled up at him. "And most won't cost that much money."

"You think you could be happy in a place like that."

"With you, of course."

"Where will you work?"

"I do a lot of my work on location, but that little shed in your backyard could be enlarged, maybe a skylight added if you don't mind. The back patio when it's not blowing hard or storming."

"There are other things we haven't talked about."

"We'll work them out as we come to them."

"We better not wait on this one. This all happened so fast, and tonight I was so caught up in you I didn't think to wear protection. What if?"

She smiled. "I got pregnant?" She smiled sheepishly. "I have to admit that not long after we first met, I visited the doctor and got a prescription for the pill. It seemed most likely that we'd eventually end up doing what we just did. I knew neither of us was quite ready for a baby yet."

He smiled leaning back in his chair as he stretched. "I can't believe we even got married as fast as we did. When you said yes,

I figured a month or two, maybe as much as a year. I never guessed three days."

"I never thought I'd hear the word marriage on your lips," she admitted. She slipped onto his lap. The air was heavy and warm, languorous in its effect. "I didn't realize it could be so fast either though. That's my aunt for you."

"She's quite a lady."

"She likes you and she's always wanted to see me married. You can bet the baby talk will be coming sooner than later." She nestled down onto his arms and ran her fingers through his tawny hair. "And I will eventually want your baby. Do you want a family, Jake? We never talked about it."

"I've never thought of it. I guess we'll see." He thought then of the man he'd never met and who had just missed his only daughter's wedding, who might someday be a grandfather. "I'm sorry about your dad. How do you think he'll feel about it, him not being here for your wedding?"

"He'll be disappointed, but he'll understand after I explain."

"I'm not so sure..." He sighed, thinking it would be a miracle if her father understood because he certainly didn't.

Snuggling against his chest, she entwined her arms round his neck. After a moment, he forgot his concern for her father. "When you took off my clothes," he said, "I thought it'd all be over right there."

"Oh Lord," she whispered, kissing his chest and pushing apart his robe. "I had been dreaming about that for weeks, since I first saw you striding across the driveway to my porch."

He stopped her. "Come on. Not that far back. You were too innocent."

"Something in me hasn't been innocent from the moment I saw you," she retorted. She remembered with renewed warmth the feeling of undressing him--oh so slowly revealing that magnificent male body, the body that was now hers. Smiling, she pushed his robe off his shoulders, revealing his broad chest. "I've had fantasies about you."

"Any I can help fulfill?" His arousal was more than ready.

Her breath was coming more quickly. "Oh I am sure you could."

He lifted his head to kiss the swelling over a breast. "Really?" he managed thinking he probably should have come up with better words, but at the moment, words weren't on his mind. Her hair hanging loose seemed to caress him with a will of its own. He'd never imagined being captive to a woman, but he was hers. He belonged to her so totally he had nothing else to want or hope for so long as she would stay with him.

"Shall I tell you some of my fantasies," she asked.

"Babe, I'm almost afraid to ask."

"Well one is to have you out on the desert and then get you to pose where I could paint you in the nude." She shifted to have her legs on both sides of his. She opened his robe and grasped his erection, making it very clear how naked she wanted him to be.

"You're thinking of that right now?" he managed as she began to tentatively stroke him.

"Well there might be more to it than painting."

"I don't like the idea of posing for you." he caught his breath as she opened her robe and their nude bodies were now pressing against each other.

"No?" He then felt her smile against his belly and tried to respond with another no, but it was taken from him by her lips, emphatically reminding him why he wouldn't say no to whatever she asked.

As he felt her settle over him, taking him within, he knew there was nothing she would ask of him that he wouldn't try to do. He had no doubt she'd have him buck naked out on the desert, getting sunburned everywhere, and he'd be loving it. It was the last coherent thought he had before their making love carried him away into that other place he had found only with her.

In the morning, she woke in his arms, stretching luxuriously. They'd have the day together. What a glorious thought. There would always be another day together.

She smiled at Jake's sleeping face, at his bristly jaw. "Jake--"

He grunted, turning over. Jake was definitely not a morning person, she thought as she slipped from the bed. With another smile she remembered how he'd carried her up the stairs, and they'd made love yet again.

She put on her swimsuit and went to the pool for a few quick laps. When she returned, his eyes were open, but barely. "Where'd you go?" he grumbled, sleepily, "I missed you." A sheet loosely covered him below the waist, and she smiled with antici- pation as she realized--the sight of those broad shoulders, that sculpted chest, those sinewy arms--were hers to enjoy for the rest of her life.

"I went swimming, and I haven't been gone that long." She kissed his rough jaw and went to shower. When she came out, he was still sprawled across the bed and showing no signs of being in a hurry to get out of it. She went back downstairs, returning with a tray of pastries and a pot of fresh coffee, which finally got him to lever himself up.

She shook her head, restraining her laughter. "Mornings are definitely not your thing."

"I manage," he grunted, coming more alive as the caffeine hit his system.

"What do you want to do today?" she asked, munching on a croissant.

"Any suggestions?" He gave her a hopeful leer.

"I mean besides that." He laughed. After a moment, she said, "I'd like to go western two-step dancing tonight."

194

"I know we danced that one time at Sandovals, but it was just moving to music a little. I don't really dance, Rachel."

"It's not that complicated to learn," she said, looking at him with that expression which meant she was determined.

"It's your risk," he growled, "but don't say I didn't warn you. I didn't learn to dance as a kid. Later there never seemed any reason."

"You danced at Mark and Maria's," she reminded him.

"That was more just shuffling around."

"You'll be a wonderful dancer," she said with assurance. "You're so graceful. There's no way you wouldn't be good at dancing."

When they got back to their room, late that night, Jake apologized again. "I did try to warn you."

She limped to the couch. "I know," she replied with a tight smile. "You did warn me."

"I just can't do it."

"You can, and you will." She reached down, pulled off high-heeled sandals, and rubbed her bruised toes. "But--just not tonight."

He sat beside her on the sofa, pulling her feet onto his lap and giving them a massage. "Such poor crushed toes." He bent and kissed the damaged appendages.

"Yes," she agreed with a sigh of appreciation.

"You're making me feel guilty."

"I can't help it. I think you stepped on every toe... at least ten times."

"I also managed to step on the toes of at least three other women on the dance floor." He massaged the calves of her legs, admiring the slimness of her ankles as he kneaded the tight muscles.

"The husband of that one woman turned around, like he was going to deck you," Rachel added with a reminiscent smile, "until he looked up--way up--and saw your face. Then he was the one apologizing." She laughed. "You'd have thought when he got through that his wife had thrown her feet under yours."

He grinned.

"It could have been embarrassing," she added, "Headlines--*Border Patrolman arrested for brawl in Scottsdale lounge.*"

"Your aunt would have had to bail me out."

"Both of us!" she retorted.

"You are my champion for sure. If I get into a mess, I just call you to come drag me out of it." The image of her dragging his lanky frame anyplace caused him to smile.

"I would," she said, laughing and sitting up to put her arms around his neck. "I am so happy, Jake. I never thought I could be this happy."

"Good."

"I enjoyed myself tonight."

"Crushed toes and all?"

"Yep, and I'm especially looking forward to what comes next." She nibbled on his earlobe to give him a clue--a clue he didn't need.

"With a night like last night," he teased, his voice growing husky, "just what do you think I have the energy for--you insatiable woman?"

"Guess!"

CHAPTER 11

Donovan grimaced as he walked into his office and saw Bannister behind his desk. The agent's feet hit the floor as he saw Jake. "Where the hell have you been?" he growled.

"You ask too many questions," Donovan responded in like tone. "What are you doing here so early?"

"It's where I have been the last three days. Waiting for you. You picked a damned strange time to be gone."

Donovan grinned. "When would be good in your view?"

"Anytime but now." Bannister stood up to let Donovan have his own chair. He edgily paced the room. Donovan leaned back in his chair, hands behind his head, trying to look more relaxed than he felt.

"We got word where the helicopter was bringing in the shipment. We were too late."

"Sounds like a story I heard before," Donovan observed wryly.

"We thought we had them. That we'd catch Ramirez and O'Brian with the goods."

Donovan began rummaging through desk drawers. There had to be a partial pack of cigarettes someplace.

"Either our source was wrong on the time, or they got wise to him. By the time we got there, everything was done but our whining. To top it off, neither Ramirez nor O'Brian has surfaced since."

Bannister pulled a pack of cigarettes from his shirt pocket and handed Jake one while he got one himself and lit them both.

"This operation has been jinxed from the word go," Bannister growled moving restlessly around the room. "When we got there, we saw tracks of the truck and where a helicopter had landed. Four or five different sets of footprints. We tried to follow the truck. Lost them on the main highway. And don't tell me again that you've heard it all before."

"Are you sure about O'Brian being in on this?"

"Geesus Jake, you are hooked on that woman, and you aren't looking at this straight anymore."

"I never jump to conclusions. Unlike some I know."

"I'm not jumping to anything. O'Brian was with Ramirez in Mexico just before this operation. We have reliable accounts of their activities... right up to when we lost them."

"Reliable? Like some creep gets a light sentence for putting the finger on whoever you boys want?"

"I don't play that kind of game. Hell, what kind of scum do you take me for?"

Jake took a deep drag on the cigarette, gritting his teeth against all the angry words he wanted to say. It was not fair to take his anger out on the agen. Maybe he was right. He couldn't say O'Brian was not in on everything Ramirez was doing. Damn, how did a man with such a wonderful daughter weave himself such a deadly web, a web that could obviously entangle her? Jake only hoped that having Rachel living with him, keeping her away from the ranch would be enough to keep her away from the worst of this. The hardest part was being unable to tell her about it, or could he?

Bannister dropped himself into the chair, staring at a blank wall. "To top it off," the agent said after a moment, "we've got another problem... or maybe I should say you've got a problem."

Jake waited as he stared at the glowing tip of his cigarette.

Bannister jumped again to his feet. He pulled his tie loose, running his finger around his collar as though finding it too tight. "The word is out. You. Delivered--$5000 dead. $20,000 alive."

"Another reliable source?" Jake retorted. Should he have been surprised? He wasn't. Nothing Ramirez would do, no matter how seemingly crazy would surprise Jake, not after having worked with the man. So Rachel was not going to be any safer with him than her father. Geesus.

"Don't take this lightly. That kind of money would turn some against their own brothers.

Jake snorted. "It doesn't take money to do that."

"He's calling in his IOU's, Donovan, and you're at the top of the list."

"Thanks for warning me. What'd you expect me to do about it?"

"Damn it to hell, big man, Ramirez is mentally deranged. Are you planning to play the Lone Ranger here?"

Donovan dragged smoke from his cigarette deep into his lungs but found little satisfaction from it. "If somebody wants to kill me bad enough--short of hiding the rest of my life--what can I do except what I always do—watch my back."

Bannister exhaled loudly. "One possibility is protective custody." When Jake smirked, Bannister gave a small laugh. "All right, the truth is, I don't know."

Donovan studied the ceiling, trying to think through his options. "You said he wants me alive," he said finally.

"We both know the kinds of things he has a propensity for."

If Rachel weren't a factor in all this, he'd be able to think more clearly. How could he protect her, maybe get her away from here for a week or two? After a moment, he looked at Bannister. "How sure are you that Michael O'Brian is in this all the way?"

Bannister gave off with a string of curses. "You are still only thinking about one thing, protecting that woman. You better wake up and smell the coffee, Donovan. It's you who has the problem here. O'Brian is Ramirez's partner, which tells me he's in on part of it at least. He will though watch out for his daughter— at least if he can. I've never heard anything to think he doesn't love her, have you?"

"No, I think he would protect her if he could. The thing is any sort of raid would leave her vulnerable, wouldn't it? Sounds like she's not safe with me or with her father."

"I don't know." Bannister paced to the window to stare out. "If Ramirez thought you and Rachel were involved, he would try to use her. That's a given. If he doesn't know... Well... Does her father know about you yet?"

"Not so far as I know."

Bannister threw himself back in the chair. "I am not as hard-hearted as you are acting like. I don't want her hurt either. I just don't know the plans-- not yet anyway."

Jake knocked his ash into an old coffee cup. "Wait a minute. I thought you had a man inside, the one you've been getting the tips from. What's he had to say?"

"We haven't heard from him for a couple of days."

Jake laughed. "Well, that sounds familiar."

"It's not funny."

"No," Jake agreed, "it's not." He drew deeply on his cigarette as he considered the facts and options. "Sounds like at this point what you have is all guesswork."

"Educated conclusions based on past experience but unless he turns up alive and soon, you're right. I'm guessing based on street talk."

"If Ramirez is after me, then maybe I should be the bait to haul him in," Jake said thoughtfully as he stared at the tip of his cigarette.

"Not a good idea."

"You have a better one? He wants me alive. That works in my favor to survive long enough for you guys to bust him. Maybe for once we could get him... if I can get Rachel out of the way first."

"Too many things have gone wrong in this operation for me go along with that kind of plan. It's like the guy is supernatural in the way he avoids traps."

"I don't know what choice you have; and for me I can't let this keep going on. I have reasons of my own to want resolution—reasons that involve looking at how innocent people like the Morrises end up paying the price for him walking free."

Bannister stared thoughtfully at his steepled fingers, then at Jake. "Let me think on it."

"I can't do it right away no matter what. I have to convince Rachel to get out of the area—one way or another. Preferably out of the state." He remembered her having a cousin in Oregon. That might be far enough.

"Well, I am saying straight out that I don't like it, but I don't like much about any of this." He shook his head, frustration etched on his handsome face. "How do you plan to get her out of town?"

Jake shook his head. "I'll think of something."

When Jake drove home from work, he still didn't know what he was going to do. How could he tell Rachel her father was a suspected smuggler of artifacts? Maybe a murderer? And what would it do to her to have him tell her that there was a contract out on her husband, possibly put there by her father? How could he protect her from the two men she said she loved most in this world?

At his driveway, he saw her truck parked in front of the house and felt a sinking sense of doom. No matter what he said, this whole thing was going to go wrong. He'd always known he would lose her, but he'd hoped for awhile longer to taste a world he'd never known.

Meeting him at the door, she wrapped her arms around his waist. Her lips were a sweet caress against his as she pulled him down for her kiss. "Mmmm I'm glad you're home."

"Me too."

"Just a minute, Jake." She frowned and pushed him back. "I thought you quit. You've been smoking again." She slapped irritatedly at the pack of cigarettes in his shirt pocket. "I don't want you dying of lung cancer."

There are more immediate possibilities, he thought darkly.

"I guess it is your business though," she muttered with a small scowl.

"I'll quit... one of these days."

She linked her arm in his as they walked into the kitchen. "I called the ranch. Dad wasn't home but should be in by five or so. Do you suppose we could drive out there tonight? "

"Uh, babe--" he started to say but couldn't find the words.

"Is something wrong?" she asked.

"We can talk later." He realized there was a tantalizing fragrance in the air. He only wished his stomach felt able to handle food. "Do I have time for a shower?" he asked, willing to postpone the conversation that he knew would cause her grief and might lose her.

"Just," she said, kissing him and walking back into the kitchen.

In the small bedroom, he grabbed jeans and a shirt. Stripping off his uniform, he stepped into the shower and turned on the cold water, hoping the shock would give him the words he needed. His problem was that he didn't want her near either him or her father. How could he manage that?

He heard the door to the bathroom open. Remembering the threat on his life, his heart rate accelerated until he saw Rachel's form through the foggy glass of the shower enclosure. He called her name, wondering what she wanted, when the shower door was opened, and she was inside with him, her bare body pressed against his.

"Ah, lady," he said, his voice almost a groan. He leaned against the side of the shower stall and pulled her into his arms.

The water poured over them as he bent and kissed her lips, feeling like he'd go crazy as she nibbled as his lower lip, her hands grasping and stroking him. He lifted her as she took him within, wrapping her long legs around him.

"If I'd known having a wife was like this," Jake said as they dried each other, "I'd have gotten married a long time ago."

"But it wouldn't have been with anyone but me," she teased. "Us-- together. We have the magic."

Just hold that thought, babe, he thought as he remembered what he had to do. Making love with her again had been beyond beautiful, but it also had solved none of the problems that lay ahead.

As they ate dinner, she chattered happily about her day, about plans she had for the backyard. He managed to hold onto his end of the conversation, but mostly with brief comments, his mind elsewhere.

She washed the dishes, he dried, then they sat on the small, brick patio, sipping a glass of wine, and watching the sun begin its color changing descent into the mountains. She was the one finally to break the silence. "What's wrong?"

He swallowed before he began, knowing he didn't have the right words but probably never would. "I was thinking you ought to take a little trip."

"Huh?" She looked at him with astonishment.

"Maybe go back and visit your aunt for a few days... or better yet fly up to see that cousin in Oregon."

She frowned. "Without you?"

"Not possible for me to go right now."

"Then why should I?" He knew she had forced the smile.

There were no good answers, but he struggled to find one anyway. "Just a few days," he said weakly. "Maybe a week."

"I don't want to leave you right now. We just got married, Jake. Are you trying to get rid of me already?" When he didn't answer, her smile faded. "I'm trying to understand what you're saying. I wanted us to go out and see papa tonight. Tell him about our marriage."

"Not a good idea, babe."

She frowned. "Why not? I have to tell him, or he'll hear from someone else that I'm living with you. Without knowing we're married, he'd be ready to kill you."

A good possibility anyway you cut it, Donovan thought cynically, tempted to reach for a cigarette. "We can't tell him just yet."

"I don't understand this. What is going on?"

He ran his fingers through his hair. His reasoning processes seemed derailed. He looked around the yard, trying to find the answer and knowing he wasn't going to stumble on it out there or anywhere else. "Rachel, you need to go away. I can't give you all the reasons. You just have to trust me."

"Trust you? When you don't trust me?"

He rubbed his forehead, trying to ease the headache that throbbed there. "Why are you making such a big deal out of this? I thought you went away now and then for visiting family, shopping or... painting."

"Not when we just got married, when we're just starting to build a life together. Not when I haven't had a chance to even tell Dad."

"Rachel, it isn't a good idea for you to go to the ranch right now either."

"Either?" Her mouth dropped open. "What are you talking about? What is really going on? You don't want me here. You don't want me there. I would like some kind of answers, Jake?"

"All right," he said finally, his voice tired as he gave up the battle to save her from this. At any cost, he had to protect her. Disillusioning her was better than having her caught in a shoot-out. If she revealed what he was telling her, his life wasn't worth anything anyway.

"You can't repeat what I'm about to tell you."

"What on earth are you talking about?"

He wouldn't wait for her promise. What the hell difference did any of it make anyway. "It's likely your father is involved in a smuggling operation. I don't want you going near him because you'd be tempted to warn him... or maybe get snared in whatever web he's gotten himself into."

She jumped to her feet. "That's the craziest thing I ever heard," she snapped glaring at him, her gaze filled with disbelief. "You don't know Dad, or you wouldn't say something like that... even as a joke."

"It's no joke." He explained, as tersely as possible what he knew of Bannister's investigation, the possible connection to the death on the desert as well as the Morrises, adding the need for secrecy, leaving out only the threat to his own life. He wouldn't accuse her father of something like that without concrete proof. Moreover, at this point, he wanted Rachel away from him. If he told her he was in danger, he didn't think he'd be able to convince her to go anywhere.

"You cannot possibly believe my father would... He'd never do anything dishonest or hurt anyone. Why are you doing this?" He could hear the little catch of a sob in her voice.

"You wanted to know why I didn't want you out there, why I really want you to get away for a week or two. I told you."

"This is ridiculous. This isn't like my father. Not him. Maybe Ramirez but..."

"Maybe. Maybe not. Sometimes people get into things before they fully realize what's involved, and then it becomes impossible to get out. Maybe that happened to your father."

"He wouldn't do that." Her voice rose with her anger as she faced the full implications of what he was telling her. "Even if he'd get into a business that was corrupt... I can't believe it, but even if he would, there is no way he'd have been part of murders." He rose, putting out his hand toward her. "No! Don't touch me!" She pushed away from him. "I don't want to talk to you right now. I need time to think... I can't understand what is wrong with you."

"Me!"

"Yes, you. You don't trust anyone. Now it's my father. What could possibly make you believe he would be a thief, a smuggler and yes, now you are suggesting a murderer? That's crazy. You don't even know him, Jake. Are you afraid I can't love both you and my father? Is this more of your insecurity?"

He nearly said that was ridiculous, but what he wanted was her away from all of this. Ideally a long way away. "Why don't you drive up to your aunt's, give it some time there to think about it. Maybe it'll get resolved while you're gone."

"You are thinking of arresting Dad?"

"I didn't say that."

"I want to be your wife," she said finally, tears running down her cheeks. "I want us to have a family, but, Jake, right now I don't know what to think about you. About why you'd say such a thing about a man you don't even know. Is there evidence, solid evidence?"

"Not that I know of yet."

"I don't know where I am going but... I need to think, get away from you for a little. Don't wait up!"

He heard the truck engine start up and pull out of the driveway, the wheels squealing. He understood how much he'd shocked her. Even worse he'd risked the whole investigation if she told her father what he had said. Despite all of the years he'd been in law enforcement, he didn't really care if she did. Pretty much that made him a bad cop, but all he could think, as he looked out the window into the darkening sky, was *she's not going to forgive me-- either way.*

∾

Ramirez snarled as he paced back and forth like an angry cat. "We cut it too close that time."

O'Brian sat at his desk, his eyes staring at the ceiling. "It's time to get out of all this."

"I told you that I have several things we must settle tonight. I know you're not happy with the way the raid went."

"That's putting it mildly. Why didn't you tell me ahead of time?"

"I didn't want it to distract you. Have you thought about what I did tell you?"

O'Brian glared at him. "You're talking about Rachel again?"

"I need a bride."

"Not her."

"She is a fit mate, and I would little interfere with her life. She could paint, go where she chose."

"Diego, why would you want a wife? I know where your true interests lie."

Ramirez frowned at him. "I must have sons to carry on. Every man must have sons, Miguel."

"Well, not by my daughter. You won't use her as breeding stock."

"So crude. You are disillusioned now by our small failure." Ramirez stared thoughtfully at him. "You wouldn't betray me too, would you Miguel?" he asked suspicion lacing his voice.

"Not betray," O'Brian said, aware men had died for even one distrustful thought planted in Ramirez's mind, but he was reaching a point where he didn't care much one way or another.

The very idea of the perverted monster touching Rachel with his dirty hands sickened him. How could he have been so mad as to become involved with such a disgusting example of humanity? "I never wanted to get into this stinking business to start."

"You didn't mind the money, Miguel."

"In the beginning I didn't understand its cost. By the time I did, you had the net tightened around me, and there was no way out."

Ramirez paced the room. "Relax, compadre. Soon, we'll be all right. With the proper offering, we can stop our enemies; then we can settle all this foolishness between us."

"Offering? What the hell are you talking about?" O'Brian felt the blood drain out of his face.

"I am taking care of that aspect," Ramirez responded with a twisted smile.

O'Brian rose to his feet. "I won't have you hurting anyone."

"This is my business, Miguel. Not yours. "

"It's mine if other people are hurt. I won't permit it."

Ramirez laughed heartily. "You thought you were in control here? You thought you had power over me. People have already been killed. It's too late for your cowardly doubts. I will do what must be done. This way we can accomplish all we need. We shall find what we need to know, and when the sacrifice has been offered, all will be well again."

O'Brian gritted his teeth in frustration. He was talking to a madman. "What sort of sacrifice?" he asked hoping by reasoning with Ramirez he could find out what was planned and stop it.

Ramirez smiled at him. His eyes vague and dreamy. "Do not worry, Miguel."

"You're not talking about Rachel?" O'Brian barely kept himself from attempting to throttle Ramirez before he got an answer to the question. Only his knowledge that Diego always carried a gun kept him under control.

Ramirez giggled. "You are being foolish, Miguel. Rachel will be my bride, not a sacrifice."

"Then what or should I ask who?" He frowned as he saw the pieces falling into place. "Donovan then?" When he saw the smile on Ramirez's face, he knew the truth. "Are you still after revenge on him? I thought I convinced you of the foolishness of that ploy. You'll only destroy yourself by trying this. It's frankly insane."

"Insane?" Ramirez chuckled. "This is not all about revenge as you suggest. There is more to it than that. It's the answer to our problem. There is a spiritual and physical answer to correcting what has gone wrong. I have been studying and saw the error of my past ways. The sacrifice has to be strong, potent. No weak, pathetic offering will solve what threatens us. We have to think more powerfully. Only a strong offering can produce the results we need."

O'Brian felt his stomach turn over. He'd heard of Ramirez's cruelty, but never wanted to believe it. With what kind of man had he involved himself? "Whatever you're planning, call it off, Diego. Let's try to get out of this while we can. We're not in so deep that we can't quit."

Ramirez only laughed again.

"This is totally crazy talk!" O'Brian snapped. His own nerves were dangerously near fraying. If he stayed around Ramirez longer, he'd be as insane as he clearly was.

Ramirez eyes were black and empty when he turned to look at O'Brian. "Soon it will be dark," he said after a long moment. Turning from O'Brian, he stared out at the purple and vermillion streaked sky, and O'Brian understood there would be no reaching him.

Michael O'Brian paced his bedroom nervously. He could hardly believe the mess he'd gotten himself into, one seemingly easy step at a time. It seemed such a little thing to begin--smuggling in a few artifacts for wealthy collectors. What did doing such a thing matter to anyone?

So a rich American owns the artifact instead of the Mexican government! It's in someone's home instead of a museum. So what! There were always more.

Then there'd been a murder, but he had justified it after he heard about it. He's salved the guilt in his heart by telling himself he had done nothing, but then there had been the Morrises? How could he justify that? What about now? What kind of attack was Ramirez planning on the hapless Donovan?

Angrily O'Brian replayed their last conversation and wondered if he could have said anything that would have reached the man. He picked up a small vase, running his hands softly over it. Rachel--his precious Rachel. The monster wanted to sully her too. Well that would never happen.

He had to stay alive long enough to get her out of this, to protect her from Ramirez, then he didn't care. If he went to the police, the likelihood is Ramirez would get off, one way or another. His fear wasn't so much that he might be nailed along with his erstwhile partner. It was that Ramirez would escape to Mexico while he would remain incarcerated. The added fear was that Rachel would be dragged into the mess.

He'd done what he could to protect the ranch from Ramirez by putting it all in Rachel's name two years before, but he wasn't confident that would be sufficient. If he was going to go down, Ramirez had to be dead first. He's seen Ramirez's unhealthy preoccupation with revenge. Nothing less than Ramirez's death would protect Rachel when his own betrayal became obvious. He sighed. He had seen Ramirez's uncanny ability to survive what would have felled other men.

He heard Rachel's truck drive in and her quick steps heading for her studio. He felt reluctant to see her, to face her with the load of guilt he was carrying, but somehow he had to convince her to get out of town for a few weeks. He wasn't sure that would be long enough to straighten out this mess, but he'd have to make it be. There had to be an answer.

At her studio door, he tapped lightly. When she didn't answer, he quietly opened the door and saw her sitting at the opposite end of the room, staring at one of her paintings, tears running down her cheeks.

"What is it, princess?"

She wiped her eyes. "Nothing, Dad." Her eyes seemed to question, but she smiled and stood up as he hugged her.

"You can't tell me. Is that it?"

"Not yet." Nervously she walked across the room.

"You look tired. Why don't you take a little vacation? Go someplace where it's cool."

"No." Her response was too loud, and he looked at her with concern. Glancing around the room, he tried to think of an excuse that would convince her when his eyes lit on the painting she'd been staring at. Tilted against the wall, it was a portrait of a man. With dawning recognition, he walked over to look at it more closely. Shocked, he recognized the tall, rugged man at the art show in Sedona. "Who is this?" he asked hoarsely.

Her answer came quickly. "Jake Donovan."

O'Brian wheeled around. "Donovan? That's Jake Donovan!" Shock took away his voice for a moment. Clearing his throat, he tried again. "I--I don't understand why you painted him."

"Jake is my husband. I married him this week." She blurted out the words.

O'Brian opened then closed his mouth, looked back at the painting, then to his daughter's white face. "I am trying to understand this. He's with... the Border Patrol?" *Please God,* he prayed, *let there be two of them, a brother, a cousin, anything.*

"Yes."

"Holy hell."

"I'm sorry to hurt you by not telling you before... We tried to call and tell you, but you were gone. I had no idea where to reach you. Please be happy for me." Tears streamed down her face.

He turned away, a feeling of darkness welling up within him. The tall, tough looking guy--so out of place at the art show—that was his daughter's husband. The man with whom he'd shared a beer... that was Ramirez's intended victim. "I don't understand," he said, gritting his teeth against his need to howl.

"It began the day I found that body. I didn't intend to keep it a secret, but--it's happened so fast and you've been gone a lot. Please try to understand. I wanted the two of you to meet, but you weren't here the day I thought I set it up."

He shook his head, staring again at the painting, thinking of the inferno that had been lit. It was bad enough before, now it was intolerable.

"I didn't want to hurt you, but I love him. Nothing in this world matters more to me than him."

O'Brian tried to think. Knowing now who Donovan was, having looked him in the eyes, he knew the man would yield Ramirez nothing, never beg and never yield. It would not change the end when that strong body would be broken, and the light in those eyes would be snuffed out.

He looked back at his daughter, saw the pleading in her eyes. How much greater her pain would be if she had any idea of what awaited Jake Donovan and of his part in it. She would hate him, and he would deserve it. *Lord*, he prayed for the first time in years, how could he make this right?

His breathing steadied as an assurance came over him. The decision of what to do suddenly seemed simple. "Rachel, you and your Donovan need to go away for awhile, take a honeymoon."

"But--"

"No, don't waste time. If you love this man of yours, get him out of Nogales. One way or another, put him in your truck and start driving. Call me in a few days, and I'll try to explain every-thing." *If I'm alive.*

He wondered as he looked into Rachel's eyes what else she knew, but he didn't want to ask. He just wanted her to be safe and get Donovan somewhere beyond Ramirez's reach. One way or another he'd put an end to Ramirez's plans; and if required, his life. He had to face the consequences for what he had done. The beginning of righting this wrong was warning Rachel.

"Look, baby, Donovan's in danger. Don't ask me how I know this. I just do. If you tell him about the threat to his life, he probably wouldn't go. Hey, a little honeymoon, everybody takes those."

He was suddenly relieved she was married. That at least ended one of Ramirez's ploys—at least as long as Donovan stayed alive. When he went to the law, they would then have what they needed to nail Ramirez. They could set a trap when he was on this side of the border.

He would do that. Nothing meant more to him than the happiness of his daughter. He only wondered why he hadn't realized that sooner. It suddenly all seemed simple. Get her away from here, and then he'd nail Ramirez permanently.

"What are you saying," Rachel begged, as he pushed her toward the door.

"Don't waste time; just get to your man and then out of Arizona—both of you."

Rachel looked into his eyes. He saw awareness grow in her eyes and then fear. Without another word or question, she ran for her truck.

"Drive carefully, baby," he said, patting her arm as she started up the truck. "But get there fast and get him out of Nogales tonight."

Sitting morosely at a table in the corner of the Lone Star, Jake was in no mood for company and anything but pleased when

Bannister came in, ordered a beer and joined him without waiting for invitation.

"I'm about ready to leave," Jake said finishing off his own beer.

"Okay, then me too."

Jake looked at him blankly. Too much had happened that day for him to play word games. "What are you talking about?"

"I'm your bodyguard."

Jake snorted. "You are joking."

"Nope. By tomorrow, I'll have authorization for round the clock protection, but tonight it's me."

"Nothing is going to happen that fast."

Bannister's smile was cold. "Something already has. Our man's body was found."

"Where?"

"Thrown over the fence, left like garbage. He'd been tortured, mutilated, you name it."

Jake sucked in a breath. "Not good."

"No, not good."

Jake lit a cigarette and took a deep draw from it. "Sorry."

"Yep."

"I don't want you watching over me like some kind of guardian angel."

"Like an angel, I'll be practically invisible."

"Oh right, sure. Remember what you said about it being more dangerous to be near me than to be me."

"Only in the short run." Bannister sipped his beer. "I have a sixth sense about things, Jake. You ever get that kind of thing?"

"No," Jake lied.

"Well, that little voice is telling me it's going down tonight. I put in calls to my superiors, but..."

"They're not big on sixth senses?" Jake guessed with a smirk.

"No, they're not. So for tonight, you just have me, baby. Tomorrow, I'll move whatever mountain is necessary to get protection for you."

"Geesus."

"Exactly."

Pulling his truck into his driveway, Donovan switched off the lights and sat at the wheel finishing his cigarette. He stared blankly into the darkness trying to ready himself for what might be ahead. He didn't need to look in the rearview mirror to know that the car, which had come to a stop down the street, was Bannister's. Jake had driven by the Sandovals hoping Rachel would be there; then hoping, when she wasn't, that she'd headed north to her aunt's. He couldn't let himself consider the possibility that she had gone to her father's ranch.

Entering the house, Donovan switched on the light. When nothing happened, he knew they were there. Instinctively, he twisted to one side even as he felt a gun barrel being poked into his back. He shoved back with his elbow, swinging his right arm hard enough to knock the gun barrel down and smash the bearer's stomach with the same move. The man grunted in surprise and pain, as the blow threw him back against the wall. A blinding pain in Donovan's head drove him to his knees. Swaying, he tried to rise to his feet only to be flattened by a brutal kick to his ribs.

"Dios, he's a bull," he heard a heavily accented voice gasp as hands grabbed him throwing him onto his stomach, and yanking his arms behind his back. Cord was tightly wrapped around his wrists binding them together. He struggled, but half stunned from the blow to his head, his efforts availed nothing.

Someone, kneeling at his side, wrapped a heavy cloth tightly around his eyes. "Open your mouth, mierda." When he didn't obey, fingers squeezed hard on his cheeks. A wad of cloth was thrust into his mouth and then tied in place with another cloth. He tried again to rise and felt hands under his arms pulling him to his feet where he swayed.

"Not so tough, now, eh Donovan?" questioned a voice with a nervous little laugh.

"Got nothing to say?" quipped another, shoving the barrel of a gun brutally into his belly. When Donovan kneed him in the stomach, he grunted in pain and hit him again.

"Quit playing around. Get him outside. We got no time for stupidness. Dios, you're an idiot."

Rough hands at his back gave him a hard shove out the door. Half holding, half dragging, they forced him toward the street where he heard a vehicle speed to the curb and stop.

He was thrown against what felt like a bumper. As he toppled forward, his legs were lifted, and he knew he was being put in the trunk of a car. A heavy blanket was thrown on top, and the trunk lid slammed shut.

He heard a shout, then three shots so close together they seemed as one. His head throbbed, making coherent thought difficult. They must've seen Bannister or the agent had moved forward to help him. Damn. What the hell had happened? As much as he hurt, he felt more anger at his own carelessness. He began twisting his wrists, trying to loosen the cord that bound them. A door slammed next door and an angry voice asked what all the noise was.

As the vehicle accelerated, he was rolled back against the metal, unable to protect himself from being tossed around. He hoped Bannister hadn't been killed, but it seemed unlikely they would have left him alive. Fighting the cords that bound his wrists, by the lack of give, he wasn't going to free himself.

The only thing he felt relief about was that Rachel hadn't been with him. Geesus, he wished he'd found a way to make her go without making her so furious. If he didn't make it out of this, he would have left her with bitter memories, leave her wondering if he'd deserted her. He'd had more than enough experience with desertions to know the damage they could do. Maybe they'd leave his body where it could be found. More likely they wouldn't. He twisted again at the cords around his wrists.

An abrupt turn of the car threw his head against the wheel

well, almost causing him to black out. The blanket had twisted around his legs, hampering him from using them in any effective way as a brace. Between the blanket's stifling weight over his face and the gag, he found it difficult to get a deep breath. He began wondering if the ventilation of the vehicle would allow him to keep breathing until they got to where they were going.

Then he wondered why he cared. He had no doubt who and what awaited him at the end of the ride.

CHAPTER 12

R achel turned into her driveway, still trying to work out
what she would say to Jake, how she would convince
him they had to both go away. It had to be tonight. They could
talk when they were away from Nogales. Outside her truck, she
heard a faint groan and only then saw a shape lying back in
the shadows. If her fear for Jake hadn't been so great, she
probably wouldn't have had the courage to run toward the
still form.

Time was suspended, until she saw with relief it wasn't her
husband. Kneeling, she recognized David Bannister, blood on the
side of his head. What had happened? She looked frantically
toward the dark house. Where was Jake?

Before she could decide what to do, she heard a faint groan.
"David," she said, putting her hand on his shoulder. "What
happened?" When he moved as though trying to sit up, she ran
back to her truck for a scarf to wrap around his bleeding head
wound. He muttered something unintelligible.

"What?" she asked, kneeling beside him.

"Lost him," he whispered. Eyes open, he looked unseeingly
at her.

She swallowed back her panic. "Jake?" she asked. "What are you talking about?"

Bannister frowned, his eyes closed and for a moment, she thought he'd lost consciousness again. Then he forced them open and said, "Ram... irez."

One of the neighbors Rachel recognized had come out of his house. "We heard something going on. I called 911. They are sure taking their time getting here," he said, looking at her and then the man lying now so still. "What happened? Hey, there's another guy over here." He came quickly back. "That one's dead. How about this one?"

Rachel felt a moment of panic until she saw the other downed man wasn't large enough to be Jake. Ramirez, David had said. Jake wasn't dead. She would have known if he was. She still felt him out there. He was alive, but where? It was Ramirez. Where would he take Jake? Her thoughts came in chaotic waves.

The neighbor's wife knelt on the other side of David. Rachel rose. "I have to go. Can you stay with him? His name is David Bannister. Stay with him until help comes?"

Her search had at least to start at the ranch. Where else might Ramirez take him? The thought of it being Mexico left her numb. She could not lose her ability to act, not now.

"Please, just explain to the police what happened when they get here." She ran to her truck, a sick feeling rising in her stomach. If Jake wasn't at the ranch, her father would know where he had been taken. That knowledge was almost as painful as the realization that Jake had been kidnapped. Quickly turning on the ignition, she pulled out of the driveway, her wheels screeching.

She felt tears rise in her eyes but angrily resisted the temptation to cry, to yield to weakness. Wherever Jake was, he needed her to keep her head. She could panic later. She thought perhaps she should have waited for the police, told them what she suspected, but it would be too late by the time anything official could happen. They might try to stop her from going.

She wished then she had remembered to charge her cell phone, but she hadn't, not for days. Who could she have called anyway? If what she feared was true, she would try to use the satellite phone at the ranch to call for help.

~

Yanked from the car, Donovan had stumbled in his darkness through a door and into a room. Hands grasped his shoulders, stopped him, held him. He sensed a man was standing in front of him before he heard the silken voice, the accent as thick as he'd remembered it. "Jacob, we meet again."

Donovan tried to assess how many men were in the room, and where they stood. Four had taken him from his home. Now there was at the least a fifth--Diego Ramirez.

"It was so nice of you to join us," Ramirez said as someone reached out and jerked the gag from Jake's mouth. He spit out the wad of cloth.

"My pleasure."

"It's been a long time, Jacob."

"Not long enough."

"Your wits are sharp as ever. It will make this time with you a delight." Ramirez walked behind him. Donovan tensed as he felt smooth hands on his wrists, checking the cords holding him. Ramirez circled slowly, coming to stand in front again. "Qué belleza."

"What's this about?" Jake asked, the blindness adding to his feelings of helplessness. Beauty? What was that about? He tried to still his breathing. Giving away fear would not help.

"So much, but we can start with information."

"Damn, too bad I don't have any."

Ramirez laughed slapping Jake's cheek. "Still joking, huh compadre? We'll see for how long. I do not like looking up at you. Sit."

Jake didn't immediately lower himself into the chair that had been shoved against his legs. "I do not want to repeat myself tonight, Jacob," Ramirez snarled. "You will obey what I tell you or the consequences will be unpleasant."

"Seems likely they'll be that anyway. Didn't your men already kill one guy tonight? Just a neighbor probably coming home."

Ramirez chuckled. "He was a good shot for a neighbor. He killed Rafe before my men dropped him." He slapped Jake hard. "From now on though forget you were a cop. I'll be the one asking questions."

Jake was shoved into the chair. He might have fought sitting in it, but he would have ended up there anyway—maybe with less teeth. Once sitting, he felt fingers at the buttons of his shirt. He gritted his teeth. The fingers were soft, gentle as they slowly worked loose buttons down to his belt, but the feeling of those fingers against his bare skin sent shivers down his spine. What exactly did Ramirez have in mind.

"I have many questions for you." Ramirez brushed the shirt off Jake's shoulders, leaving it to hang from his bound wrists.

With his upper torso bared, Jake tried to brace himself for what was coming. It would be torture at least to begin. Ramirez liked it too much to pass up any opportunity. He remembered warnings from training sessions on how to withstand what now faced him. The words then had been so dry. *Prisoners are often stripped. Psychologically it breaks a man, makes him feel vulnerable to be nude when others are clothed.* Straightening his shoulders, he forced boredom to his voice. "Ask away."

"Who was the man watching at your house tonight?" Ramirez asked.

"Geez, there was somebody watching my house?" He felt something brush his chest, stroke down his belly.

"I must be more exacting in questioning you, I can see," Ramirez purred. "I will have my little friend help me." The object moved up Jake's torso to his shoulder. He realized it was a whip, likely a riding crop. This was not going to be much fun. At least not for him.

"I want the name of the man, and I know you have it," Ramirez repeated. "My foolish men didn't take time to check his ID. They claimed it was too risky to stay. The neighbors were yelling, trying to find out what happened. They feared your cops would arrive. The man was not an innocent neighbor. I want to know who he was."

"What was that again?" The whip slashed through the air before it struck his bare shoulders.

"Perhaps with time your memory will improve," Ramirez suggested smoothly as he struck again with the whip, this time across Jake's chest. The lashes were painful but bearable, intended only to show him what was coming. Jake kept his body rigid, did not flinch at any of the blows that followed.

"This one will not break easily, *patron*," a voice said from another side of the room.

Ramirez laughed, his voice filled with exultation. "*Bueno, bueno.* I've dreamed of this. I want to enjoy every moment. Now, are you remembering anything, Jacob?" The whip struck again. "Just his name. This all can go easy for you or hard. I would prefer hard but you will prefer easy, I'm sure." The lash came down across his cheek.

"Let's see. Hey maybe it was the boyfriend of my hot neighbor." This time the whip descended with more force, striking his bare belly. Swallowing hard, he gritted his teeth, suppressing a grunt of pain. "She has a couple of them," he managed.

"I don't like hurting you," Ramirez purred in his ear. Jake recoiled at a soft touch on his chest, as Ramirez's fingers stroked the painful welts, seeming to caress. He had resisted Ramirez's advances when he was undercover; so he had no illusions about what the man wanted along with the torture.

"You know," Ramirez said contemplatively, "if I did as my ancestors, I would tear your heart from your chest with my bare

222

hands." He stroked across Jake's chest to a flat male nipple and pinched it hard.

"Go to hell," Jake snarled, as losing control, he leaped to his feet. Lashing out with his boot, he caught someone solidly with the kick. He twisted to the side, using his shoulder on another who was rushing at him. He heard air whoosh out and a hard fall. Bound and blindfolded, he had no chance to overpower them all, but he could make them pay something for their victory.

A savage blow to his head flattened him. Half conscious, he struggled to his knees, only to be struck again. When he regained awareness, he was again in the chair. "Take off his boots," he heard Ramirez wheezing. "No more boots to our bellies."

Jake felt hands on his legs, pulling boot and sock off first one foot and then the other.

"Can I have those boots, patron?" one of the men asked.

"You could put four of your feet in those boots," another joked.

Ramirez yanked on Jake's hair, forcing his head back, his voice an angry litany against Jake's throbbing head. "Wake up, carrion."

A door opened. "What's going on?" another voice demanded, American and soft in everything but the steel at its core.

"Keep out of this, Miguel," Ramirez growled.

"This is stupid even for you, Diego." The voice, which sounded strangely familiar to Jake, moved across the room until the man stood only a few feet away. "Let him go."

Water was thrown into Donovan's face. "All in all, I'd as soon drink it as wear it," he muttered, working to lift his head.

A laugh came from one side of the room, but the remark infuriated Ramirez as he took his whip and lashed Donovan across his chest again. There was the sound of a brief struggle, and Ramirez angrily snarled, "Give it back to me, Miguel."

"No," came the soft voice and the sound of something hard snapping in two. "I won't stand by and watch you whip a man like a dog."

"Mateo!" Ramirez yelled.

"Would you shoot me, Mateo?" the soft voice asked.

"If el patron told me I must, I would have no choice."

The American voice sighed but backed off. Donovan's only card had been dealt, and it wasn't enough to save him. Whoever this man was, and he had to believe it was Michael O'Brian, he didn't have a strong enough hand to pull him from this fire.

~

The drive to the ranch was interminable as Rachel played over again and again the argument she'd had with Jake, the warning from her father. Jake had to be alive. He just had to be. If he was, and she could think no other way, how could she get him away from Ramirez? She had seen how effective Jake was in a fight. They had to have taken him off guard, hurt him. In what kind of condition would he be?

At the beginning to the long driveway into her ranch, she stopped her truck before anyone inside would hear its approach. Until she was certain where Jake was, what they had done to him, better no one know she was there.

Roughly she turned the truck into a dry wash a hundred yards from the house. Her breath coming uneasily, she opened the truck boot and pulled out her 9mm pistol. She knew how to use it--on targets but what about men? She checked the magazine and found it held only spent shells. Reaching into the box for more, she stopped and in the darkness felt again. Only three bullets. Why hadn't she bought more? They would have to do as she loaded the weapon and thrust it to her back under her shirt.

Tears running down her cheeks, she walked as quietly and quickly as possible toward the house. When she saw Ramirez's vehicles parked by the porch, she felt certain Jake was also here.

If they'd been confident enough to bring him here, there was no doubt about her father's complicity. Still there was that cryptic warning he had given her.

She swallowed hard, putting aside her sorrow over her father's betrayal. For now, she would find Jake. What she would do then, she didn't know. She prayed he was still alive.

At the house she looked in the window, saw Jake in the chair, realized his hands were tied behind his back, a blindfold over his eyes, then she watched with horror as Ramirez landed his fist punishingly in his belly. The marks of torture were on his skin. She saw her father standing by and letting it happen.

She wouldn't panic. What could she do? Her gun with only three bullets would not free him. There were too many men, and one of them was her father. She didn't deceive herself into believing that firing a gun at any man would be so easy for her as for them. No, she couldn't go breaking in there, hoping to rescue Jake. That would only get both of them killed.

If she drove back to a phone, it would take an hour-- and then convincing the police to come, putting together a team. It would be more hours before anyone could be back while Jake was being beaten or worse. He could be dead or taken elsewhere by the time help could arrive. In an attack, he'd have no way to protect himself.

An idea came to her. Get inside the house. Call the police and then be there to help Jake when they attacked. If she drove up as though she knew nothing, would Ramirez kill Jake in front of her? She was going to be taking a risk. There was no way to know that they would not beat her alongside him, but Ramirez didn't know she and Jake were together--she hoped. If he did know about the involvement, perhaps she could convince him they'd had a fight and broken up. He knew little of her character. Might she convince him that even if he knew she and Jake had been seeing each other that she didn't really care what happened to the man?

She would have to be smart and play it all by ear, not revealing anymore than was necessary to trick Ramirez. She was counting on his monumental ego to help her and that her father would not give away her secrets. Then she would take her first opportunity to get to the phone to call for help or-- She had no idea what the 'or' was.

Running lightly across the rock strewn terrain, she got to her truck. Backing Matilda quickly over the rough ground, she continued backing down the driveway without headlights. Sometimes the wheels edged off, almost into the brush, but she couldn't take time to be careful. She had to get to the end of the long drive, then make them believe she was driving in for the first time.

Stopping a moment to steady her nerves, she was going to live or die with her husband. There was no other choice. Turning on the headlights, she drove down the driveway.

Ramirez's blow to the side of Jake's face, snapped his head back. The crooning words were nearly as harsh an assault on his nerves. "I've imagined this day, Jacob. You can't know how eagerly I've awaited the time when I had you under my power—totally under my control."

"No, and don't give a damn either," Donovan said, spitting blood from his mouth.

Ramirez chuckled. "Spirit, ah how I like in you. Too bad you didn't stay with me, Jacob. What a team we could have made." His hand caressed Jake's neck, making him feel more repelled than the blows from the whip. "You must cooperate with me though. I need names. Names I know you have. Let's start again with the man who was shot tonight."

"Go to hell."

"Patron, I have seen a cigarette help a man remember much."

"Your ingenuity pleases me, Mateo."

"Sí, patron?"

"Most definitely."

The voice Jake assumed to be O'Brian's gave a grunt of disgust.

"Hey gringo, want a cigarette?"

Donovan felt the heat near the bare skin of his belly. Cringing back against the chair, he gritted his teeth as the burning stub ground into his skin. *Rachel was right,* he thought with a black humor he never would have believed he could dredge up, *cigarettes are no damn good for you.*

His faint smile evidently infuriated Ramirez. "Don't be a fool, Jacob. You are hurting yourself for nothing. Think, man, how it would be to be home, to be lying in your own bed with a beautiful woman."

Donovan froze. Did Ramirez know about Rachel? God, he prayed the monster didn't. He tried to think how to divert him but the pain, the blows he'd taken had left his mind confused, unable to come up with anything coherent.

"You're going to kill him," O'Brian said with a forceful tone, "and what good will that do you?"

"I won't kill him. I have other plans. Plans for which he must be alive—at least for awhile."

Donovan tried not to groan as a fist jabbed into his stomach, snapping his mouth shut with the force of the blow. It felt like a rib had gone that time. Only half conscious, he prayed to pass out. As if in a haze, he barely heard the questions and repeated the only answer he could remember--*Don't know.*

"Patron, I hear a car," cried Mateo.

"It's my daughter's truck," Michael O'Brian snarled, "you're not going to drag her into this, Diego."

"Too late," Diego argued, then stopped. "Put away the gun. You know you wouldn't shoot me, Miguel," he said, his voice turning to a wheedling tone.

"Don't try me. I've seen all I can stomach here tonight. This gun will be where she can't see it, but don't forget where it's pointing, Diego."

"A gun battle would kill her too," Ramirez said softly.

"Which does not suit your purposes either and why we will all be good."

Donovan heard the door open. Half dazed by the beating he'd sustained, he felt a panic he'd not known when he heard Rachel's angry voice. "What's going on in my kitchen?"

"Rachel," Ramirez said, "we..."

She interrupted in a cold voice. "That looks like that lousy Border Patrolman from that day. What's he doing back? They're always snooping around somewhere they don't belong."

"Exactly. That's what he did," Ramirez said.

Rachel laughed, and the sound seemed to cut right into Donovan's heart. She had been angry at him earlier but not to this extent. She wouldn't protect her father at his expense. He had thought he could never trust a woman, but he knew otherwise with her. Whatever she was doing, his fear for her was worse than the torture.

"I can believe that." He heard her voice sounding irritated. "Cops are always poking their noses into places they don't belong. What are you going to do with him?"

"We'll let him go after we teach him a little lesson," Ramirez said. He laughed. "Isn't that right, Miguel?"

"Absolutely."

Donovan could hear Rachel's footsteps as she crossed the room, caught her scent as she passed in front of him. He kept his mouth shut as anything he could say could only endanger her further. All he wanted was for her to be out of this and back in town. She didn't understand these men. This was a game beyond her experience. If she didn't do it all just right, she'd die with him.

"Well, just make sure your actions here don't bring anything back onto me. Any bad press would be bad for my gallery sales."

She laughed again. "When you finish your business," she said, her voice soft with the tone Donovan remembered so well, "I'll be in the living room having a little glass of wine." With that, she walked out of the room.

When she had gone, Ramirez laughed. "Your daughter amazes and delights me, Miguel. Perhaps she shouldn't though. Like father, like daughter, eh? I suppose she likes the money our little enterprises bring in. Mateo go make sure she has what she needs." There was a hard edge to the last sentence.

"She is my daughter, all right." O'Brian had moved to stand near the door. Jake could hear the smile in his voice. "What are you going to do with him now?"

"What I want cannot be done here. In the morning, my helicopter is scheduled to come for us. For tonight, I'm no longer in the mood." Viciously, he yanked Donovan's hair, forcing his head up. "Do you hear me, Jacob? But in the morning, after a night of love, I'll have all the time in the world for you." He turned away. "Diego, yank the lines to the satellite."

"Why?" O'Brian interrupted. "You heard Rachel. She has no interest in what happens to him. Why yank the lines? We may need them."

"I take no chances," Ramirez said. "You can have the satellite hooked up again tomorrow. I have lived as long as I have by being leaving nothing to chance."

"Maybe so, but yanking out the phone is stupid," O'Brian argued.

"Stupid or not. It is the way it will be." Ramirez's voice seemed to carry a threat directed at O'Brian. Donovan didn't suppose O'Brian's pulling a gun on his partner would soon be forgiven and from his own experience, never forgotten.

Ramirez laughed. "Let's have a glass of brandy and see if your beautiful daughter is in the mood for some pleasant conversation." He bent low over Donovan, his breath against his forehead as he brushed his hair back. "In the morning, I'll take you where I will not again be interrupted. There we can finish what we started. Gag him again, then secure him well in the shed out back," he barked out the order, then was gone. From what Jake could tell, O'Brian with him.

Jake didn't bother to resist the gag being tied again over his mouth before he was yanked from the chair. He stumbled but managed to right himself. When he nearly fell, hands went under his arms, and half carried him.

"Dios, he's one big hombre," one of the men grunted with a painful laugh as he staggered under even part of Donovan's weight. A door opened and cool air was on Donovan's skin. The ground was rough under his bare feet as he struggled to stay erect, to place one foot in front of another. Another door opened, and he was given a brutal push. He crumpled to the dirt to the accompaniment of more laughter.

"Should one of us stay and guard him?" the voice of Mateo asked.

"You want to stay out here all night?" There was more laughter. "We'll brace it closed from outside. He's in no shape to do anything."

Donovan felt hands on his ankles, then cords binding them tightly together. The effort seemed pointless since he doubted he could stand even if he miraculously got the door to the shed open.

When the door slammed shut, Donovan was left lying on the dirt floor, his ability to think muddled by the pain, his thirst and the suffocating heat of the shed. Sweat rolled down his torso, and he alternated between feeling a fevered heat, a shivering cold, and a blinding fear for Rachel.

People had told him that when his time came, when death came for him, he would pray. If he had thought praying would do anything, perhaps he would have. Nothing was going to save him. If he had thought it would work, he'd have asked for Divine help for Rachel. He had no such comfort.

In pain, dazed and confused, he held onto only one thing. He had been betrayed by everyone he ever cared about, but that wasn't Rachel. It might have sounded like it, but he didn't believe it. Even if she had turned on him, wanted to leave him, it was not in her to see someone beaten and not care. She was obviously determined to help him even at the risk of her own life. If she died, nothing else mattered. He had brought her to this, and the guilt was killing him more than anything Ramirez could do.

He didn't know what he could do to help her, but he struggled against the ropes binding his wrists. All that availed was blood and sweat. There was no give in the cords. He wouldn't stop trying. Even if he got free, he didn't know what he could do. It wasn't the first problem.

Donovan woke, startled to realize he had slept and that some noise had wakened him. Were they coming so soon? The door opened quietly, causing him to shrink back, even as he knew there was no escape from what was coming. Despite the useless-ness of it, he struggled to get an elbow under him. He wouldn't face his end flat on his back.

There was silence then as the door closed, but he heard breathing at the same time he smelled her scent, felt her gentle hands at his head, loosening the knots that secured the blindfold and then pulling the gag away.

"What have they done to you?" He could hear the sob in her whisper.

He was unsure if he was more afraid he was dreaming or that he was not. He felt her hands on his face, then moving down his arm toward his wrists. Fear quickly replaced relief. There was no safety for her with him. "Rachel, you got to get out of here." His voice was little more than a raspy croak.

He felt cold against his wrists and then the sound of a knife slicing through the ropes.

"Can you walk?" she asked after she cut through those at his ankles.

Barely restraining a groan, he shrugged his shirt back up over his shoulders. He rubbed his hands to try to restore circulation, as he struggled to his feet. His head throbbed, body ached, but worse, he nearly blacked out. Her arms quickly came around him, steadying him.

"Jake, can you do this?" she whispered. She flicked on a small flashlight, running it up his torso to look at his face.

"Turn it off unless you need it to see."

"No, there's just enough light from the moon."

When they got outside, he stopped. "Secure the door however it was. If they check tonight, we want them to think I'm there."

She left him long enough to replace the wooden brace, then threw her arms around him. "They were drinking and fell asleep," she whispered, "but in the morning, I heard them say a helicopter would be coming. It's almost midnight now."

A few steps told Jake that he wasn't going anywhere fast. "Rachel," he started to whisper before her fingers came up and pressed against his lips.

"If you're going to tell me to leave you, don't waste what energy you have," she ordered, her voice low but firm in resolve. "We go together, or we don't go."

He tried to think of words that could convince her to leave him. It would be a waste of his limited energy. How she had gotten to him, where Ramirez was, those questions would have to wait.

He straightened, determined to find the strength to keep moving. Except where could they go? The unconsciousness he had craved earlier seemed to threaten him now with each step, only sheer will kept him on his feet. His body, slick with sweat shivered as the cooler night air hit it.

Rachel stared across the yard to the barn. She couldn't carry Jake far. They needed supplies, which she had not taken from the house. She had to find a temporary refuge for him to recover enough to make it to the truck—on the other side of the house. The men, who had all been drinking, were unlikely to realize he was gone before daylight. They had time. Not much but hopefully enough.

When he realized to where she'd led them, he groaned but couldn't find the strength to argue. Slowly they made their way to the back and a pile of straw. Bracing herself, Rachel helped Jake lower his body onto it.

She knelt beside where he sprawled. "You need to rest and I need to get us supplies before we try to leave here."

"Babe, take your truck and get out of here, call for help when you get to town. I'll hide in here. They won't find me. Don't come back until they have them. I'll be okay."

"Don't bother lying to me, Jake," she said, the smile in her voice.

"Don't be crazy." Before he could think of another argument, she was gone.

Hell, he groaned, feeling more helpless than when he'd been Ramirez's prisoner. At least then it had only been his life on the line. The thought of anything happening to her was more than he could stand. Shivering, he lay back, gritting his teeth to stop them from chattering as he tried to think of a way out. Nothing came to mind as he listened for the sound of her return. If anything went wrong, he'd be all but useless to her. How had he let this happen? For all the intentions he'd had to keep her safe, he was her greatest source of danger.

It seemed an eternity before he heard movement again in the barn. Raising himself on an elbow, he strained to see through the darkness. He didn't see her until she was at his side, then she was kneeling, a canteen at his lips. The water was tepid, stale, but it wetted his throat and took away the hellish thirst that had been tormenting him for what seemed hours.

"Take it easy," she whispered, "not too fast."

She poured a little onto a rag she'd brought and in the dim light of the flashlight, began washing some of the blood from his face, assessing his injuries. "Jake," she whispered, her lips kissing where the cloth washed, tenderly bathing his injuries with her caresses, "I'm so sorry." Her tears tell on his face.

"None of this was your fault."

"I should have believed you when you said... Well I do now. My father... well he did one good thing."

"He wasn't part of what Ramirez was doing. He tried to hold him back. He just didn't have... enough clout with the others."

"Then two because he knew when I came into the kitchen that I was lying. I had told him earlier tonight that we were married."

He groaned. "You took too big a risk coming in like that."

"I'd have taken more for you."

He knew that and it scared him more. "Where is Ramirez now? He didn't touch you did he?" The thought of that would drive him insane, but he had to know.

"When he came into the living room, he had a drink, and then he seemed to doze off. I don't know. Maybe Dad put something in his brandy. Whatever the case, I didn't have to do anything."

"You shouldn't have come back."

She managed a little laugh. "Of course, I should have," she said her tone inflexible. "David was shot but managed to tell me who had you. I didn't want to take time to call the police, but I thought I could do it when I got here, but the phone didn't work."

"Ramirez had the lines pulled. He trusts in nothing."

"If I'd been with you, this wouldn't have happened."

"How badly was Bannister hurt?"

"I don't know. It's a head wound. Not good but he was alive when I left him with help on the way."

The thought of her in Ramirez's hands left him unable to think straight. "Geesus, I wish you hadn't come back."

"I had to come back. You know that." He could hear the smile in her voice. "Through all the mistakes and anger, and least now we're together." She reached into the back pocket of her jeans and brought out a tube of ointment. "I found this. Maybe it'll keep some of the cuts from infecting and ease the pain."

As she doctored the welts and burns on his torso, cleansing a deep cut across his chin, and carefully washing away the blood from the lump at the back of his head, she forced herself not to think about the danger they faced. She didn't deceive herself that if she was found with Jake that her fate would be any different than his.

"All right then, we need to get out of here," he said with a groan of frustration. Could he make it anywhere? She sure couldn't carry him.

She felt of his forehead, trying to determine if he was becoming feverish. "We will. Just rest a few minutes first," she murmured.

"There is no time for that."

"You need to be able to walk. Just a few minutes." He lay back with a groan of frustration. As she watched him try to sleep, she found it hard to believe any of this night was real. Things like beatings and shootings didn't happen to people, not people she knew. She had to get a grip on herself or her sorrow over her father's perfidy would make her incapable of action.

Holding Jake against her, she knew that if he didn't walk away from this, she didn't want to either. If she had not known how desperately she loved him before, she knew now.

CHAPTER 13

Aﬁer what seemed hours but she knew had been half an hour or less, Jake opened his eyes. "We have to go."

"Where are your boots?" she asked as he sat up.

"One of them thought he could fill them." Jake got to his feet, swaying but steadier on his feet than he'd expected. "These boys have a thing about shoes."

"I could try to find them," she suggested.

"No, it's time to go."

"I have to go back to the house." She had thought this through while he rested. "I heard Diego set out a guard out by the main road. We'll have to take the old wagon road. It's longer, winds down into Mexico before it turns north. I haven't been on it in years. It may even be washed out. We need more water. There is some water in Matilda, but not enough if anything went wrong..." She stopped and added, "If they see me, "they'll only think I got up for a drink."

He hated the idea of her going back in there, but she was right. It could be a greater risk of her life to start out without emergency water.

"All right, but no place but the kitchen. No sneaking around the house. Forget the boots. And Rachel," he added, his voice brooking no argument, "if they do see you, I don't want you coming back. You go to bed and forget you saw me. I'll hot wire one of their trucks."

She started to argue, but he put his hand over her mouth. "It's the only way I can let you do this."

Frowning, she lied. "Okay, but you sit down while I'm gone. Rest!"

As if he would be able to rest with her in that house, but he had no choice. He was still dizzy, not remotely capable of fighting any battles. He did as she ordered, waited on a feed box, feeling useless, and knowing the next minutes would be the longest of his life.

By the time she got back with three large canteens, a loaf of bread, cheese, cookies and three apples in a backpack, Jake's nerves had been stretched to their limit, his jaw clenched tight as he had fought back the stupid urge to go after her.

Seeing the muscle throbbing in his jaw, Rachel kissed him. "I brought dishtowels. We can wrap them around your feet."

After she had helped him tie the ends of the thin towels to his ankles, they slowly inched their way around the house. With the crescent moon still above the horizon, there was some light. "Can you make it?" she whispered, looking back with concern.

"Is there a choice?" he hissed, wincing as he made contact with a rock through the cloth.

The distance they had to walk was probably only a few hundred feet, but Jake felt spent. At the truck he called on the reserves that had never deserted him.

"Put it in neutral and steer," he directed. "I'll push you away from the house."

"You can't do that. Just get in the truck."

"I can and will. We have to be away from the house when the engine starts up. We can't afford to take a chance on alerting them just yet." He tried to give her a reassuring smile unsure how

237

well he succeeded as he shoved her gently toward the driver's side. Because the driveway sloped a little, it was easier than he'd expected.

When the truck was rolling, he gave a little jump and was in the passenger side. Everything seemed to be going their way as no lights came on in the house. When the engine came to life, it purred like a baby. Keeping the lights off down the narrow lane, Rachel drove from memory and dim moonlight.

"It beats all, the way you see in the dark," Jake said as they circled around past the barn.

She glanced over. "With those cougar eyes of yours, you ought to see in the dark." He just smiled. When they were finally pointed away from the house, she put on the low beams and accelerated a little.

Jake sighed, leaning back in the seat, letting himself relax for the first time in what seemed days but which in reality had only been a matter of hours. They weren't safe, but they'd made it away from the ranch buildings, and they were together. When the wheels of the truck bounced in and out of a pothole, he held his side against the stabbing pain. He figured a rib must have been cracked if not broken from the beating Ramirez had administered.

He heard her crying. "I am sorry, babe. It's going to be okay," he said, wishing he had words to reassure her. He was a long way from sure they would be okay.

"After you and I fought," she said, "I came out here to sort through what you'd said. My father came into the studio. He warned me you needed to get out of town. I didn't want to believe it, but I finally accepted everything I had believed about him had been wrong." She fought back tears. She'd cry later. Now was no time to break down, but she was also angry at herself for not believing Jake when he tried to warn her.

Jake wished he was better at words. He wanted to comfort her but the words didn't come. He reached into the pocket of his shirt and with relief found half a pack of cigarettes. As he drew deeply on the cigarette, blowing the smoke out the window, he thought again about Michael O'Brian's voice trying to remember where he'd heard it before. "Your father did try to help me, before you got there."

"I guess there wasn't much he could do by then, but if he hadn't gotten involved with Ramirez..." She stopped when she heard Jake wince with pain as the truck bumped through a pothole. She had to put the past behind her at least for now. No self pity. No questions. Just get them both somewhere safe.

"Ramirez was out to get me from before this. It would have happened someday anyway." When she didn't say anything, he added, "Your father pulled a gun on him to try and stop him. That won't be forgiven." He again thought of O'Brian's voice, about the strange sensation he'd had that he had heard it before somewhere. No use, the thoughts were too jumbled, his own situation too pain-filled to put together any puzzle. He closed his eyes, trying to forget his discomfort as he had managed to do so many times in his life.

She reached out to touch his shoulder. "Shall I slow down?"

He shook his head. "The more distance we put between us and them, the better I'll feel."

Rachel fought her impulse to push her foot harder on the accelerator. They could ill afford an accident. Several miles from the ranch, when the road forked, she turned left. Logic should have had her turning right but she was nearly sure she'd been told that road had been wiped out in one of the floods. She could only hope she remembered the way as well as she thought. When the road turned into a washboard, she shifted down again in an effort to make the ride smoother for Jake.

Some miles farther, she frowned as she saw a red, dashboard warning light blink on. The truck seemed to struggle up a slight rise even though Rachel pressed her foot more firmly on the gas pedal. Worried, she looked at the gauges beside the dashboard.

The temperature needle was rising rapidly. Shifting down again, she knew they had a real problem.

The needle on the temperature gauge had traveled as far as it could go. Letting off on the gas a little, the truck's engine began to sputter and, then to Rachel's cold horror, stopped dead. "Merde," she swore, her nerves frayed as she pounded on the steering wheel.

"What happened?" Jake asked thickly, having closed his eyes for what had seemed a second and fallen asleep.

"She's quit. I can't believe it. Matilda's never done this to me."

"Leave the lights on so I can see." He yanked the passenger door open smelling the sickening smell of hot coolant. Not encouraged, he lifted the hood as he swore succinctly.

"What's wrong?" Rachel asked, peering into the engine. "I don't know anything about mechanics."

"Find me a rag if you have one." He waited a moment, then with the rag wrapped around his hand, gradually opened the radiator cap. "Stand back," he ordered as he stepped back himself to allow the steam to shoot straight up.

"What is it?" she asked, her voice edged with worry, torn between concern for them being on foot and her beloved truck. The geyser of steam didn't bode well.

"I'm guessing, but likely the truck hit something, sprang a hole in the radiator or maybe it's just plain old age." He swallowed, leaned back against the hood, and tried to think. They didn't have enough water to share with a truck that had a radiator with a hole.

"How serious is it?"

"Not good, not good at all, babe," he said with an attempt at a reassuring smile, "especially when you're running from the bad guys."

She couldn't believe he was able to joke at a time like this, then she realized this kind of danger probably hadn't been as unusual in his life as it had been in hers. "What shall we do?" she asked, putting her hand lightly on his arm and glad that now the answer to that question, to the problem, was shared with him.

He ran his other arm across his forehead, wiping sweat away. He stared at the distant mountains barely outlined in the pre-dawn hour and seemed to consider for a moment. "Unless you've got a better idea, we walk."

She looked at him, then down at his feet, barely covered by the dish towels, which might have been adequate for a short walk to the truck but would hardly take him across the barren waste around them.

"You can't do that."

He gave her a look that said it all. He'd have to do it. Then she saw him taking off his shirt. "Hand me your knife."

"What are you doing now?"

He knelt, using the knife to rip the sleeves from the shirt. "I got to make a choice here between maidenly modesty, sunstroke and footwear."

She smiled and slipped up behind him, running her fingers seductively down his bare chest. "Whose maidenly modesty are we talking about here?"

"Why mine, of course, babe," he drawled, kissing her fingers and tearing the rest of the shirt into two pieces. She handed him the few paint rags she had stashed in the truck boot, then sitting on the ground, he took the material and padded, then tied cloth over his feet putting as much barrier as possible between his soles and the rough terrain. When he'd done what he could for his feet, he told her to grab her own hat from the truck as he wrapped his sleeves around his head to create a rough turban.

"Jake, there are miles out there before we'll find anybody to help us. No ranches. Nothing. You've been beaten, tortured. You can't walk that far with just cloth covering your feet." She remembered the bloodied feet of the dead man. "I think you should hide in the brush, and I'll walk for help."

She couldn't believe it when she heard him chuckle. He didn't argue with her, just stuck her knife into his belt. "Grab those canteens and whatever else you think we can use," he said as he stared into the distance. "We will head for a desert tank I remember. We have enough water to get us there. With the recent storms, it'll have water."

"We'll die like he did."

"Don't give up on me, babe. We know the country. He didn't."

"But..."

"We're on our own with this. You think David was going to be able to tell anybody else what he saw?"

Reluctantly, she shook her head. "Unlikely." She hoped he wasn't dead.

"So it'll be a few days at the least before anybody comes looking and even then with no idea where to begin. You think sitting here that Ramirez won't find us? Come on. Help me push the truck into the brush. We won't make it easy on the bastard. When we head more or less northeast, after the tank, we won't be far from Esmeralda."

"How will a ghost town help us?"

"I heard a guy from California bought the whole shebang. He was going to put a caretaker up there to keep people out."

"That is a tenuous hope at best. What happens if nobody's there?"

He raised his eyebrows. "You want to wait here for a ride?"

She shut her mouth and quit arguing. He was right. They couldn't stay where they were. She felt lucky she had worn jeans, a light cotton shirt and her good tennis shoes. She pulled on her cotton hat.

They pushed the truck into the brush, turning off its headlights. "Shouldn't you rest before we start out? You are not invincible, Donovan."

"We have to get as far as we can from the road and truck." He smiled. "I know it's an iffy plan, but I don't much like the idea of falling back into Ramirez's hands. He didn't think highly of me before. I doubt my running out on his party is going to endear me more." He couldn't avoid a shudder as he thought of those hands touching his chest. The thought of them touching Rachel was worst.

"I have a gun." She reached under the front seat of the truck and handed him the 9mm. "Only three bullets though." She patted the seat telling her truck that she would be back for her... she hoped.

"It's a lightweight weapon." He didn't need to add that three bullets weren't going to give them much firepower against Ramirez and his men.

"It's something."

"It is." He shoved it under his belt. "There's another possibility here," he began softly. "If we split up, you could head back to the ranch. It's not so far from here. Tell them I kidnapped you--forced you to go with me."

She gave a short laugh. "I hope you're joking," she said, that chin going into the air.

"It would be your best bet. You might get a chance to call for help--send somebody after me."

She narrowed her eyes. "Donovan, whatever happens, happens to both of us. I left you once. It was the worst mistake of my life. I won't do it again—ever." She put her arms around his waist. "This is not negotiable. I don't want what Ramirez has in mind for me either."

He turned away, not wanting to think what that was. One way or another the man would know she had tricked him. The monster's vengeance would be as great on her now as on him. He couldn't afford to think about that. She was right. They would stick together. He knew the desert; so did she. They would do better out here than the softer men chasing them.

Jake willed his strength to be enough to carry him through the ordeal ahead. His body had never failed him, but he'd never asked so much of it. He clenched his jaw. From now on he couldn't make any mistakes and feeling sorry for himself or losing hope would be the worst he could make.

Breaking off a long, mesquite branch, he began brushing out the tracks of the truck. "Let's make them work for it," he said, trying to make the roadside look as it had before the truck had been pushed off its shoulder. "If we're lucky, they might not notice it right away. That will buy us some time. They might send someone to town hoping to catch us there. The less coming after us, the better."

She made sure she still had the tube of antibiotic ointment. It was a pathetic thing to put her security in-- a slim comfort against the odds against them. Within a few hours, Jake's feet were going to need whatever help she could give them. The food went into a lightweight backpack, which she put on her back. "Don't go macho on me," she said before he could argue. "I've seen the welts across your shoulders."

He smiled with chagrin only arguing when she tried to carry all three canteens as well. "I'll take those," he said, his tone brooking no argument.

For some distance, Jake brushed out their footprints as they walked up the arroyo. At the end, when he felt they had to change direction, he looked up at the sky trying to get a fix on where they were. Their goal was Esmeralda, but they needed not to miss the desert tank first. Three canteens wouldn't take them all the way in the summer heat. They had no choice in the beginning except to walk under the hot sun, to put as much distance as possible between themselves and those searching for them. After that, they would travel at night.

"We'll stick with the arroyos as much as we can where there are live oak and some shelter. If we hear the helicopter or a jeep, we'll get under what we can but most important, sit tight until they're gone," he told her. "If they don't see movement, they'll have a hard time spotting us."

She nodded, looking back until she tripped on a chunk of

granite. From then on, she kept her eyes in front of her. With morning, the sun rose red in the sky, which meant a scorcher of a day ahead. She looked futilely to the south, hoping to see the beginning formations of thunderclouds. An afternoon thunderstorm would not only wipe out their tracks but cool the land if only for a few hours. Of course, it would also mean lightning with no shelter to protect them from its possible strikes.

As the sky brightened, they kept as close to cover as possible. Shifting from one rock strewn arroyo to another, Jake set a steady pace. As long as the arroyo headed east, they stayed in it, only climbing out and finding a new direction when necessary. As the morning went on, Jake lost some of the desperate concern to hurry that had dogged his steps with their first hours.

Rachel kept a watchful eye on her tall man. Were his steps a little slower, was he favoring his left side more than he had? How many thorns were now embedded in the soles of his feet? She would have given a lot to see his eyes. Those golden eyes couldn't hide much from her, but he kept them on the ground, only looking up to adjust their direction.

"Are you all right?" she asked as she took a couple of quick steps to catch up with him.

"Listen, in case I go out on you." At her expression of panic, he smiled wryly. "I don't mean permanent like, just spacey. Sometimes when I've gotten exhausted or--well, the body can keep going when the brain quits. If that happens, I will keep moving if you just tell me. Then you keep your ears open for the helicopter they may use to hunt us. Remember what I said if you hear it or see it in the distance, hide under the edge of a bluff, tree or whatever shelter is possible. They shouldn't be able to see us from the air if we aren't moving. See that rock formation." He pointed to a high rocky crag in the distance. That's roughly the direction we need to go. Keep heading that way."

She put herself in his path and placed her hands on his chest. "How often can we rest? You need one now." He nodded and leaned back against a rocky bluff as they both drank from the canteen. She'd never appreciated the taste of water as she did now. Tepid it might be but so welcome.

With the sun now well above the eastern mountains, they kept moving, one foot in front of the other. It seemed to Rachel the arroyo went forever; sometimes the shade of the undercut cliff provided a respite from the heat of the sun; other times she felt the full power of the Arizona sun, making her grateful for her cotton hat.

"We have to find a place to stop," she said when she heard Jake stumble and catch himself for the dozenth time. "The sun's too high to keep going."

She saw then that he was past thinking. There was no expression in his dazed eyes. Only the mettle of the man had kept him moving. Looking around, she saw a shelter that seemed promising. Taking Jake's arm, she guided him toward the shade of a large mesquite under the overhang of the embankment. She stuck a stick in it to assure herself no rattlesnakes had thought likewise.

"Lie down," she ordered, easing him to the ground. She put the canteen to his lips and let the water trickle into his mouth, grateful when he swallowed. With her fingers, she gently smoothed the precious liquid over his cracked lips before she drank.

She felt so tired, so drained that all she wanted to do was lie down beside him; but before she could do that, she had to erase whatever signs of their presence she could. He was right about the helicopter. Nobody was likely to be following them on foot, not where they had gone.

She used the broken branch to brush out their tracks, then hide their presence as much as possible, she decided they could get a little further under the sheltering lip. "Jake, you have to move." He seemed able to respond to her voice, to force his body to obey even when he was barely conscious; and she was able to ease him into the precarious shelter.

She looked at him carefully, trying to assess his physical condition. Large bruises, burns, and welts on his chest and stomach were painfully obvious in the light of day. One cheek was swollen. The gash across his jaw was at least not bleeding. Seeing clearly for the first time the injuries Ramirez had inflicted on him, she applied more of the antibiotic cream as she wondered how he had stayed on his feet. She ought to remove the rags and cleanse and doctor his feet, but she was tired, so tired. She hadn't slept in two days. With a sigh of resignation, she gave into the sleep her body desperately needed.

CHAPTER 14

R amirez ranted and raved as he stalked around the empty shed. "Where is he? You were supposed to secure him, you dolts." He shoved his men aside and walked back outside, turning to glare at each of them in turn. He then faced O'Brian, who had been leaning against the side of the shed. "What happened to him?"

"I haven't the foggiest notion," he said restraining the urge to grin.

Scowling, Ramirez stalked into the house, screaming at his men as he went. Following, Mateo muttered to himself. Ramirez turned on him. "What? You coward, say what you're thinking?"

"Just someone had to have helped him."

Ramirez glared at him, then at O'Brian. "Where's Rachel? Where is *she* this morning?"

O'Brian shrugged. "Rachel doesn't report her every move to me, but I'd guess, since it's early, she's gone out onto the desert and is painting or sketching."

"I didn't hear her drive away."

"You wouldn't be likely to. Since she leaves before I wake up, she's learned to be quiet about it." O'Brian stared thoughtfully toward the dawn-outlined mountains as Ramirez paced the kitchen floor.

"He can't get far without his boots," Mateo suggested backing up when Ramirez took three quick steps. Not quick enough to avoid the hard slap.

"You don't know the man. He would walk through fire if he had to," Ramirez snarled. "Diaz, look through the buildings, make sure he's not hiding in the barn." All three henchmen took the opportunity to escape Ramirez's wrath and ran for the door pushing at each other as they went through it.

Ramirez drummed his fingers on the table. "They won't find him," he said, almost to himself. "He's gone."

"We should get out of here too, then. He'll bring an army back with him," O'Brian said, pouring a cup of coffee.

Ramirez acted as though he hadn't heard him. "When my helicopter gets here, we will make certain he isn't still out there somewhere. Maybe his luck won't be so good. Maybe my energy is stronger." He was silent a moment before his voice returned to the eerie one that set O'Brian's teeth on edge. "Never mind where he is, I will find him and next time take him directly to my citadel. No one will get him away from me again."

Not saying a word, O'Brian took his coffee out onto the patio. If only he could enjoy the clear morning air. How long had it been since he'd enjoyed anything? He knew all too well. It had been since he sold his soul to the devil. It was time to take it back. He stared into the sky and thought of how he'd let down his beloved Marguerite. She had counted on him to protect their baby, and he had let his drive for profit blind him to what he was doing. He could only hope that by now Rachel and her border patrolman were safely back in Nogales and police were on their way to arrest this nest of vipers, but inside he feared that wasn't the case. If they had made it that far, forces should have already arrived. Something had gone wrong on the drive east. So it was up to him to do what he could to right his wrongs.

From the moment he had walked into his home, had seen Donovan being beaten, he'd felt as though a bucket of cold water had been thrown in his face. It was as though he suddenly awakened from a nightmare and found it still surrounding him. Vividly he had perceived the irony of the situation. The last time he'd seen the tall man, they had laughed and shared a beer. Who would have thought he would stand by and watch him be tortured? For one wild moment, he'd considered shooting Ramirez, but man had a seemingly inhuman talent for recognizing threats and stopping them. A blindfolded and bound Donovan would have never survived reckless gunfire.

When Rachel had walked through the door, he'd felt a horror that almost made him ineffective in helping her carry off her charade. He had followed her into the living room, as she laughed and teased Ramirez filling his glass.

O'Brian had gotten out his best brandy and dropped a powder into it that insured a good night's sleep. To be certain of her successful escape, he'd stayed up all night watching to see that she was not disturbed as she got Donovan away. He could have gone with them, but he had believed he might help more by staying and doing what he could to stop Ramirez if he discovered what had happened too soon. If they had made it to Nogales, then he'd have been here also to help with the arrests—including his own.

O'Brian looked in the kitchen window and saw Ramirez pacing like an angry cat, shrieking out threats at the empty room. The only real security any of them would ever know would come when Diego Ramirez was no more. O'Brian had no personal or moral hesitance about shooting the man, but he couldn't take the chance he might fail. If he tried and failed, it would leave Rachel and Donovan with one less hope. No, this was a time for patience, never one of his long suits.

When O'Brian walked back into the kitchen, it was to hear Ramirez cursing the helicopter for not having already arrived.

"Thanks to your trick with the phone he couldn't notify you if he had a problem." O'Brian didn't resist the jibe. Ramirez glared at him.

Mateo came in, slamming the door. "As near as we can tell, patron, he went from the shed to the barn, then around the front of the house."

"And there is more, isn't there?"

"We think... someone was with him, helped him to--" He glanced nervously at O'Brian. "Señorita O'Brian's truck is gone."

O'Brian shrugged casually. "Which is unrelated. She went out to paint."

Mateo stared at him. "We think that is where Donovan went too then."

Ramirez shut his eyes with his anger and fury. "Explain this," Ramirez growled, turning to glare at O'Brian.

"I don't have to explain anything. Rachel didn't care what happened to him last night. Why would she help him?"

"She had better not be with him is all I can say."

"That sounded like a threat," O'Brian said, rising to his full height. "You will not hurt my daughter. If she's with Donovan, she was kidnapped. You heard the contempt she had for him."

Ramirez gave an ugly laugh. "I see. He forced her to open the shed, to free him, to help him to the barn, then to the truck!"

"If we find them together, we'll ask her what happened. You *will* give her that much."

Ramirez stared at him, his eyes as ugly as his laugh. "When the helicopter gets here, we'll follow the tracks. And we better find them. If Donovan makes it to Nogales, we're finished here." He reached inside his shirt to finger the medallion he wore around his neck. "Everything is going wrong. It is Donovan's fault. I will find him out there or follow him into whatever hole he has crawled. If I go down, he goes with me."

"Your failure has had nothing to do with Donovan," O'Brian

said knowing reasoning was impossible but interested now in delaying Ramirez starting his search.

"It has everything to do with him." He looked upward making the sign of the cross. "It has been seven years. This is the right time. The right day. When he is sacrificed, I will have my power restored. I will not allow him to escape again."

O'Brian looked at him, acknowledging that the man had gone completely mad. "What kind of sacrifice?" he asked finally not because he wanted to hear the answer.

Slowly Ramirez turned and looked at him. "Only through blood can power be gotten. Surely you know that. Isn't that what you Catholics believe--that a man must be sacrificed."

"Catholics believe God made the sacrifice," O'Brian corrected.

Ramirez laughed. "Well, I am a god," he said malevolently, his smile enough to cause a chill to travel up O'Brian's spine. "Donovan is my chosen sacrifice. He has escaped me twice. I have waited for the stars to show me the time to reclaim what is mine. It is now. It will be my luck now—not his."

"I see. That is very clever," O'Brian said forcing a smile. He had debated arguing with him, trying to reason with him, but it would have been wasting his breath. If Ramirez was listening to anybody other than himself, it wasn't human.

Outside he heard the whirr of helicopter blades. So, it was to begin. He followed the four outside and watched as the giant bird settled to the ground. He listened as Ramirez gave his pilot instructions and with the sun rising higher in the east, climbed into the helicopter with the others.

As they followed the old wagon road, O'Brian felt his nerves being frayed by the continuous string of curses coming from Ramirez. Then, looking to the right, he caught a glimpse of metal reflecting sunlight. *Hellfire and damnation,* he cursed, recognizing Rachel's truck and praying no one else would see it.

"Hey, I see something," Mateo, staring out the same side, yelled.

The pilot dipped low, and they could all see the truck pushed back into the arroyo. Ramirez smiled. "So," he crooned, "it is my luck today and not Donovan's. There is open ground over there. Land!"

Out of the helicopter, they made their way to the truck. Ramirez scanned the ground, and then cursed. "No tracks. Diaz and Mateo, you stay here and look for some sign of which way they went. Circle wide and eventually the tracks will start. Chaco will take us back up, and we'll make sure he didn't go down the road."

"He is without boots, patron," Mateo reminded him. "He can't get far."

Ramirez laughed, his good mood momentarily restored. "You're right. His feet will be cut to ribbons."

"I'll help Diaz and Mateo," O'Brian offered. "I'm better at tracking than either of them." He slung a water bag over his shoulder.

Ramirez stared at him a moment, then agreed.

O'Brian pointed down the road. "If you don't see them, head back to the ranch for more water. We can't stay out here long without provisions."

"It will waste time."

"Unless you want to die the same torturous death you're hoping for Donovan, it's time well spent."

Angrily Ramirez slapped his own fist but didn't argue.

With the helicopter gone, O'Brian put the two men with him to searching in the opposite direction of where he thought Donovan and Rachel would head. He smiled when he saw the scars of a freshly broken branch. Donovan might have been beaten but was obviously not broken. Although Rachel knew a lot about the desert, it was Donovan who understood a hunt.

"Be careful as you look," O'Brian yelled to Mateo. "This man is desert trained. Keep your eyes open for traps."

"Traps?" Diaz questioned.

"Snares, sharpened sticks set to hit a man, things like that. Just take it slow. I wouldn't want either of you with a spear through his heart."

Diaz nodded, his eyes wide as he looked around him.

O'Brian smiled as the two would-be trackers proceeded more slowly. Though they had lived in this country all their lives, they were of the city, not hardened by the harshness of the desert. They would not hold up well to the blistering, mid-day sun, the thorns and stings that were waiting for those who took a careless step.

He smiled as he thought how lucky these two weren't coyotes, the kind of men who knew this desert better than he. When these two made mistakes--and he would see that they did make mistakes, accidents would result, accidents that would cut the odds for when and if they found Donovan. As he followed the men into a draw, he checked the load in his gun.

~

As the sun began its descent in the sky, Donovan woke, Rachel in his arms. At first he lay trying to remember where he was. The pains throughout his body helped to remind him all too quickly that this was no picnic, no desert idyll. It seemed impossible to believe he'd escaped Ramirez's clutches, that Rachel had somehow pulled him from the pit he'd been sure was going to swallow him. It wasn't over though, and now her risk was as great as his.

A dull roar grew, the sound drawing nearer, finally penetrating his musings, and he knew why he had awakened. He saw Rachel's eyes fly open, and he smiled reassuringly at her, lifting his eyebrows to signify what they both knew was flying in search of them. Looking at the sheltering overhang of the bank, the deep, black-green canopy of the mesquite, he saw that only a fluke would reveal their whereabouts to whoever was in that helicopter.

"You did well." He knew he'd been of little help to her. Although the beginning of the walk was clear in his memory, he had gotten beyond that to a point where he had quit thinking as his body had just kept going.

"I did what I could to erase our tracks, pile up brush around us."

"Good girl. They won't see us."

When they heard the sound recede, Jake reached down and lightly kissed her mouth, their chapped lips making the meeting a mixture of pleasure and pain.

"I have ointment," she murmured as she reached into her pocket and spread some thinly on his lips, kissing him to coat her own.

They lay back, their arms around each other. "You know," he said after a moment, "you saved my life."

"I did, didn't I?" she whispered as she kissed his neck. "I think that means you belong to me now."

"I already did."

Her lips moved lightly onto his chest.

"We'll wait for dusk, then travel as long as we can through the night. Lucky you've got those cat eyes. All we'll have to do is watch out for snakes. Personally I prefer the kinds that crawl on the ground to Ramirez and his bunch." When he kissed her cheeks, he felt the tears. "Don't worry, babe. We're going to make it."

"I was thinking about my father. I thought he was a wonderful man... and now I have to wonder if I knew him at all."

He drew her tightly against his chest, stroking her head soothingly. "Sometimes when a man gets involved with somebody like Ramirez, things happen before he realizes it."

"I don't know what to believe."

"Earlier I kept thinking I had heard your father's voice before. Then I remembered. It was at your art show in Sedona. He and I talked, had a beer together, but had never said our names. "

"You never said anything."

He nodded. "I didn't know who he was. Just a nice old guy, well not all that old. I liked him, and I'm usually pretty good at judging people. My bet is his business dealings with Ramirez were like riding a roller coaster--no backing up."

"I find that hard to believe. You're just trying to make me feel better."

He kissed her forehead. "I've seen it before. I told you about my brother, how he got snared into it. You know he got into illegal deals to pay for us to live."

"It seems different."

"Not as much as you think. It's a road people head down, and sometimes there is no turning around. I don't think he was a bad man either, but the crimes got bigger. At a certain point, he wanted me to join him. It was when he and I split. You ever wonder why Ramirez hates me so much that he would risk everything to get me?"

"I never really knew he did until this."

He told her about the work he'd done, the end of it, and Ramirez getting away. "In the end the little fish got caught, but he got off as he always has. He sets it up and manages to leave others the fall guys."

"Thank you for trying to make me feel better but..."

"It's the truth. With a man like Ramirez, it's hard to turn around. It becomes more dangerous than staying. When I went undercover, I got a taste of how it could be as I saw the ones he used. Other people had nothing, no chance, and a lot ended up with him because it seemed there was no other way."

Rachel shook her head, tears coming to her eyes again. "I want us to wake up and find out none of this happened." He bent to kiss her, working his way down her neck. "Nothing matters but you," she whispered fiercely, pressing herself against him, kissing his lips and every other bit of flesh she could reach.

She slid her hand down his torso, felt his hands similarly stroking over her, caressing her breasts, her buttocks. In moments, they were naked and locked in each other's arms. They made love with the kind of fervor only those who have narrowly escaped death can know. She took the lead and straddled him, setting the pace. Letting a woman control the lovemaking was a first for him, but with Rachel, he liked yielding control.

As their breathing returned to normal, he whispered, "I never thought I'd hold you like this again."

"I was afraid you wouldn't either," she said, kissing his chest. "Are we going to make it out of this?"

He nodded, hoping against hope that he was right. He'd die to save her but was that going to be enough?

Walking through the night, the air was cooler, but the darkness demanded caution and didn't allow them to move as fast as they would have wanted. There was a strong need to put distance between themselves and Ramirez but an equally strong need not to have an accident that would end their hopes. Rachel used her little flashlight only when necessary, but the thought of falling down an embankment or being bitten by a rattlesnake prodded them to proceed with some caution unless the way ahead was open. Although they heard the helicopter once in the distance, it didn't come near and wouldn't be nearly as effective in seeing them with just a spotlight.

When they rested, Jake smoked one of his rationed cigarettes, and they drank more of the water. "How far do you think we have to go?" Rachel asked.

He looked up at the crescent moon and tried to get his bearings. "I lost track of how far we got that first morning, but I think in a few hours we'll be at the water tank and with enough water, we ought to get to Esmeralda by tomorrow night."

"What if we don't find the tank?" she asked worried at their low supply of water and aware of how big this country was, how every hill could look like the one next to it. Could Jake really find one small pool of water?

"We will."

She suddenly felt full of doubts. So much was at stake. Not just being caught by Ramriez but the pitfalls of the desert were all around them waiting for a careless move. This was her home. She knew it well. She loved it; but because she did know it, she also knew how dangerous it could be. She didn't need to express any of those doubts to Jake as he knew it as well or better than she. He was right. They would make it. They had to make it.

"I'm still not sure what good that ghost town is going to do us," she said as a new problem occurred to her.

"If there is no caretaker on duty, maybe we'll get lucky and find sightseers or relic hunters."

She looked up at him, the moonlight illuminating his large body, the bare, sweaty chest, the battered face, unshaven jaw, and the rags tied around his feet. "Who do you think would give us a ride?" she asked with a rueful smile.

He patted the little gun shoved into his belt. "Anyone who's feeling charitable," he responded with a wolfish smile, his teeth gleaming white in the moonlight.

As the night wore on, Rachel found it an increasing effort to put one foot in front of the other. It had to be worse for Jake. He was limping, the cloths around his feet stained with dirt and blood. How much longer could he keep moving?

"There," he said with a relieved grin. Beyond where Jake pointed, Rachel saw the glimmer of water in the faint light. They walked down the hill and stood at the side of the round pool, two cottonwood and a scrub oak above them. "An oasis for the lady," he said, kneeling to cup water into his hands.

"What about giardia?" she asked as she knelt beside him.

Jake laughed. "The lady could die of dehydration or get shot, and she worries about dysentery. When we make it out of this, I'll take you straight to the doc."

She laughed aware she'd been silly. Giardia was treatable, would not strike right away, and wasn't fatal, although sometimes sufferers thought it was going to be. Old habits of being careful with water sources were hard to break, but as she cautiously drank the water, it tasted sweet.

When they had refilled their canteens, Jake looked up at the sky. "We've got about two hours before first light. We'd hear the helicopter from a distance. A quick dip shouldn't hurt anything."

She'd wanted to soak in the water so badly she'd nearly been able to taste it but had been sure they didn't dare take the time. "Does Ramirez know about this place?"

"Unlikely. He hasn't spent any more time out in the desert than he has to."

She was stripping off her clothing before he finished the words. In moments she'd waded into the water up to her waist. "Oh Jake, this is heaven."

He followed her, his own clothing left behind and as she turned to watch, his strong body outlined by the moonlight, she knew again the desire be one with him in all the ways possible. She also wished for her paints. It wasn't possible for her to separate her art from her life. The two fed off each other and even here with danger all around them, she felt the itch to paint what she saw.

"What are you thinking?" he asked as he came up to her.

She reached out to stroke his chest, laving water over his body but she only shook her head. Then she laughed.

"Now I really have to know," he said as he performed similar ablutions for her. There was no soap but just to have the water cascading over their skin was refreshing.

Rachel undid her bedraggled braid, then ducked under,

wetting her hair, before she turned to float on her back, her hair all around her on the water surface.

"You are so beautiful," Jake said, smiling.

"I wish we could stay here."

"There's a lot of things I wish," he said with a sigh, "but we don't have time for any of them as they could stumble across this place. When we leave, even with all the animal tracks, we should erase ours as best we can."

"We could come back."

"It's possible. You have horses."

Her smile answered his as she rose from the water at his side. "I could make it worth your while."

His smile broadened. "Oh I don't doubt that for a second."

On the little beach again, they stood a moment, letting their bodies mostly dry before they dressed. Before Jake could tie back on the nearly shredded dishrags, Rachel stopped him. "Let me look at your feet."

Jake looked toward the sky. A few minutes more shouldn't matter, and his feet had gone beyond painful. He laid back as she looked at the soles in the moonlight then with the flashlight. He stared at the dark branches of the tree overhead, trying to be stoic. He had no doubt what his feet looked like and was equally sure there wasn't much they could do for them out here.

She moaned at the cuts, thorns, bruises and gashes. This was as bad as anything Ramirez had done to him; yet she'd not heard a word of complaint.

"I don't know how you kept on your feet--let alone walked," she muttered as she pulled out the thorns she could reach.

"You offering to carry me," he asked, clenching his jaw against the pain of her ministrations.

Pushing her hair behind her ears, she shook her head and spread ointment over his soles. "Blasted macho man," she muttered adding a few expletives that seemed to fit the occasion.

"What'd you say?" he asked with a wry grin.

"Never mind. You should have let me look at these earlier." She took a pocket knife from her pocket. Stripping off her shirt, she sliced into the sleeves, then did the same thing with her jeans leaving her wearing shorts.

"What are you doing?" He propped an elbow under himself to watch her put back on the now sleeveless and tail-less shirt.

"I'm adding padding to the mess you've made of your feet," she growled, her eyes daring him to argue with her.

He grinned appreciatively at the slender waist revealed by the cropped top. "I'm not complaining."

"I wish we could rest here longer," he said when she had tied the last knot. "It just wouldn't be safe."

"I understand."

As they left, retracing their steps, Jake brushed out the marks of their visit. Although, since javelina, deer and assorted small rodents had recently visited the tank, discerning one track from another would be difficult for all but expert trackers. Ramirez might have those in Mexico, but it was unlikely any of the ones with him up here would be that good.

By the time the sun had risen in the sky, Jake looked for and found a hollowed cavity in the side of an arroyo for shelter from the heat of the day.

In the afternoon the helicopter woke them. Jake smiled with a genuine look of amusement. How he could do that with their dire situation, she had no idea. "Ramirez must be having a fit." He pointed toward huge black thunderheads moving up rapidly from the gulf. "Looks like he won't be up there much longer either," he added as the wind began whipping up. Within an hour, the sky had turned a bilious green, then almost black, the wind was a gale and the storm was upon them. Nestled together, they watched as lightning struck the hills around them.

"Good thing you're not scared of a storm." The crash of

thunder almost wiped out Jake's words as three prongs of lightning struck the ground seemingly right above where they lay.

"Well-- I didn't say I'm not the teensiest bit nervous when I'm
right under their path."

He grinned. "You mean I'm not the only one who's been
playing macho?"

Nodding, she moved so that she could lay against him
shoulder to thigh.

"Hmmm, it's okay to be nervous." He bent to kiss the swell of
her breasts.

"It is?"

Rain was falling hard, huge drops pounding in the ground as
they undressed. Picking Rachel up in his arms and ignoring her
protests, Jake carried her out into the downpour. "Put me down,"
she muttered, sure he would hurt himself by carrying her.

He did as she ordered, laying her on the sandy river bottom
where they clung together, the rain plastering their hair to their
heads and running down their bodies. Forgotten were the
thunder and lightning and anything but the joy of touching and
kissing.

His lips tasted of rain drops and tobacco as she nibbled them.
Jake brought her chin up and caught her lips with his as his
tongue delved into her mouth, tasting the honey of her
passionate response. The excitement of the storm increased the
intensity of their lovemaking as once again they found forgetful-
ness from all but each other-- the drive to be one stronger than
any other.

As the storm passed, they stood back under the overhang to
dress, taking time to kiss and surprisingly, given the situation, to
laugh. When Jake first heard the distant roar, he thought it was
the helicopter, but it didn't take long for him to reassess his judgment. "Quick," he yelled, "grab the stuff!"

"What is it?" she screamed, helping him grab canteens and throw their gear on the bank above them. He gave her a powerful boost. He was scrambling after her when the water of a flashflood hit his legs.

Her own feet on solid ground, Rachel grabbed Jake's wrist, pulling with all her strength. Wheezing for breath, he flopped onto the bank to lie beside her. Below them, muddy water, filled with debris, shot past them.

"That was too close," he gasped, looking down at what could have been the end of them both.

"We escape Ramirez, make it through the desert heat, and end drowned in a flash flood," she agreed wryly.

He shook his head at the absurdity of it. "Pretty ironic. Although," he added, "I've seen more drowned bodies on the desert than you'd believe."

"Lucky the water didn't come sooner," she teased, remembering their ardent lovemaking.

He chuckled. "I can see us now--walking into Esmeralda jay-bird naked."

"Try talking some nice, old couple into giving us a lift into town then. Even the gun wouldn't have convinced them." She laughed at the mental picture.

"Unless they were men," he quipped, "then they'd have offered you a ride and left me behind." His eyes traveled with appreciation down her slim figure.

"Or women, who'd leave me behind." Clad in jeans and little else, she knew how quickly she'd offer him a ride--battered or not.

CHAPTER 15

"Nothing's gone right since we brought Donovan to the ranch," Ramirez snapped as he paced back and forth like nothing so much as a mindless, angry animal. "Now you tell me Mateo simply fell like some clumsy idiot."

"Just one of those things, Could've happened to anybody." O'Brian shrugged his shoulders from where he sat on the edge of the porch, watching the erratically pacing man.

"The storm's wiped out any hope of tracking them. Now my pilot tells me the rotor is damaged--the copter will be down for hours, maybe 'til tomorrow."

"Lucky it happened while we were at the ranch," O'Brian said benignly.

"I can't believe our luck! It has to change." Ramirez reached into his pocket and pulled out a small leather bag. First he removed a bundle of dried herbs, holding them close to his nose and drawing the pungent fragrance into his lungs. Seemingly in a trance, he pulled out small pieces of bone. Throwing the objects onto the table, he studied them as though reading something invisible to O'Brian.

"Even you can't control storms, Diego," O'Brian said, feeling edgy at the strange behavior.

Ramirez smiled, an unearthly smile of knowledge and power. "I can't?" he said, not asking a question so much as offering a challenge. Carefully he gathered the objects into the leather sack meticulously retying it before he said, "I will have Donovan in my hands again. It is a mere matter of time. Believe me when I tell you this. I need to stop and just let myself hear the answer," he muttered. "Where would he go? Where is he heading?"

O'Brian looked off toward the mountains. "Maybe by now he's in Nogales."

"No. He's in those hills. I feel it."

O'Brian looked up as Diaz came out of the house. "How is Mateo?"

"Still unconscious."

"Actually, the way it happened, him losing his balance trying to grab at me, it was lucky we didn't both fall off that cliff," O'Brian said.

"I think he needs a doctor, patron," Diaz suggested hesitantly. "It is bad how he is hurt."

"Not now!" Ramirez glared at him before stalking into the house.

Diaz looked at O'Brian hopefully, but he only shrugged. They followed Ramirez into the kitchen, watching as he opened a map and stared at it. He traced a line with his finger and muttered but without words O'Brian could understand.

"What do you see?" he asked finally.

"Why not? Why not?"

O'Brian eyes narrowed as he studied where Ramirez pointed. It was indeed possible.

"I know where they will be," Ramirez said with a sudden, wolfish smile. "Get the truck."

"Give it up, Diego. Go to Mexico and forget Donovan at least for now." Later he'd make sure it was a permanent forgetting.

"Never," Ramirez sneered, removing the gun from the holster that hung from his belt. "I will never let the carrion go. He is my only hope."

"If you must, then I'll go with you," O'Brian said. Smiling faintly, he would not stand by and allow his daughter and her husband to be gunned down. If Ramirez did find them, it would no longer matter if he survived. He would save Rachel. In that, at least, he would not fail.

Looking down at the ramshackle, weathered remains of Esmeralda, it was hard to believe this had once been a town filled with people. When Donovan saw no vehicles, no sign of a new caretaker, he knew there would be no quick rescue. This was in a rarely traveled part of a little populated county, and soon the sun would be below the horizon. If they left the protection of the hills, would they be safer or in more danger?

He looked down at Rachel, her eyes red-rimmed from exhaustion and the dust of the desert, but her chin still held proudly high. Despite her courage, neither of them could go much farther. His feet had passed from being painful and were now complete agony, the pain running up his legs. He had only been able to keep moving by reminding himself of the alternative.

They had to find a refuge, but Esmeralda might not be that. At times Ramirez had seemed to have an almost superhuman capacity for outguessing his enemies. Would this be one of those times? Esmeralda could be a haven or a trap.

Donovan realized he was deciding not only his future but also that of his wife. He was just beginning to understand what together meant. She had proven herself his partner as well as mate. By trying to protect her from the deadly options, he was not trusting her. He was too used to going it alone, to being responsible only to himself. It was time to change that.

He looked around them, noting the lack of trees, of overhanging cliffs, of dry washes. "We can find shelter in those buildings, but I don't think help is going to come before morning." If then. "And Ramirez could figure out where we've been heading."

"How do we decide?"

"I don't know. If he comes, the buildings might be a trap for us or him." He didn't need to remind her, with only three bullets against possibly at least five men, any ambush on their side would have to be a beaut. "One advantage in the buildings would be that this gun won't fire far with stopping power. We need to be closer and that could give us that possibility."

"Maybe he's given up," Rachel suggested as another consideration. "Maybe when he didn't find us right away, he decided we got help; and he will have gone back to Mexico."

Jake didn't say anything, but he didn't believe Ramirez was capable of making such a rational choice.

"Jake," she said tentatively.

"Yeah?"

"We could pray about it."

He considered that. "Rachel, I'm not a believer."

"Well if you're not, it can't hurt either, can it?"

He smiled faintly. "Probably not."

"Then?"

"Go for it, lady. Just don't remind him or her who you're with." As he gave her that moment, he stared down at the town that had died years before, the sun slowly sinking as the day went with it.

"So we go," she said as she took a deep breath and looked down at the mining camp remains.

"One way or another, I think it'll end here," he said as they began to make their way down the hill. Cautiously approaching the shacks, Jake pointed to a dark blemish on the earth. "Mine shaft. Watch where you walk. They usually have been boarded up, but nature has a way of opening them."

The building in which they sought shelter was small. Perhaps at one time someone's home or store. Now although it had four walls still in place, its two doors were in various states of disintegration. There were two intact window panes and a tin roof, which although it originally protected its inhabitants from the desert rainstorms and the unrelenting sun, now barely protected half the deteriorating floor.

Pushing open the half hanging door cautiously, Jake peered inside to make certain it held no desert denizens. "I know I promised I'd carry you over every threshold... but I'm going to renege on that."

She smiled as she followed him, slumping down against a wall. "Not luxurious," she said as she studied the room, "but it does have a certain something."

"Think you could fix it up?" He eased his aching body down beside her.

"With a little money and adding on a few rooms. Oh and a roof."

"Not just couple of trips to Mexico?" he asked, closing his eyes on his weariness.

"Well that and visiting a garage sale or three--"

"I'm just trying to take you to different places. You been to all those fancy venues, had champagne and caviar. But with me you get dry bread, stale cookies and tepid water." He grimaced as he stretched out.

"Donovan, that isn't the only thing you've given me," she murmured, reaching up to kiss his neck.

"No?"

"You've given me love."

He looked up at her. "And," he said finally, "you gave me hope. I didn't think that was possible." He smiled. "It sounds crazy in a place like this, with a madman after us, but... I wouldn't change a thing. Well maybe I'd have been a little more careful coming back home."

She shifted, intending to examine his feet, but his hand came like a band of iron around her arm, pulling her back to him. "Let 'em go," he said. "You rest. This isn't over."

She lay back, unable to find the will to argue. "Why do you suppose," she asked, looking at the broken furniture in one corner of the room, "this town was here? It's so in the middle of nowhere for anybody to even find it." She yawned as her eyes closed.

"Silver, maybe copper, a hope of gold. For most it was just a place to sleep while they worked for somebody else's dream."

Unwilling to take the risk of sleeping himself, he cradled her body to his as he tried to read the graffiti on the opposite wall. Giving up, he decided it was just as well. He'd never read anything good when it was written by someone who liked to deface what they couldn't own. A piece of torn wallpaper still clung to a wall, faded, a faint design of a flower.

Jake thought about what lay ahead. The immediate future looked tenuous at best. He hadn't wanted to seem a pessimist to Rachel, but he was thinking he might not have many hours left to live. He was in pain, facing a madman and yet he'd not trade any of it for any of the riches some might have sought in Esmeralda-- except the part that endangered Rachel. He wondered if Michael O'Brian could protect his daughter if he fell.

If Ramirez came, it would be either in the helicopter or by truck on the dirt road. Either way he'd be ready for them. How many would there be? Too many for his three bullets. Would the stack of broken wooden furniture at the other end of the room protect Rachel from the bullets that would inevitably fly?

He considered the possibility of surrendering to Ramirez in exchange for Rachel's life. But he knew how foolish an idea that was and instantly discarded it. Rachel would never agree; but even if she would, Ramirez would be as brutal to her in the end as to Jake. Rachel had betrayed him, and she knew too much for him to allow her to walk free.

Not attempting to think more, to reason or plan, Jake lay watching as the sinking sun turned the sky to crimson. When he heard the sound of a truck, he eased Rachel from his lap and walked with frustrating slowness to the window, gritting his teeth against the pain. Leaning against the wall, he watched silently as a truck drove into what had once probably been the center of town. It stopped, dust swirling out from it to form dust devils. When the doors opened, four men emerged.

Crawling back to Rachel, he put his hand over her mouth. "Babe, wake up." Her eyes blinked open as she looked up at him. With awareness came the fear he hated to see in those beautiful eyes. "They're here," he whispered, "and I don't mean the cavalry."

He pointed for her to crawl to the other end of the room and lie down behind the broken furniture and loose boards. She shook her head angrily, and he scowled back. "I can't be worrying about you getting hit or being someplace I don't know." Relieved, he watched her obey, still arguing with her eyes.

Jake moved back to the window to watch the progress of the men as they began to search the few standing buildings. Although there was no way Ramirez could be certain they were here, there was equally no way he wouldn't eventually find out.

At the pile of wood, Rachel found several pieces that could be used as clubs. Picking up one after another, she examined them for strength. It would be useless to hit a man over the head with a piece of rotten wood. She finally selected what looked to have once been the leg of a table and settled back with her weapon.

Seeing the traces of blood on the floor, Rachel looked at Jake's feet, wondering how he was able to stand. How long could he remain upright--let alone move fast enough to fight off men intent on capturing or killing him?

Through a dirty window she glimpsed a face. She had never seen the man before but he had to be one of Ramirez's paid hoods. She grasped her piece of wood more firmly. Before the man could cross the threshold, Rachel heard Jake's low growl. "Far enough."

The man turned, centering his gun on Jake's chest. Jake's bullet caught him before he could pull the trigger. Staggering backward, the man spun, stumbled a few steps and fell well beyond the building.

"Damn," Jake cursed.

"Did he hit you," Rachel cried.

"No." Jake shook his head. "Just mad that his gun fell outside with him." When he saw her start to edge forward, he glared at her. "Get back behind that pile or so help me to your god, I'll walk out there and let Ramirez take his best shot."

She glared at him but obeyed.

Shots at the other end of the buildings made Jake duck back. He strained to hear what was going on. Then caught a glimpse of Ramirez running low and heading for their shack.

Taking a chance, Jake fired, cursing as he missed. Three men appeared to be left. One bullet. He wasn't ready to answer the question of how he would face Rachel's father with a gun, even to save his own life. Gritting his teeth, Jake moved across the room to position himself where he could watch both doors. Stepping down on his left foot, the sudden pain caused him to stumble, nearly sending him to his knees. Choking back an oath, he fought the blackness that threatened. When his head cleared, he decided not moving was the best course. Situate himself and wait--with one bullet.

"Hey Jacob!" Ramirez yelled. "You don't know how good it is to see you here."

"Hey, me too," Jake retorted dryly.

"We can make a deal."

Jake only laughed.

"Rachel's with you, isn't she?"

"Rachel who?"

"Let her go."

"Nah, I needed an insurance policy, and she was it." He ignored the angry hiss from the other end of the room.

"Let her go. You want an innocent woman caught in the crossfire?"

Donovan knew Ramirez hadn't believed him for a second. He glanced over at her, saw the stubborn expression on her face. "I have one bullet," he said. "It'd be the smart thing. Maybe your dad could keep you safe."

"Not a chance," she retorted, then yelled, "Hey, Diego, did I mention I got married? Jake's my husband. Surely *even* you aren't stupid enough to think I would leave him!" Jake scowled at her, but nothing he could say would take back those words.

Ramirez hissed a crude curse. "Donovan, come out. We can work something out."

"I remember how your deals work out," Jake said. "But just for fun, what's the offer?" He knew he was stalling, not that he could imagine anything that could significantly change any of this.

"At least let Rachel come out. I swear it; she'd be as safe as if she was my sister."

Jake laughed harshly. "Not even your own mother would be safe--if it benefited you otherwise." He prepared himself for an onslaught from outside and edged cautiously to the opposite side of the room.

When Ramirez burst through the door nearly beside him, Jake fell back, steadied his gun and fired. The force of the bullet threw Ramirez against the door jamb where he began to slide down the wall. On hands and knees, Jake crawled toward him, intent on getting his hands on a gun with bullets.

Ramirez gave a little laugh, straightened, and lifted his gun. His smile was cold and evil as he looked at the gun Jake had leveled on him, "Ah Jacob. Don't you think this is all just a little funny."

"Drop your gun," Jake ordered.

Slowly, holding his shoulder with one hand, Ramirez began advancing across the room. "Should I do that? Or... should I take a chance that the reason you only fired once, was because your little gun is now empty, heh?"

As Ramirez walked toward Jake, who had pulled himself up to half lean against the wall, Rachel came up behind Ramirez and hit him hard across his neck with her table leg. Although it didn't really hurt him, it startled him sufficiently for Jake to launch himself off the wall, tackling him and sending them both through the door and into the yard.

Rachel followed, watching them viciously pound each other as they rolled across the ground. All she could think was that Ramirez seemed to have suffered only a flesh wound and was in better condition at this point than her battered husband.

Then she remembered the man Jake had killed. Jake had wanted that gun. Running around the building to where he'd fallen, she saw his body. The staring eyes and blood caused her to hesitate only a second before she grabbed the gun.

When she came back around the building, she froze. Jake was lying half stunned as Ramirez rolled away from him. Rachel felt paralyzed as she tried to bring up the gun, brought it to bear on Ramirez's back. Her hands were shaking so badly she was afraid if she fired she might hit Jake, who had managed to get to his knees.

Heaving for breath, Ramirez scrambled for the gun he'd lost in their fight. Rachel stood frozen, as she watched as though in slow motion--Ramirez raising his gun, pointing it at Jake, her father appearing from seemingly nowhere, yelling threats at Ramirez as he ran toward them. The sound of a shot was deafening.

"No," she screamed as her father was propelled back by the force of the bullet. Ramirez turned his revolver then back to Jake.

Grasping her heavy gun with both hands, Rachel leveled it.

273

She felt a sense of peace come over her. "Diego," she screamed as she watched him bring his gun up and then stop.

He turned, and then smiled at the sight of the gun in her hand. "Beautiful Rachel, even after all you've been through, a fit mate for a god." His smile was a travesty.

"Put down your gun," she ordered. She trembled with fear and horror.

"You won't shoot," he said and began to walk toward her.

"I will. Put down your gun." She began to back away as he steadily approached.

"I can give you everything. Everything you've ever wanted," Ramirez purred, still smiling that ghastly smile.

"Don't come a step further," she ordered, trying to keep the gun leveled on him. He seemed not to hear her words and continued to force her back. Suddenly she remembered the mine shaft. Her quick glance behind her was all the opportunity he needed to leap for her. Mindlessly, she pulled the trigger, the recoil from the shot throwing the barrel into the air as it bucked back against her hand.

Feeling disconnected from reality, she watched Ramirez stumble, try to rise and despite his new wound, lunge for her again. Rachel stepped to the side, barely aware that Jake had found enough strength to lunge forward and hit Ramirez, sending him to the edge of the mine shaft. He struggled for a moment to keep his balance, then let out a shriek as he fell into the pit. She could hear the sound of a heavy body falling, seemingly forever, before there was the hard thud of a something hitting the bottom.

After the noise, confusion and the lingering smell of gunpowder, the total silence was a shock. Numbly, Rachel stood with the gun hanging from her right hand. She turned, tears running down her cheeks as Jake stumbled to her. "You all right?" he asked his voice a croak.

"I think so. Ramirez... is he dead?"

"Even he can't survive that." He turned back then to her

father as Rachel went to kneel at his side. He ripped open the wounded man's shirt to bare the bloody wound in his side, high up.

"I'm sorry," O'Brian choked out. "I really made a mess of this."

Jake gave him a wry smile. "You do have a way though of jumping right in after it." He lifted him slightly to see his back, pressing a compress made from the torn shirt against the bleeding exit wound.

Jake looked up at Rachel, only now beginning to get control over the panic he'd felt, the sense of helplessness when he'd seen her facing Ramirez with that gun. "Sweet Jesus," he whispered, "you scared me so bad, babe, but you saved us all."

"I froze. I couldn't stop shaking and took too long to pull the trigger."

"You did though and gave me enough time to get my feet under me," Jake said, not letting up on the compress he'd pressed to her father's side.

"Ramirez would have killed you, except for--" She couldn't finish her sentence. They both knew Michael O'Brian had saved Jake's life.

O'Brian groaned. "So he's really dead?"

Jake gestured with his head toward the other building. "Unless he can survive a hundred foot fall. Him and the one behind the shed. There was a third."

"I... had to kill Diaz," O'Brian said. "I tried to get him to drop his gun, but he wouldn't listen."

"I don't understand any of this, Dad," Rachel cried, tears running down her cheeks. "Why?"

"I'm sorry, princess. I didn't know... then didn't know how to get out of it." He coughed.

"Well," Jake said with a cynical twist to his lips, "I hope you weren't counting on checking out as a way of doing it now."

"Huh?" Both father and daughter looked at him and at the hard expression on his battered face.

"Your bullet wound won't keep you in bed a week. So there won't be any tearful funeral oratories."

Rachel smiled with relief.

"Princess, you've got yourself one hard man there," O'Brian muttered.

"I definitely do," she said as she put her arm around Jake's waist.

"We've got to get help," Jake said. "Was there a CB in Ramirez's truck?" When he tried to get to his feet, he was nearly pushed flat as Rachel thrust him back down.

The air hissed out of her lungs in an angry rush. "Donovan, you are not moving. Tell me who to call, and *you* sit here!" She glared from man to man before Jake meekly gave her instructions, and she stomped off to the truck.

Jake's gaze followed her until she was out of sight. "I hope you realize what you've got there," O'Brian said. Jake looked back down at him seeing the older man's eyes intently on him.

"More than most," Jake said, and then glared at him accusingly. "The only question I got now is--how do we keep the mess you're in from causing her more pain?"

EPILOGUE

"Jake," Rachel's soft melodious voice called from the bedroom.

"Yeah?"

"Could you help me?"

He rose and said, "I'll be right back." Heading in, he saw her leaning over the baby, while a toddler tried to grab the powder from the table. Jake came up behind her, putting his arms around her newly slender waist. "Got a problem here, babe?" he asked, nuzzling her behind the ear and nipping her lobe teasingly.

"Maybe I now have two," she moaned, leaning back against his arms before she said, "If you expect us to ever be ready for her christening, you have to take Johnny out to Grandpa."

Jake grinned, letting go of her as he reached down to scoop up his dark-haired son. "We aren't appreciated here, son." He whispered in the toddler's ears, "I bet Grandpa is doing something more fun than this anyway."

Back in the living room, Michael O'Brian was sitting comfortably on their sofa, his arms outstretched to receive his grandson. "I haven't seen you in a month," he said as he took the squirming boy.

"Where Grandpa been?" Johnny asked giggling as his grandfather swung him up in his arms.

Jake sat down, listening to the explanation and grinning. Looking about the room as the younger and older generation talked as only they could, he couldn't believe the changes in not only his home but himself.

The living room had the same four walls but that was about the only thing that remained--except for two pieces of Mexican folk art, a man and a woman, who stood forever on the mantle. Colorful Oriental rugs covered tiled floors. Furniture had been replaced or reupholstered. Over the fireplace hung the portrait she had painted of him four years before. Although it still made him uneasy to see his face in the tough looking man who gazed across the desert, he had to admit the colors were good in the room.

The changes in the man he was had gone beneath the skin and into his inner being; they had been so great that at times he barely remembered who he had once been. Jake still wasn't that sure about any heaven, but on earth, well he had as close as it could be. Still staring at Rachel's painting, he smiled wryly as he remembered the other portraits she had painted of him during the intervening years. Fortunately they were stored away in the shed he'd turned into a studio for her. She had managed to convince him to pose several times in the desert wearing less and less until finally he'd given up, stripped to the skin and allowed her to have her way with him. Of course, after that he'd had his way with her--which had probably led directly to the bundle, which she was now carrying in from the bedroom to meet her grandpa.

With Johnny on his lap, O'Brian admired the pretty baby. "So what's her name?" he asked the toddler with a happy grin.

"Rita," Johnny said proudly.

"Fully Marguerite Esmeralda Donovan," Rachel added,

pulling the blanket back a bit from baby's face so he could see her full head of dark blonde hair.

O'Brian glanced over at Jake, who lounged across from him. "She looks like you, Donovan."

Jake got a shocked look on his face. "Good Lord, I hope not."

As they laughed, Johnny, bored at baby talk, jumped down to go outside and play in the fenced backyard.

After Rita had been properly admired, Rachel laid her in a cradle at one end of the living room. "How are you?" she asked her father, coming to sit on the arm of Jake's chair, draping her arm around his shoulder, love a visible presence in the room.

"I'm okay... I miss not living closer, but under the circumstances, it's definitely healthier to the north." He grinned ruefully.

Jake's thoughts turned inward, back to the aftermath of the battle at Esmeralda. It had taken nearly an hour for emergency services to get to the ghost town. While paramedics did what they could to doctor their injuries, the police officers went to look into the hundred-foot deep shaft where Ramirez had fallen. They decided it would take special equipment to bring up the body.

The next day when they returned, they found the mine had caved in. Hundreds of tons of rock and beams had closed its opening forever. Possibly a fitting resting place for the man who had sought power at any cost and ended his life in a pit. Donovan would have felt more confident if he had seen the body. He knew in his mind that Rachel had heard the sounds of the fall, the landing thud; but with no body, a small part of him would always wonder.

Because David Bannister's wound had required a lengthy recuperation before he regained strength and wit, his superiors had been left to settle the issue of what was to be done to O'Brian. They listened to his confession, and in exchange for what he knew about the smuggling pipeline, his total non-involvement in any murders, an agreement was reached. The whole thing had been kept remarkably quiet while arrests were made. O'Brian's full cooperation had meant a long probation and many hours of community service far to the north, away from the border and any threat it might have represented in case Ramirez's confederates decided to seek revenge for the closing down of their operations.

Since ownership of the O'Brian Ranch had previously been turned over to Rachel, they had had to decide what to do with it. With Jake still working for the Border Patrol, they had hired a ranch manager, letting the land further heal from those years of overgrazing. Lately Jake's work had seemed less rewarding, the long hours away from Rachel less tolerable, and they had been talking about moving back to the O'Brian land and running the ranch themselves. For many generations of O'Brians, it had been a good place to raise families.

A tap at the door and Aunt Flo pushed her head in. "Sorry I'm late," she said as she entered. "The traffic was terrible in Tucson. An accident or something. Father Renaldo dropped me off and headed straight for the church."

"Don't worry," Jake told the old woman as she bent to admire Rita, "we have plenty of time. David isn't here yet either."

"You know," Aunt Flo said, grinning at Jake, her eyes twinkling, "I think she looks just like you--" Rachel winked at him as Aunt Flo added, "She is beautiful!"

The End

Character David Banister shows up as the hero in "Bannister's Way" set in Oregon. The O'Brian family story is told in three earlier historical novels. Arizona Sunset, Tucson Moon, and Arizona Dawn.

REVIEWS

Desert Inferno

This was a fun read. I especially like how well Rain evokes the atmosphere of the desert Southwest. Her hero and heroine are smart and likable, and there are some great action scenes. Looking forward to reading another of these entertaining novels. *M*

What a wonderful, wonderful book. It kept me engrossed for hour upon hour and I had trouble putting it down. I would definitely recommend it and any other books by this author. *B*

Tucson Moon

Rain Trueax's TUCSON'S MOON was a page turning, warm romance .... Priscilla stepped up and rescued the clueless guilt ridden (Marshall Cord and Grace). I loved her strength. *P*

A Montana Christmas

Rain 's first novella added a high note to my Christmas. I turned off the news. Sat down with a hot drink by a wood fire stove!! I was transported to Montana and could believe a ranch could be the instrument for Helen to bring a family once broken back together again. It made me feel good about the season. I highly recommend it for a quick read, which is perfect for this time of year. I just would like Rain to write more of these. *P*

From Here To There

I wasn't sure what to expect from this indie offering. The book description sounded promising however, so ... I was glad I did. I found it well written, formatted and edited. In fact, once I got into the book, it felt like I was reading a romance novel from a traditional publisher. ... I would recommend this book to adults who like romances, in particular those who would enjoy a modern version of the prairie romance. Pleasantly surprised ...*H*

Her Dark Angel

Wow love this Book. Keeps you on your toes, can't wait to see what's next. Really enjoyed it. recommend to you all....M

ALSO BY RAIN TRUEAX

ARIZONA BASED

Arizona Sunset

Tucson Moon

Arizona Dawn

Rose's Gift

Echoes From The Past

Lands of Fire

Bound For The Hills

Frederica's Heart

NORTHWEST CONTEMPORARIES

Moon Dust, Evening Star

Bannister's Way, Second Chance

Hidden Pearl, Her Dark Angel,

From Here To There, Montana Christmas,

Diablo Canyon, Luck of the Draw

OREGON HISTORICALS

Round The Bend, Where Dreams Go

Going Home, Love Waits

www.ingramcontent.com/pod-product-compliance
Lightning Source LLC
Chambersburg PA
CBHW061548170626
46811CB00001B/137